Turn up the heat with Terry Spear's paranormal romance

"Dark, sultry and primal romance… The chemistry is blazing hot and will leave readers breathless."

—*Fresh Fiction* on *Savage Hunger*

"A sizzling page turner. Terry Spear is wickedly talented."

—*Night Owl Reviews* Reviewer Top Pick,
5 Stars for *Savage Hunger*

"The vulpine couple's chemistry crackles off the page."

—*Publishers Weekly* on *Heart of the Wolf*

"Intense and swoon-inducing… The chemistry is steamy and hot."

—*USA Today Happy Ever After* on *Dreaming of the Wolf*

"Crackles with mystery, adventure, violence, and passion."

—*Library Journal* on *Seduced by the Wolf*

"Sensual, passionate, and well-written…Terry Spear's writing is pure entertainment."

—*Long and Short Reviews* on *Wolf Fever*

"This novel has it all… Hot doesn't even begin to describe it."

—*Love Romance Passion* on
Heart of the Highland Wolf

Also by Terry Spear

The Jaguar Shapeshifter series

A SEAL
WOLF CHRISTMAS

TERRY
SPEAR

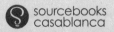
sourcebooks
casablanca

Published by Sourcebooks Casablanca, an imprint of Sourcebooks, Inc.
P. O. Box 4410, Naperville, Illinois 60567-4410
(630) 961-3900
Fax: (630) 961-2168
www.sourcebooks.com

Printed and bound in Canada.
MBP 10 9 8 7 6 5 4 3 2 1

To Donna Fournier who, for years, has sent me inspiration to write about wolves. She lives near the International Wolf Center and has been sending me articles about the wolves in her neck of the woods in Minnesota, along with wolf CDs so that I can tell which of my sexy wolves is making a call of the wild, as well as hunks she's sure are some of my wolves— pictures of hunks, that is. And now she's even getting into the jaguars! Thanks, Donna, for sending me so much inspiration!

Chapter 1

Amazon Jungle, Colombia

DESPITE BEING DEEP IN THE JUNGLE ON A LIFE-OR-DEATH mission, Bjornolf Jorgenson couldn't rid himself of the refrain of "Jingle Bells" playing over and over again in his head. He'd just come from an assignment in snowed-in Minnesota where he'd heard the song. For now, he was shadowing his favorite retired SEAL-wolf team and one female operative in action, and Christmas should have been the furthest thing from his mind.

Their mission: rescue a kidnapped family. His mission: watch the team's back.

They were getting paid as private contractors. *He* was doing it as a favor to Meara. Neither her brother, leading the operation, nor her mate, serving as one of the team members, would appreciate that she'd asked Bjornolf to watch over them.

So he was serving in a covert way, which he preferred over any other.

Bjornolf was also doing this for Anna Johnson, who had intrigued him during their last hot encounter. Straight ahead of him, she was keeping low as she made her way through the jungle with the rest of the team.

It was dusk, and high above them in the canopy, the cacophonous cries of black howler monkeys sent a jarring noise through the trees, warning other monkeys that this was their territory. The air was heavy with moisture and the scent of fragrant orchids as moths fluttered around them.

Bjornolf crept close to the ground. He trailed the team unseen, blending in with the feathery ferns, hibiscus, mimosa, and bromeliads, one kind sporting sweet pineapples that he'd had a bite of earlier in the day. Massive spaghetti-like creepers of lianas crisscrossed the jungle floor underneath his boots where insects and lizards moved about.

Up ahead, Hunter Greymere led the group. A highly decorated SEAL team leader, he was also the alpha pack leader of the Oregon-coast gray wolves.

Finn Emerson, Hunter's brother-in-law, and Paul Cunningham were to Anna's left, and Allan Rappaport, now hidden from view, was somewhere off to her right. While all wolves, none of them were members of Hunter's pack.

Bjornolf shifted his attention from the team to the jungle and, hearing no human sounds, he focused on Anna. Because of his enhanced wolf sight, he saw her in the twilight as clearly as if it were daylight. She was svelte and sexy, even when covered from head to toe in camo gear. She was all curves and hotness, her face painted in a pattern of greens, browns, grays, and blacks to hide her in the foliage. Anna had silky auburn hair tucked under a jungle hat, though straggles of it curled about her shoulders.

He admired her stealth, courage under fire, and resolve. He had to admit he liked watching her a lot better than the men. No matter how dangerous she looked, bristling with weapons, some hidden, she was still all woman. And one who could fight.

He listened again to the noises all around him, attempting to hear even a hint of human voices. Colorful yellow-crowned parrots and red and green macaws made their noisy cawing and chattering, frogs croaked as in a mating call, rather than higher pitched in distress, and insects rustled everywhere.

Then two men began speaking in the distance— complacent, unaware that highly skilled men and one woman were about to descend on them. The men spoke in Spanish, talking about the hostages, so Bjornolf knew the team was targeting the right people. The men appeared to be serving guard duty on the perimeter.

The odor of bitter smoke drifting to him told him the men were smoking.

Although Hunter's team members were all in human form, they moved like a wolf pack, working together, moving slower now, more cautiously, determined to see the hostages freed without causing any casualties on their side.

A jaguar roaring in the jungle not too far away made the kidnappers' chatter die instantly. The call of a second and then a third big cat's roar rent the air.

Anna and the others paused mid-crawl… listening. They continued to stare straight in front of them—their focus on the mission. Allan moved up closer to Hunter and Finn.

Uniformly camouflaged like her, Bjornolf crept nearly parallel to Anna, far enough away in the jungle and slightly behind her so that he could keep an eye on her. He was effectively in her blind spot. He'd broken his cover the last time he'd been assisting the team, but he hadn't needed to this time. Yet. He was half hoping he could get through the mission without revealing himself and half wishing he could let Anna know he had her back.

Like a wolf stalking its prey, Anna crept toward one of the two guards. To her left, Paul matched her careful pace. The last time Bjornolf had seen him, Paul wore a scruffy blond beard, but now he was clean shaven. Wiry and thinner than Bjornolf and Finn, Paul was quick in his movements, an economy of force to be reckoned with.

Bjornolf was torn between wishing he was in Anna's place so she didn't have to risk her neck taking down the guard, and wanting to replace Paul so he would be the one at her side. *Him, a ghost.* He was known throughout the SEAL community as a super-wily deep undercover operative who never revealed himself to anyone. For years, body counts would add up during a mission that no one else could account for, all attributed to him, whether he was in the vicinity or not.

So why was all of his damnable interest in the she-wolf's welfare now potentially blowing the carefully concealed part of his business-as-usual attitude?

She was fully capable of handling herself just fine.

When she was close enough, she popped up from the jungle floor like a woodland sprite, framed by massive trees, twenty feet in diameter and reaching toward the heavens like skyscrapers. She whipped out a *shuriken* and threw it. The stainless-steel, five-pointed throwing star slid through her fingers, heading straight toward the guard's forehead. Without making a squeak, he collapsed with a thump in a cluster of vines and ferns.

Before the other guard could react, Paul had him in a chokehold, jerked his head to the side, and snapped his neck, then dropped him where he stood.

Hunter and the others hit the camp just as two relief guards headed for Anna and Paul. Not normally impulsive, Bjornolf was having a devil of a time curbing the urge to intercept the man targeting Anna, but he knew to keep his attention focused everywhere else—anywhere that someone might be hiding with dark intent.

Anna moved forward in attack mode as gunshots rang out in the camp. A woman screamed and kids shrieked as Anna dropped the relief guard with a rapid barrage of bullets. Paul took down the other man with a burst of gunfire before the guy could retaliate.

Mission accomplished, Anna and Paul raced toward camp, running at a crouch.

Without warning, a man jumped out of the brush, his rifle raised to shoot Anna. Bjornolf leaped from where he'd been running and slammed into the man's back, taking him to the ground. Startled by the surprise attack from behind, the man yelled out. Bjornolf slit his throat, then jumped to his feet. He looked up to see Anna watching his back, her gun ready, mouth pursed in annoyance.

"You could have let us know you're with us," she said, her voice hushed. Her green eyes narrowed as she sent him a caustic glare.

He gave her half a smile and a small salute. "You're welcome," he said quietly back.

She turned slightly, aimed her gun as fast as she could, and fired off a round. Before Bjornolf could turn and see what she'd shot, a thump sounded as a body fell from a tree. He stared at the dead man, bullet hole in his temple.

"We're even," she whispered to Bjornolf.

He could read her plainly and smiled. They would never be even.

After confirming there were no more surprises waiting for the rescue team, Bjornolf followed Anna into camp where the rest of the team had gathered.

"Look what Anna dragged in," Paul said, his brown eyes widening. He gave Bjornolf a small smile.

Last time Bjornolf had observed him, the SEAL had just arrived on the Oregon coast from Florida, dressed in blue jeans and a Hawaiian shirt with hot-pink palm trees and green flamingoes that was the most god-awful thing he'd ever seen. If Bjornolf hadn't witnessed Paul in action before, he would have wondered if the guy could handle any kind of a mission. He was less muscled than Bjornolf, but he was quick on his feet and where Hunter's sister, Meara, was concerned, Paul had been protective and wary of Bjornolf before he knew him.

So he chalked that up as good points in Paul's favor.

Hunter and Allan glanced his way, both checking the rescued family over for injuries, both smiling a little at Bjornolf.

William Wentworth III and his brother, wife, and five-year-old twin daughter and son were dirty, disheveled, gaunt, and tired, but otherwise unharmed. Mom and the kids were crying, and Bjornolf wanted to slap the husband for bringing his family here. Sometimes rich folks had more money than sense.

All the family members had raven hair, their eyes

varying shades of blue. The two men looked similar, except that the brother was a little taller and a little skinnier. All wore jeans, the guys attired in Western shirts, the woman in a once-clean white shirt, now stained green and brown. At least they were wearing boots. Deadly venomous snakes could cause fatal consequences for humans who weren't properly dressed out here.

Next time, maybe they'd plan a normal trip for a couple of five-year-olds this close to Christmas. Like a vacation at Disney World where the bad pirates wouldn't threaten to kill them if someone didn't pay a ransom. Bjornolf would have felt sorry for William Wentworth III, but the adults should have known better. Not only that, but their ignorance had also put the team in danger, just to bail them out.

"Who are you?" William asked.

Hunter said, "Special ops contracted to take you out of here safely."

He didn't explain any more than that; he didn't need to. The man nodded. The woman sagged a little with visible relief. Brows furrowed and looking pensive, the brother glanced at William.

Bjornolf watched the interaction between the two. The brother, Jeff, was younger, the follower, he could tell from their nonverbal actions. But something else passed between them. A guarded communication. Worry. Doubt. *Something*.

"Seems Bjornolf can't stay away from us. Maybe we ought to make him one of the team, Hunter." Paul sounded like he was half joking, half hopeful, maybe getting used to the SEAL joining them on missions without Hunter's approval.

Bjornolf working for someone else and with a team now that he'd retired? Not likely.

He did find some appeal in the way the team worked together. After they arrived at a safe destination, they'd share beers or tequila, whatever was easy to obtain, thanking their lucky stars that they made it out alive after another difficult mission. They'd joke and let down their hair, commiserate, blow off some steam.

While he went his own way. They never even knew he'd shadowed them on another mission, taking down the bad guys they hadn't realized were after them. He meant to revert to his old way of doing things. As a loner on his own, no family to worry about, no pack obligations.

A team like this would soon become family. He didn't need or want the distraction.

The problem was that he couldn't have taken out the guard who targeted Anna without her seeing him do it. So he was stuck being part of the team this time around. Just like the last time.

"Glad you could join us," Hunter said to Bjornolf, his expression mostly somber because of the still precarious situation they were in. His dark brown eyes studied Bjornolf, judging him. Bjornolf could almost see the wheels in Hunter's mind working furiously through the situation. Did Bjornolf want to be part of the team now? "We can certainly use your help in getting the family out of the jungle and safely home."

"Couldn't have my favorite SEAL team, and *others*," Bjornolf said, making a point to slide his gaze Anna's way, "come to harm."

She cast him a quizzical glance over her shoulder, their gazes locking.

Unable to stop himself and amused at her reaction, he winked at her. He swore she had to be blushing under all that jungle paint as she gave him an annoyed look and continued on her way to provide security with Finn.

Catching sight of Bjornolf's reaction to Anna, Allan snorted and folded his arms. "More likely Anna's got his attention."

Yeah, he was ready to spar again with the woman to prove to her that one alluring she-wolf would never get the upper hand with a SEAL. He'd wanted to kiss Anna ever since he'd met her during his last mission, gotten the best of her, and tied her up with her pantyhose, but he couldn't make himself do it.

He shook his head at Allan. The man had a boyish charm. When he turned ninety in human years, he'd probably still have that look—wide-eyed innocence, dimples, raised brows. The look was totally deceiving. Under that charming appearance, he was all hardness like the rest of them.

"I don't know about the rest of the guys, but I missed you, Bjornolf. Good to see you're still kicking." Paul clapped him on the shoulder, then crouched down and talked to the five-year-old boy. "What's your name, son?"

"Jimmy." Tears left a path of white streaks through the dirt on his face and his lower lip was trembling, but at least the question stopped his and his sister's bawling.

"I'm going to give you a lift as we move through the jungle, okay? Piggyback ride?" Paul asked Jimmy.

The boy looked at his dad, who nodded. As dehydrated and fatigued as the dad and his brother appeared, Bjornolf knew they would have a hard enough time

keeping up and staying on their own feet without having
to carry a couple of kids.

Allan didn't offer to transport the little girl. Finn safe-
guarded them from some distance away, leaving the others to decide how to handle the logistics of the situation.
Hunter was in charge of the operation, so he needed to keep
his hands free and his thoughts on the team and the freed
hostages and couldn't haul the girl himself. Anna didn't
seem to be into kids, but even so, she couldn't carry a child
that far without the effort putting a real strain on her.

Bjornolf sighed and stepped forward, towering over
the tyke, and said, "Wanna horsey-back ride?" He
thought a horse sounded much better than a pig.

She gazed up at him with wide, blue, tear-filled eyes.
She was wearing tiny snowman earrings in honor of the
season, reminding him again how she shouldn't be here.
The girl glanced at her mother.

Mom nodded. "Go with the man, Elsie. He'll help get
us out of here safely."

"I'm Bjornolf," he said, carefully pronouncing his
name *Byee-or-nulf* so she'd understand it. His name
meant bear-wolf, but she looked frightened enough
without him sharing that additional information.

He probably should have met her eye to eye, like Paul
had done with her brother. Then again, his face was covered in camouflage face paint like the rest of Hunter's
team. The strange streaks of olive green, black, muddy
brown, and woodland gray markings all over their skin
had to look scary.

Her lip trembled and he was afraid she would begin
to bawl again. He quickly crouched down in front of her
and dug out a camouflage face-paint stick.

"You want to wear some of this so you blend in with the jungle like the…" Bjornolf was going to say "snakes," but he didn't think that would appeal to her. "Jaguars who are covered in rosettes, spots," he clarified. "It makes them almost invisible in the shadows of the jungle trees."

Allan chuckled. Turning to look at Bjornolf, Anna raised her brows. With her mouth curved up and her eyes sparkling with humor, she looked highly amused. He wanted to ask if she needed any of her camouflage makeup redone because he'd be glad to help her out.

Finn glanced over his shoulder at him, a wry grin tugging at the corners of his mouth. Paul swore under his breath.

"Could we all look like the jungle cats?" Mom sounded hopeful that if they blended into the jungle more, they might get out of this alive.

Grinning, the boy nodded vigorously.

Before the party got under way, four of the SEALs were face-painting the humans, making them blend into the woods as much as possible, while Anna and Finn continued to provide security. Once that was done, the men made sure the family had enough to drink and eat. Then Bjornolf crouched, letting Elsie grab on to his field pack. He held on to her scrawny legs to keep her in place.

Vulnerable, he thought. Both he and Elsie were at a disadvantage, should they be attacked en route to the location where they would be transported out of the country. He felt his stomach tighten with disquiet. He liked being the ghost of a backup. No one knowing he was there. The bad guys died, never getting close to the team. No one to say thanks. No getting emotionally involved.

Except for the last mission he'd had with them, and he hadn't believed he'd ever get that involved with the team again. That would have suited him fine.

To physically transport a human child out of a potentially volatile situation was also something foreign to him. He was the lone wolf, the hidden security, which fit his personality perfectly.

Paul carrying the boy and Bjornolf the girl, they walked in the center of the group. Mom and the dad led the way, while the dad's brother hiked behind Bjornolf. Hunter was out in front, Allan bringing up the rear, while Anna and Finn flanked them in the jungle, providing cover to the left and right. Bjornolf couldn't see them, but he kept thinking that was where *he* should be.

Elsie whispered, "Did you tell Santa what you want for Christmas?"

Anna instantly popped in his mind. He smiled to himself.

"Have to make up my list," he whispered.

"I wanna iPad and a phone and a…" Elsie began listing all the colors, brands, and kinds of toys she wanted for Christmas while Bjornolf nodded absently, all the while attempting to listen for trouble.

He smiled to himself. He had to admit the idea of Anna sitting pretty under his Christmas tree sure appealed.

The going was slow, not because of the difficulty with the heat and humidity or the terrain, but because the two brothers and the mom were struggling to keep up. They huffed and puffed as he felt Elsie's tension-filled legs loosen their grip on him. She'd fallen asleep.

Worrying that she might slip off, he paused. The uncle pulled the sleeping child off Bjornolf's back and offered to carry her, despite his obvious lack of strength. He looked about done in with his shoulders stooped, sweat pouring off his face, and his eyes heavily lidded.

Bjornolf declined Jeff's help and continued to carry Elsie in his arms. She was a dirty-faced little angel, her nearly black hair tangled and sweat plastering her bangs to her forehead. He felt a strange pang in the pit of his stomach.

Probably hunger. He hadn't eaten in hours, he reminded himself.

He caught sight of Anna watching him. He couldn't tell from her camouflaged expression what she thought. He shouldn't have cared, but he was curious—as wolves were known to be. Was she amused by what he'd been roped into doing? Or maybe she felt a little sorry for him.

They had traveled for a couple of miles—although the thick jungle made it seem much farther—when he heard a startled male cry come from Anna's direction. Everyone immediately crouched down. Heart pounding, Bjornolf knew to stay where he was and protect the child at all costs, but he damn well wanted to ensure Anna was okay.

She finally made a bird call, letting them know she was all right and to continue to move the family.

Still caught up in the anxiety that had seized him, he moved with the others, keeping alert, every muscle tense, ready to spring into action in the event of new danger.

Trouble didn't take long to manifest itself.

The rat-ta-tat-tat of a spurt of gunfire off to his right meant Finn had his hands full. Then Bjornolf heard rustling to the left where Anna was watching their flank. Suddenly, Hunter was fighting a man in front of the group in hand-to-hand combat. Everyone came to an abrupt halt and crouched. Bjornolf handed the child off to the uncle, while Paul left the boy with his father. Bjornolf's and Paul's gazes met. Bjornolf motioned with his head toward Anna, indicating he was looking after her. Paul raised his brows a little.

Allan stayed with Hunter to safeguard the family while Paul joined Finn.

Bjornolf stealthily made his way to where he had last heard movement in Anna's direction. He couldn't find her. His heartbeat was racing when he heard her soft curse nearby. Even making that much of a sound seemed to be an effort for her.

Hell. He dove through the jungle in her direction.

Chapter 2

FURIOUS THAT SHE WAS CURRENTLY INCAPACITATED and needed help, Anna Johnson heard a man crashing through the jungle like a tapir on steroids.

Damn, that's all she needed—another terrorist coming for her after the last one she'd eliminated had collapsed on top of her, crushing her. The brute had to weigh over two hundred pounds and with fallen tree trunks on either side of her, she didn't have any wiggle room to free herself.

She stayed very still, barely breathing, her heart pounding. With all the jungle noise around her—the bugs, the birds, the frogs, the sound of a river flowing nearby—none of the terrorists would hear her even if she struggled to free herself. *If* she could move at all. Hopefully, the dead body would hide her, and the approaching man would move along, looking for another target.

"Anna," Bjornolf whispered some distance from her. She couldn't see him, but she'd know his voice anywhere, gruff, worried. But he couldn't see her, either.

Exasperated, she closed her eyes and cursed to herself. Of all the men who could have come to rescue her, she didn't want Bjornolf to see her like this.

Swallowing her pride, she whispered, "Here." Her voice came out muffled and barely audible. The dead bastard crushing her made it difficult to draw in a deep breath to say much more.

She thought she heard Bjornolf move closer, but it couldn't be him. Whoever it was came from a different direction.

The person's boot pulled away from the suction of mud on the jungle floor nearby, one step at a time. Then the boots moved onto drier land, with more of a crunching sound, slowly growing closer. She barely breathed.

A shadow suddenly blocked out the scant trickle of light through the canopy. A dirty-faced man with cold gray eyes peered down at her. Instantly, a chill swept up her spine. *Not Bjornolf.*

"You killed Juan," the grungy man said with a thick Spanish accent. He aimed his pistol, and a gunshot rang out.

Her heart stuttered, and she expected to feel the bullet's impact. Only she wasn't shot.

The man fell face forward right on top of the other already resting *heavily* on her. The new dead man felt like he weighed nearly two hundred pounds himself.

"Anna, you okay?" Bjornolf asked, pulling the top dead body off her, then rolling him to the ground on the other side of the fallen tree.

She was filled with overwhelming relief when he moved all the additional pounds off her.

God, it was good to see Bjornolf, lips thinned with worry, high angled cheekbones giving him a rough, rugged look. In his camo gear, he was formidable, his clothes hugging his tall frame and his broad shoulders blocking her view of the canopy above. He was one sexy, virile wolf. His amber eyes were tinged with sage green, his burnt sienna brown hair cut short as if he was still in the Navy. No matter how much she needed to focus on the mission, she watched him with some envy, the way his muscles strained, showing the power in that tightly controlled body, while he tried to move the second man off of her. "Yeah," she said, breathing a little easier, but still feeling light-headed.

"Get you out of there in a sec," Bjornolf said, his voice rough. Despite Bjornolf's strength, the other man took some time to move. The man was big, and the deadweight made it even harder for Bjornolf to lift. He finally managed to pull him off of her enough so that she was able to shimmy out from underneath him. She was still sandwiched between the two massive downed trees. As soon as she was free, Bjornolf dropped the man into the place where she'd been lying flat on her back.

He quickly leaned over the fallen tree and offered his hand to Anna, his gaze lingering on hers. She clasped his large hand, letting it engulf hers, which seemed suddenly tiny in comparison. In a flash, the jungle felt steamier, as if the temperature had risen another twenty degrees and the humidity levels had increased just as much. He pulled her up while she used her boots to dig in for purchase. After he helped her climb the rest of the way over the dead tree, she landed on the other side and took another deep breath.

"You okay? No injuries?" he asked, his words hushed. He focused on her expression, reading it, reading her.

Pride was all that had been injured, but she wasn't about to admit that. She was sure he knew it already. She shot him a thumbs-up. Given the dangerous situation they were in, talk could prove deadly.

Everything was quiet as far as weapon fire was concerned, the jungle noises again reigning. Bjornolf headed back with her to where the team had been. Everyone was waiting, watching, protective of the family, but not moving until Bjornolf and Anna had been accounted for.

The men looked over Anna, worried. She gave them a thumbs-up and headed out again to provide security. Before she moved, she saw Bjornolf and Hunter exchange glances. She was certain Bjornolf wanted to switch places with her, but she wasn't about to give up her job. She liked providing security on the outskirts, making certain that no harm reached the family they were attempting to get to safety.

She couldn't help but respect Bjornolf for carrying the little girl, and she had seen the other team members admire him for it. Bjornolf might not be willing to admit to himself that he was quickly becoming part of their team, but this cinched it for her. A more disquieting thought came to mind—him as a father, protecting one of his own.

And her… the reminder that she had lost her own.

She shook her head at herself for such a fanciful notion concerning Bjornolf having kids of his own. He would never be the kind of man to settle down. Of course she'd thought the same of Hunter and Finn, and look what had happened to them.

Watching for any sign of movement, Anna resumed the slow, tedious trek with the team. They traveled for another couple of hours, took a break, then moved on until Hunter stopped them and went exploring on his own. When he returned, he led them to the base of a hut on stilts.

Anna looked up at the thatched-roof hut, which was silent and vacant. She sniffed the heavy, wet air. The area smelled strangely of jaguar and tangerine-scented soap.

Hunter said to her, "You and Bjornolf can take turns on guard duty inside the hut."

She noted then that Bjornolf had already carried the girl up the wooden steps.

Anna frowned at the odd scents so close to the hut and then said, "All right."

She normally did whatever Hunter said. He was the team leader, and she respected him. But she couldn't help feeling that Bjornolf had said something to him about giving her a break. Sure, she was dead tired. So were the rest of them. But she wanted to hold up her end of the mission.

"Need a hand up?" Bjornolf asked, peering down from the screened-in porch, a small smile on his self-assured mouth and his eyes lit up with amusement.

She gave him a scathing look and climbed the steps. She tried not to show how difficult that was with all the gear she had on and as tired as she was.

When she reached the top of the rickety wooden steps, Bjornolf gave her a hand and pulled her into the enclosed porch—without her permission. Reminding herself that he would have done the same for any of the guys, she gave him a quick nod and thanked him.

Before she could remove her field pack, he was doing it for her. His large hands deftly moved to the buckle around her waist and began unfastening it. The experience was way too intimate. She felt as though he was going to strip her down the rest of the way. She was certain he would not have offered to help remove one of the men's packs for them. Unless the man had been wounded.

She was annoyed with herself for having no control over the way her heartbeat increased or the way her temperature shot through the canopy, making her feel as though she was sweltering in an overheated sauna. Worse, her thoughts were straying to carnal possibilities instead of remaining where they should—that he was just being helpful.

With her sensitive wolf's hearing, she could hear his elevated heartbeat, and the heated gaze he gave her said he was feeling it, too. Thankfully, he didn't say anything to her. He didn't need to. She smelled his interest in her. A wickedly lascivious thought came to her—wouldn't it be nice to relieve some of the tension from the past couple of days by indulging in a sexual frenzy with a really hot guy like him?

She smiled at the notion. His brows rose as if he was interested in what she was thinking, and she smiled even broader. He'd never know.

Once the buckle was unfastened, the weight was instantly withdrawn from around her waist and she could breathe easier. He pulled the heavy weight off her back and laid the pack on the wooden floor of the hut.

She peered through the screen door and saw the two kids and their mother huddled on cots, sound asleep. The two brothers were settling down on sleeping bags, courtesy of two of the SEALs. She was glad the family had a place to sleep off the ground and more comfortably tonight.

"You want the hammock or your sleeping bag?" Bjornolf asked, motioning to the hammock tied to the ceiling of the porch.

The hammock would be cooler, she thought as she sat down on the floor to take off her boots. "I'll sleep on the hammock."

"Good." He sat down on the floor next to her and began removing his boots. She frowned at him. "What are you doing?"

"The same as you. Getting ready to lie down for a bit."

"I thought one of us was going to have first watch."

"I am. Believe me, if anyone tries to come up here, he won't know what hit him."

He would shift into a wolf.

She stared at him, then glanced at his pack. He didn't have a sleeping bag. "Where's your…" She looked over at the screen door to the main room. He'd given his to one of the men. Great. So he planned on sleeping in *her* bag. Bjornolf's heady male scent of sandalwood and hot hormones and sexy wolf would be all over her bag when she had to sleep in it later.

Then again, he'd breathe her in all night as well. She stifled a groan.

"Why are you here, watching them and watching us on this mission?" she asked with a heavy sigh.

He shrugged and pulled off his camo shirt and laid it next to his boots. He yanked his T-shirt off after that, baring his beautiful chest and all those ripped muscles. "I wasn't supposed to tell anyone under threat of death, but I figure the secret is safe with you," Bjornolf said.

Anna looked up from his sculpted abs, dying to know what the secret was and more than surprised that he would reveal what it was to her and nobody else.

"Meara asked me to watch over Hunter and Finn."

Anna chuckled under her breath. "Sounds like Meara. The guys are glad to have you here. And little Elsie, too."

"What about you?"

She didn't know how he managed to fluster her so, but she felt her whole body flush with renewed heat. "Yeah, thanks for the help back there."

"You're welcome." Bjornolf stretched his arms behind his back. She watched as his muscles moved. "Elsie and her little brother shouldn't have been put through this hell."

Anna glanced at the room, wondering if the parents were asleep.

"There's only been one time that I remember being that small and frightened," he said, his voice more hushed this time.

She took a gander at all of him again. She couldn't imagine him ever having been…small. *Or* frightened.

"My friend and I were in the woods when we were twelve. I don't know how we ever survived all the near-death experiences we had before then. Right before Christmas, we were hiking up a mountain, and we startled a momma black bear that only thought to protect her two young cubs." He looked away and took a deep breath. "Gregory was mauled to death, and I couldn't do a thing for him."

Anna swallowed hard. She could see the grief he still felt for his friend, the feeling of helplessness, of being at fault.

"I ran away before she took notice of me. I didn't leave the area, though. I went back as soon as the mother and her cubs moved off. I was the same size as Gregory, and I was sure that mother bear would come back at any moment. I had to carry Gregory's body home to his parents. They were grief-stricken; it was awful. And I got hell from my own parents who were furious with me for hiking without adult members of the pack to keep us safe."

Anna closed her gaping mouth. Even when he was young and terrified of facing his own mortality, he'd been honorable.

"Even today, the sound of a bear roaring in the wilderness gives me flashbacks about that horrific incident. After that, I resolved to be as tough as I could. Take no prisoners. Kill before being killed. Law of the jungle. I never wanted to have to rely on anyone else to get me anywhere safely." He took a deep breath and exhaled it. "I had convinced my friend to join me on the hike. I was responsible."

"You were just a kid, Bjornolf," she said. "We all make mistakes. But the bear killed your friend. It could have been you."

"Yeah." He sounded like he still felt he was at fault. "These kids are with their parents. In this case, the mother and father are responsible for putting the children in harm's way. Who the hell does that to their kids?"

Anna nodded, unsure what to say. Sometimes lending a sympathetic ear was enough.

Yet, she wanted to hug the young boy in Bjornolf who had suffered such a traumatic experience. And immediately thought how dangerous that would be.

She slipped out of her shirt and spread it next to her boots. He stood and unbuckled his belt while she watched. She couldn't have taken her eyes off him at that moment for anything.

He unbuttoned his pants. She rose to her feet and unbuckled her belt, unfastened her pants, and slid them down her legs. The pants were caked with mud, stiff from the knees down, and it felt good to get out of them. If she had the time, she'd wash them in the morning.

Wearing only a pair of black boxers, Bjornolf lay down on her spread-out sleeping bag, his arms behind his head, his eyes on hers. He looked sexy, his tan muscled legs spread out, his chest lightly dusted in dark hair, his pecs remarkably toned as if he got a regular workout.

Which made her think of women and Bjornolf getting a really good workout that way.

Anna definitely didn't want to ponder that further.

She climbed onto the hammock, wearing a clingy olive-green tank top over her bra that showed a little skin between the top and her low-cut matching bikini panties. As Bjornolf's gaze lingered on the skimpiness of her undergarments, a heated blush crept up her chest and neck and stretched down her torso.

Sure, the other guys looked when she stripped partway to climb into her sleeping bag—they *were* hot-blooded men of the wolf variety, after all—but she didn't think they appeared quite as predatory as Bjornolf did when he swallowed her up with his gaze. She'd noticed that the other men looked her way but then looked away again.

The hammock swung back and forth for a moment before it settled down. She sniffed at the canvas and smelled a feline scent. *Jaguar?*

"They kind of grow on you, don't they? The team, I mean," she asked softly so as not to wake the sleeping family.

"Kinda," Bjornolf admitted.

For a man who was as tough as a tortoise shell and as reclusive as a jaguar, he had to have had a hard time admitting that, but he seemed to trust her at least that much.

"They're growing on me, too," she said.

They were silent for a long time, then he said, "That bruiser who buried you weighed a ton."

She smiled. "Yeah, but when you took the other one out and he landed on top of me, I felt like I was buried beneath tons of rubble."

"Sorry. He was supposed to drop the other way."

She chuckled, then stretched out on the hammock again and closed her eyes. She was getting sleepy.

She heard a howl from the jungle and an answering howl back. *Paul and Allan.* They must have shifted into wolves to provide security while on guard duty.

An hour later, she heard whispered words between William and his brother, Jeff, inside the hut. Her ears perked up and she listened hard.

"It wasn't supposed to go down this way," Jeff whispered.

"Someone got their noses into the business instead of leaving well enough alone," Wentworth said.

"Now what happens?" Jeff asked, his voice hushed but angry.

"I don't know. Hell, it's not my fault that these people killed our kidnappers."

Chapter 3

ANNA'S BACK STIFFENED. WHY WOULD THE SEAL TEAM be at fault for killing the kidnappers in an effort to free the family?

Her thoughts shifted in another direction, more sinister in nature. What if saving them hadn't been part of the agenda? What if Wentworth and his brother had arranged the whole thing?

She leaned over the hammock to peer at Bjornolf. In the sweltering night, he looked hot and sexy resting on his back as he spread out on her sleeping bag. His eyes were closed, but the way he was breathing, she could tell that he was wide awake.

Good. She liked having verification when she believed some skullduggery was in progress.

"We'll have to come up with another plan," Wentworth whispered to his brother.

"You'll still have to pay the guys," Jeff said.

"Cost of doing business."

"What about that other situation?" Jeff asked.

"I left a trail straight to his door. He'll take care of it if he wants to survive."

"Except we won't be there to help him this time," Jeff said, his voice still hushed.

"Perfect for us."

When they didn't say anything further, Anna assumed they must have fallen asleep. She soon followed them, drifting off to nothingness.

Bjornolf knew he had to speak privately to Hunter about what the brothers had revealed. Once they were all on the trail again, it would be harder to get the word to Hunter without the family overhearing. Bjornolf threw on a fresh set of clothes and left the hut.

Finding Hunter stretched out on a hammock nearby, Bjornolf explained what he overheard. "All I know is that you had to rescue this family, and from the research I did, I learned that William Wentworth is a multimillionaire with more than a dozen businesses. Some have to do with pharmaceuticals and trying to discover new medicines from plants in the Amazon. He also has other more diversified businesses, including computer technology. What I don't understand is why they were here in the first place. Dragging two little kids and a wife on a trip to the jungle this close to Christmas?"

"According to family friends, they came here on a special tour—to get a look at the jungle that has made so much money for them. What we were told was that the adventure went bad when their tour guides were murdered and the family was taken hostage. Their lawyer received a ransom message and he was concerned that if he paid the money to the kidnappers, they'd take the payment and kill Wentworth and his family. The lawyer relayed the information to my source, who got in touch with us, knowing we could handle the mission.

"We all believed he brought the family here to prove he wasn't just a desk jockey. That he could handle the Amazon jungle as well as he did a corporate jungle, but then he found himself way out of his element here. What you overheard blows that theory all to hell. What *I'm* not

clear on is how *you* came to be here." Hunter waited for
Bjornolf to respond.

"Truth is, it needs to remain a highly kept secret,"
Bjornolf said seriously, though he was having the
damnedest time keeping a straight face.

Hunter shook his head. "*Meara* sent you."

Bjornolf smiled a little. "Yeah, she *emphasized* that
both you and Finn were needed home for Christmas.
Good thing I don't have a sister. *Or* a mate."

"Speaking of that…"

Bjornolf wondered where this little talk was going.

"Listen, Bjornolf, I know you don't do team projects
any longer. I know about your team being killed on a
mission and you being the lone survivor. I know what
that kind of thing can do to a guy, so don't think I'm
unsympathetic. But I could really use your help for a
job. Right after we arrived in Bogota, I got a call from
Tessa. She said Nathan—you remember the teen you
brought home after he'd run away?" Hunter asked.

"Yeah, sure. Good kid. Troubled."

"Yeah, well he's working at a Christmas tree farm
and smelled a couple of dead *wolf* bodies. Tessa has our
police officers looking into it, but they haven't found
any bodies, and we have more of a problem than that."

Bjornolf wondered why Hunter would ask him to
work a job instead of going to his own team members.
"What is it?"

"Actually, I need a couple to handle this," Hunter said.

"A… *couple*," Bjornolf said slowly. It didn't sound
like Hunter meant a couple of men.

"Yeah, like you and Anna. You both know each
other already to an extent, and I need a highly trained

team that can handle a situation that might get ugly real fast."

"A situation?"

"Tessa said the police officers are certain that two of our wolf kind were murdered at the Christmas tree farm."

"Hell. Why do you need a couple?"

"We need you to take Nathan in for a bit, serve as his guardians, while you search for clues about the murders. It would be a good cover and would help to safeguard him. We'll provide one of our beach homes for you to use as you and Anna play the role of being newlyweds. Tessa is having the boy stay with one of the cop families in our pack in the meantime. But Nathan wanted you and Anna to watch out for him. Of course, I told him I hadn't seen you since the last trouble we had there. So I explained I'd tried to pair up either Allan or Paul with Anna."

Bjornolf wasn't sure what he was getting into. "Have you spoken to Anna about the mission?"

"No. I asked Paul or Allan if they wanted to work with her on the assignment, but they both had other contracts after this mission. I'm sure if I told them I had no one else to serve as her partner, one of them would have stepped up. But before I tell Anna, I want to ensure I have someone lined up to watch her back."

"Watching over the boy?" Bjornolf was surprised. Somehow he didn't see her stepping in to take care of a teenage boy.

"No. Trying to solve the murder mystery."

Bjornolf nodded.

"I wasn't about to assign her the job unless I could

find a man I trusted to keep her safe. Then here you are all of a sudden. The two of you could be perfect for the job. Especially since you know Nathan already. And he asked for you specifically. Paul and Allan have never met the boy. If you don't have any other plans for Christmas and you don't mind working with Anna—I know she has no plans for the holidays—it could work. Or I'll ask the other guys again and see if one of them can break his contract."

"I'll do it." Bjornolf couldn't believe he'd just accepted a mission to work with Anna as a team. He wondered how she'd view it.

"Good," Hunter said. "As to our current mission, the team intends to get this family safely to the American embassy in Bogota. Whatever other agenda is playing behind the scenes is not our business. Although I fully intend to have my source and others check into the matter to learn what the truth is. I don't like being played for a fool. And I sure as hell don't appreciate getting my team shot at when a mission isn't necessary. For now, we'll conduct the undertaking as we'd first intended. The family needed rescuing. Eliminate the threat. Get the family to safety unharmed."

"Sounds good to me."

"All right." Hunter settled back in his hammock. "Got to get some rest."

"Night." Bjornolf headed back to the hut and climbed the ladder. All he could think of was serving in wedded bliss with Anna—in a pretend role. During Christmas? That should be interesting. He hadn't done Christmas in eons. Having Nathan around would keep the business more professional, but hell, maybe Anna and Bjornolf

could get in a few sparring sessions—just to keep in
shape when they had some spare time. When he retired
to her sleeping bag and took in her sexy fragrance, all he
could think of was "I'll Be Home for Christmas" with
Anna in his bed.

———

Anna slept until she heard Bjornolf's approach. The
blue-gray light of day hadn't yet appeared, but the birds
were beginning to call to each other high in the canopy.
Bugs—from the buzz of mosquitoes to the chirping of
crickets—added to the raucous noise.

"Time to go," he said quietly, his voice rough with
tension. His gaze focused on hers at first, then drifted
over her scantily attired body.

"What… wait, what happened?" She frowned, feeling disoriented about the time. "I was supposed to have
guard duty at some point. And I should have had some
outdoor time."

"You had indoor duty, watching these folks. Hunter
wanted you to be here for the woman or kids if they
needed you. That was the most important job you
could have."

She snorted. "I slept, you mean." She couldn't believe she'd slept soundly through the night.

He smiled gently. She didn't remember him ever really grinning or laughing out loud. He was more subtle,
cool under pressure, all mission-oriented. He was also
damned hot, with his chest bare and still only wearing
boxers. She thought about spending the night with him
and what a real treat it would be to wake up with him
first thing in the morning.

After climbing off the hammock, she crossed the small porch and peered through the screened door to the hut. William Wentworth's brother was still asleep. She yanked fresh camo pants, another olive-green tank top, and a camo shirt out of her backpack, and then began to dress. She noticed that the muddy clothes she'd removed last night were hanging off a bamboo rod, the articles washed and still damp.

She frowned at Bjornolf. "Who…?" She waved her hand at her clothes. She couldn't imagine Bjornolf had washed them. Nor any of the other men, for that matter.

"I couldn't sleep," he admitted, looking like he was fighting a smile.

She envisioned him scrubbing the mud off her pants in the dark next to a stream and couldn't believe it.

"Thanks." She looked back at her clothes. What he'd done had been nothing short of heroic and thoughtful. "You took an awful risk. A croc could have gotten you," she scolded.

"I killed him. Well, technically it was a caiman, a smaller crocodilian."

She frowned at him, then seeing he was totally serious, she shook her head, trying not to chuckle. This was a side of him that was appealing and so unexpected.

She finished buttoning her shirt, needing to be fully clothed before she got too close to Bjornolf's half-naked body, and whispered, "Did you hear the brothers talking last night?"

Bjornolf looked into her upturned face, his own expression dark, and nodded. "I spoke to Hunter about it already."

"What did he say?"

"You know him. He has to ponder it for a while. He let the others know. We're all mulling it over, coming up with different scenarios."

"Blackmail?" she whispered.

"Possibly." Bjornolf glanced at the hut. "We have to get them on their way." He dressed, then walked toward the screen door. "I'll wake and feed the family. You go do whatever it is you have to do, and we'll all be ready to leave in a little bit."

"All right." She sat down on the floor and quickly pulled on her boots.

When Bjornolf rapped on the door to the hut, Wentworth answered in a tired voice, "Yeah?"

"Rise and shine, folks. Time to eat a bite and get on the road."

Bjornolf walked inside the hut, speaking quietly to the dad, telling him about the next phase of the journey.

"What do you mean I need to give up my cell phone?" William asked, highly agitated.

"The men who took you hostage might be able to track you using the signal from your cell."

"Can't get a signal out here."

"Just hand them over." Bjornolf was no longer playing Mister Nice Guy. In truth, they had to make sure the brothers didn't use them to contact someone to institute a new plan as soon as they *did* get a signal. "All of them."

"I don't have one," Jimmy said, his voice small.

"That's okay, Jimmy," Bjornolf said.

Anna didn't envy Bjornolf the job. She climbed down the ladder and found Allan standing partially hidden by the floor of the hut that served as a roof on stilts. He was chewing on a piece of meat and smiling at her.

He always looked cute, his cheeks dimpled, his eyes full of mirth. "Have a good sleep?"

"You should have woken me up for guard duty," she said, annoyed.

"Hunter's orders. You had babysitting duty along with Bjornolf." At the last comment, his eyes narrowed a little as he looked up at the hut.

She snorted. But she wasn't about to tell Allan that she had slept through the night. She also couldn't believe Bjornolf had actually washed his clothes and hers, too. She'd have to do something good in turn for him.

Then she saw the black caiman stretched out over a fire. The reptile had to be at least thirteen feet in length! A *little* caiman? She looked up at the hut. That's what he'd killed just to wash her clothes?

⁓

A few minutes later, the family descended the steps to the forest floor. Bjornolf carried the girl down, and Paul, the boy. Anna came out of the jungle to join the group, giving Bjornolf a look.

He wasn't sure what was up until she said, "Little caiman?"

Loving that the she-wolf was in awe of his hunter prowess, he just smiled back at her, which earned him a shake of her head.

After roasting and eating the caiman that Bjornolf had slaughtered by the stream, they were on their way. As soon as they headed out, Jimmy asked the question no one wanted to answer. Not: *When will we get home?* Or: *How long will this take?*

"Are we gonna be home in time for Christmas and

see Santa coming down the chimney? We have to leave milk and cookies out for Santa," the boy continued.

Paul frowned, not responding.

"Will we be home before Santa comes?" Jimmy asked again, not about to be ignored.

"Sure, you'll make it home in time for the jolly old elf to climb down the fireplace," Paul said. "But we've got to be real quiet like before, okay?"

His eyes wide, the kid nodded.

That had Hunter wishing he was home with his family. His wolf pack celebrated the holidays like many packs did, although some years in the past he'd been on missions with his team. Christmas was only a couple of weeks away, and he looked forward to spending his first Christmas with Tessa and helping her decorate for the holidays. Finn and his sister had now become mates, so it would also be their first Christmas together. With Bjornolf and Anna sticking around? It would be a real SEAL holiday.

Using a machete, Hunter whacked through the thick foliage impeding their way, creating a narrow path through the jungle that would be swallowed up again soon, as if the humans hadn't passed this way. Black howler monkeys called to each other, grew quiet as they listened for return calls, then howled again.

As daylight broke, the heat quickly elevated, and the buzz of winged insects filled the air. Thousands of cicadas added their noisy songs, the jungle sounds intruding on Hunter's thoughts of hearth and home. As he and his team traveled through the dense jungle, Hunter cut through thick vines and branches, while he kept feeling as though someone was following them. The family stumbled over roots, the mother sobbed once, but the rescue team moved silently like wolves in a territory not usually their own. This was jaguar land.

Anna's warning bird call sounded. Hunter stopped the group and waited, protectively shielding the party as Bjornolf lurched forward.

Remembering he had the girl on his back, he stopped long enough for the uncle to take hold of her before Bjornolf charged forth to rescue Anna again.

Chapter 4

WHEN BJORNOLF REACHED ANNA AT A LOW CROUCH behind a bank of ferns, he found her safe, his own heart hammering with worry for her. He tried to catch his breath as he drew close to her to see what she was observing.

She bowed her head in greeting as his arm brushed against hers, having to touch her like a wolf would and have the reassurance she truly was all right before he looked further into the matter that had concerned her.

Two men were attempting to drag a young native boy of maybe eight or nine with them. The kid was kicking and hitting and biting. She motioned to Bjornolf that she wanted him to draw the men's attention so she could take them out and the boy could get away. "Involved with Wentworths," she whispered.

One of the men said to the other in Spanish, "Where the hell are the Wentworths? I thought we were supposed to be done with this business by now. And be paid. Get that kid out of here."

Bjornolf was planning on being the one to attack the men—and keep one of them alive for questioning—while Anna drew their attention instead, but before he could do anything, the men slapped at their necks, released the boy, and collapsed in dead heaps on the ground. The boy glanced in Anna and Bjornolf's direction, gave them a big smile and a wave, then tore off into the jungle.

"*Shit*," Bjornolf said under his breath.

"What just happened?" Anna whispered to Bjornolf. "I thought we could wound one and question him."

"Poisoned darts, hunters, natives in the area," he whispered into her ear. He jerked his head toward the path he'd taken, telling her that they needed to get back to the team.

She nodded, thanking him silently, but he could tell she was just as disappointed as he was that they couldn't have learned more from these men—now that they needed to question them concerning what the Wentworths were up to, and not just eliminate the threat.

Bjornolf admired her for attempting to rescue the boy and alerting the team for help, not jumping in to do this by herself. It showed a side of her that she tried to hide behind her camouflaged suit of armor. He swore she flushed a little under all that camo paint when the boy smiled and waved at her.

Sighing, he hated leaving her to continue to provide security for the team, hated that every time he thought she might be in danger, his heart would nearly stop. Everyone had a mission on the team. For now, his was transporting the little girl. He still didn't like that he'd have to let Anna fend for herself, no matter how good she was at her job.

When he returned to the group, Hunter gave him a quizzical look. Bjornolf couldn't tell him in front of the family how they had overheard that the men knew something about the Wentworth's kidnapping. Bjornolf instead gave Hunter a thumbs-up, and he took the girl in his arms again. First chance they had, either he or Anna would let Hunter know what had happened.

The team traveled with the family for four more days through the jungle in the same manner as before—sleeping with guards posted, eating and drinking all together, and keeping a low profile. At the end of the fourth day, they reached the outskirts of a village and, before anyone saw them, they scrubbed the camo paint off of each other with soap and water from a nearby river, not wanting to give the villagers the impression that they might be trouble.

Anna smiled when Elsie scrubbed the paint off Bjornolf's face, dragging a wet soapy cloth this way and that over his skin. He exaggerated his expressions of pain and surprise, groaning and moaning, making Elsie giggle. He caught Anna's gaze and grinned at her. Leaving the girl to her mother, Bjornolf advanced on Anna.

As he closed in on her with a feral gray wolf's heated look, she felt her body temperature elevate in the steamy heat.

"You didn't quite get all *your* makeup off," he said, pulling a cloth out of his sack and soaking it with a container of soapy water. He stood too close—*way* too close.

She gave him a skeptical look, not wanting to believe him, but since she didn't have a mirror, she wasn't certain. The parents were washing their kids' faces and Wentworth's brother was working on his own, but her team watched Bjornolf as he washed her face.

Feeling her cheeks heat, she folded her arms and silently entreated him to hurry it up.

But he didn't. He took his time wiping every inch of her face, her lips, her ears, and neck so gently, she didn't think he could have removed anything.

When he was done, she said, "Let me see the cloth."

His eyes widened a bit. "You don't trust me?" he asked with feigned innocence.

She knew he was all pretend when he was balking at showing her the cloth. She stretched out her hand, raised her brows, and waited.

He let out an exaggerated sigh and handed the cloth to her. "See, what did I tell you?"

A faint green cast covered a section of the white cloth, and one dark brown smudge colored another spot. This time *she* sighed audibly. "Thanks. Good job."

"You've got to learn to trust your partner," he said.

She looked at him, trying to read the meaning behind his words. She swore he was trying to tell her something.

The show over, Hunter moved the group through the village to a couple of cabanas that he had rented— all the buildings decked out in Christmas lights, decorated Christmas trees sitting in front of some of the windows. Despite the Christmas decorations, the jungle atmosphere reminded them they were still far from home.

"Anna, you'll stay with the mother and the kids tonight. Paul, Allan, the two of you also. The Wentworth brothers will stay with Bjornolf, Finn, and me," Hunter said. "Better protection for all concerned."

"I want to stay with my wife," Wentworth said, looking cross and obviously used to getting his way.

"Sorry, Mr. Wentworth," Hunter said, his tone curt, not the least bit sorry. "You're under my orders until we drop you off safely at the embassy. After that, it's your decision."

"Honey, do as he says," his wife said as she held

her kids' hands. "They got us this far without any of us being hurt."

He gave her a murderous look. Anna saw a flicker of relief on the woman's face when her husband didn't get his way.

Hunter was clearly giving Anna a chance to question the mother without the husband being present. Paul and Allan slid looks in Bjornolf's direction. His expression was neutral, but he was totally annoyed. Bjornolf couldn't stop thinking about staying with Anna at the hut, and he definitely didn't like the idea of being in a separate cabana away from her. All his protective instincts were on overdrive.

He loathed the idea of Anna being out of his sight, and that was beginning to annoy him, too. Bjornolf thought of himself as a quintessential loner, and now he was anticipating a mission with a partner. If that wasn't bad enough, the partner was someone he was getting way too personally interested in.

Before bedding down for the night, Hunter sent Bjornolf and Anna to buy meals from a local eatery. The owner of the cabanas had recommended three of them. Eating at the others was at the customers' risk. They chose one that looked a little less rustic than the others. Small wooden tables filled a flagstone patio surrounded by rough, yellow stone walls topped with white Christmas lights. More lights wound around vines and hanging plants, while the smell of arepas wafted outside. Friendly chatter and the clinking of bottles of beer filled the air. Chickens clucked and pecked at bugs scurrying around on the pavers. A donkey brayed in the distance—adding to the South American–style holiday ambience.

Anna surveyed the surrounding area again, watching for any sign of danger while they waited for their meals. Bjornolf caught Anna looking at him, which made him smile a little. Garbed in civilian clothes to fit in with the other tourists, Anna wore a jungle-print, see-through blouse over a green tank top. A pair of black jeans and heeled boots were a lot sexier than the combat ones she'd had on, though he knew she could use those boots as weapons. He had to admit anything she wore looked damned good on her. She appeared as beautiful as the colorful birds and flowers of the jungle, he thought.

She quickly looked at the patrons again. Like any good operative, she'd been observing the patrons as well as the jungle. When their gazes collided, he watched her cheeks flush. All fresh and clean, she fairly sparkled. Her auburn hair hung in damp curls around her face, her green eyes widened a bit when Bjornolf continued to look at her, taking her in, every delicious part of her.

He'd never seen her dress in anything but camouflaged clothes, or on that last mission when he'd first run into her—close-fitting black for cat burglar–type operations—so this was a new look for him. The colors were still dark, but he couldn't pass up another look at the sheer blouse that hinted at a playful suggestiveness. She might not be suggesting anything, but he liked to believe she was teasing him a bit.

"What?" she said, casting him an annoyed glance, arms folding defensively over her chest.

"You look nice."

Her mouth opened as if she was about to give him a smart-assed reply, then she closed it, eyes narrowing.

"*Really*," he said. He wanted to tell her that it was okay to accept the compliment, that it wasn't demeaning or anything for someone who tried so hard to be just one of the guys. "*Really* nice," he said, in a way that meant his appreciation of her beauty had nothing to do with wanting to get her into the sack.

Not that he wouldn't love that, but he hadn't meant the compliment in that way.

"Thank you," she said, her voice sounding a little suspicious.

Okay, so maybe the appreciative look he gave her did border on lingering, and definitely indicated that he was interested.

"*Señor?*" a young dark-haired woman called, coming up to him and handing him the bags of food, the spicy scent making his stomach rumble with anticipation.

"*Muchas gracias,*" he said, thanking her.

His mouth was watering, too, but that had more to do with the way Anna looked than anything to do with the food.

Anna quickly took some of the bags, then they left the eatery.

"So… about the sleeping arrangements…" Bjornolf began.

She glanced his way before they crossed the narrow dirt road. "What about them?"

"I couldn't help but notice that both Allan and Paul jumped right in to protect the woman and her children," he said, unable to keep the sarcasm from his voice. He knew they also wanted to protect Anna, though he wouldn't say so because he figured that wouldn't set well with her.

She smiled at him, the warmth of that wicked expression going straight to his groin.

"Hunter made the assignments. But… you wanted the job?" Her brows were raised, her eyes wide with innocence, but he knew she was feigning that virtuous look.

"Nah," he said, "but Finn or Hunter could stay with them, and you and I could eavesdrop on William and his brother again."

"I doubt they will say anything more to each other. At the hut, we were apart from them on the porch so they probably figured we couldn't make out anything they said. They may be a bigger threat to our mission than the mother and kids are. That means you should stick with them. The reason I was asked to come along was to offer female companionship for the mother and to be a surrogate mother for the daughter and the son, should their mother have died."

That was the first he'd heard of the role she was supposed to play. He really hadn't thought she wanted to be around the children. But if the battle had gotten out of hand, she would have stepped in to mother them. That put a different spin on her part in the operation. He would like to see how Anna interacted with the children.

Lively salsa and pop music began to drift from a couple of bars catering to locals and foreigners alike, while Christmas carols played somewhere off in the distance as Bjornolf escorted Anna to the cabana where she'd stay the night. Allan opened the door to let her in.

Bjornolf took the opportunity to lean over and kiss her ear, still annoyed they were able to stay with her and not him. Wouldn't it be better for Anna and him to spend more time together before they had to play the role of husband and wife on the next mission?

He wondered if Hunter had already told her about it.

"Sleep tight, Anna," he whispered, and he saw a shiver go through her.

She smiled at him. "I will miss sleeping with you tonight," she teased, winking at him.

What the hell. He needed a good night's sleep for as much time as they'd have to sleep. He moved the bags of food to one hand, quickly slipped his arm around her back, and kissed her. He felt her tense ever so slightly. Not enough to stop him, and she didn't make any move to shove him away.

His mouth covered hers, and she kissed him back, tentatively. He licked the seam of her lips, pressed his body against hers, and showed her what she did to him, even if she wasn't going to encourage his kiss.

A small smile curved her lips, and the most devilish sparkle lit her eyes as she looped her arm around his neck, the bag of food resting on his back, and kissed him as if the world would end tonight. He growled against her mouth, feeling the way her rigid nipples pressed against his chest, her tongue sliding into his mouth, probing, tasting, teasing him.

"Ahem," Allan said. "Our food is getting cold."

Bjornolf expected Anna to pull away, and she did move her arm down from around his neck. But instead of stepping inside the cabana, she handed the bags to Allan, her gaze still on Bjornolf.

Freed of the bags, she wrapped both arms around his neck and kissed him again. "For helping us out back there." Then she pulled away and said, "Night."

She closed the door to the cabana and he heard the lock click.

He wanted to howl! He stood staring at the door for a minute, still wondering how he'd gotten so damned lucky. He'd thought it was going to be like the first date he'd had when the girl had slipped inside her parents' home before he had a chance to give *her* a kiss. Only Anna was one hot she-wolf.

He chuckled and headed next door. Next time, he'd plan the logistics better so he didn't have his hands full of anything but Anna. Finn unlocked the door for him, and Bjornolf left the food on a table while Hunter gave them the guard schedule. They ate the spicy tamales and mango-pineapple cranberry sauce—typical South American fare for the holidays—and drank the beer, and then it was time to sleep. Bjornolf took first watch.

Afterward, Hunter took Bjornolf's seat at the window while Bjornolf lay on his sleeping bag by the door. But he found sleep wouldn't come. He finally got up and looked out the window, watching the cabana where Anna was staying, unable to quit worrying about her.

Still observing the street, Hunter said to Bjornolf, "Sleep. You already had guard duty. You need to be well rested for tomorrow. The women will be all right. Hell, you couldn't have gotten much sleep last night."

Bjornolf frowned at him. "I don't need much."

"Anna is a big girl, and she will be just fine." Hunter continued to watch their surroundings.

Bjornolf smiled to himself. He saw Finn watching him from his sleeping bag, nodded to him, and retired to his own, wishing he was sleeping on Anna's bag and smelling her delightful scent instead.

———

Still feeling her lips swollen from Bjornolf's hot kiss and wishing she could have had a lot more, Anna climbed into the double bed nearest the window, thankful that both Paul and Allan insisted she take the bed—while the mother and kids slipped into the one closest to the wall of the cabana.

Anna turned to Helen Wentworth. "What are your plans for Christmas?" she asked softly so she wouldn't wake the kids.

The woman turned around on the bed and looked in Anna's direction. The room was dark, but because of Anna's wolf vision, she could make out the woman's facial features perfectly.

"The usual. Christmas party at the company. Open a present Christmas Eve with the kids. The rest of the presents Christmas Day. You know. Because Santa will have left their gifts after they've fallen asleep that night."

"Yeah," Anna said, forgetting that was the way it was supposed to be.

"You?"

Anna only wanted to ease Helen into talking about what was going on with her husband and his brother. She didn't want to get drawn into a discussion concerning *her* Christmas plans. Which meant avoiding the holidays as much as possible. "Haven't decided yet. So what do you have to eat?"

Helen took a deep breath and expelled it. "Turkey, ham, sweet potatoes… too much food, really."

"Yeah. Wreaks havoc with a diet."

Helen smiled a little.

Now for the tough part. "So what were you doing in the Amazon exactly?"

Helen didn't say anything. Paul was watching Anna, a frown furrowing his brow. Anna didn't expect the woman to know what her husband and his brother were up to, but if Helen had heard anything at all suspicious or out of place before they were taken hostage, she might have a clue.

"One of the major firms my husband owns has to do with pharmaceuticals. He had a business trip down here, and he wanted to take the family on a vacation at the same time. I would have preferred somewhere else, honestly. My idea of a pleasure trip is visiting the Swiss Alps or the Riviera. He said we'd have a fun adventure."

The mention of a business trip surprised Anna. "So he had some business meetings before you all took the trek into the jungle?"

"Yes. A couple of meetings. The cottages had a swimming pool. I took the kids swimming. We were there a day before we went on the trip into the jungle."

"Who all knew you were going to be here?"

"Everyone. It wasn't a secret." The woman closed her eyes, then opened them. Her eyes shimmered with tears.

Anna glanced at Paul. He was still watching Anna, his eyes meeting hers, waiting for her to say something that would encourage the woman to speak the truth.

Time to drop the bombshell. "I know that we weren't supposed to rescue you." Anna let that information sink in.

Helen's heartbeat kicked up another notch. She was barely breathing, as if she was afraid she'd give her rattled emotions away.

"My team knows, too," Anna added, to emphasize that they *weren't* about to be bamboozled by William Wentworth.

Helen swallowed hard, then bit her lip.

"You don't want to lose custody of your children," Anna prodded, shifting the focus so abruptly that Helen's eyes widened.

"What do you mean?" Helen asked, trying to sound innocent, her words choked by unshed tears.

More silence. Heavy pauses were important, unsettling to someone being interrogated. The time gave the person being questioned a few seconds to reflect, to sweat, to make mistakes.

"We came here to rescue you, but your husband and his brother had some *other* agenda. We were set up, Helen."

"No," Helen gasped.

Anna studied her, unable to ascertain whether the outburst meant Helen couldn't believe the team had figured that out, or that she hadn't known what was going down.

"If anyone on the team dies during this mission, it's on your and your husband's and his brother's heads."

Helen had turned into a statue, her expression horrified.

"You'd be an accessory."

"I didn't know anything about it," Helen said hastily.

She hadn't denied that her husband and his brother had set the whole situation up, Anna noted.

"Until when?" Anna asked.

Helen didn't say.

"At the hut where we stayed several days ago?" Anna asked. Had Helen heard her husband and Jeff whispering that night? "Before that? When you were first taken hostage? When did you know this was a setup?"

Helen backtracked as if she'd finally managed to get a grip on her thoughts. "They didn't set this up. We were with tour guides on a trek through the Amazon to see the kinds of plants my husband uses in his pharmaceuticals. They… the men… barged through the jungle and killed our guides."

"You weren't with a group of other tourists?"

Helen turned up her nose. "Of course not. We always have private tours when we go on vacation."

"Okay, well, we know your husband and his brother are involved in something underhanded. Just be forewarned that if we get you and your family out alive, the team isn't letting this go."

The woman's face hardened. Then she finally said, "You won't discover anything more than what really happened." But she didn't sound sure of herself. She turned her back to Anna and settled down to sleep.

"Your kids could have been shot and killed. They could have died."

Helen didn't say anything. Anna was dying to know what she was thinking, feeling. Anna let out her breath, exasperated that she couldn't get a confession out of the woman.

If Helen hadn't known, or only suspected something more was going on, she might try to speak with her husband about it sometime soon. Paul, Allan, and Anna would watch William and Helen's interactions tomorrow. One way or another, they'd eventually learn the truth.

"Maybe you don't know what this is all about," Anna said. "For your sake, I hope not."

Let Helen try to sleep on that.

Chapter 5

"FINN AND I ARE GETTING BREAKFAST FOR EVERYONE," Hunter said to Bjornolf early the next morning. "Go ahead and rouse the Wentworths. We'll be right back. Vehicles will be here momentarily."

Neither of the brothers had said a word to each other last night. Jeff and William had taken turns snoring, but the team still didn't trust them.

When Bjornolf woke them up, they both had sat up in bed looking a little dazed.

Jeff was still sitting on the bed, not making a move to leave it. "When do we get our cell phones back? I need to make a few calls. Let people know we're all right."

"When we get you to the embassy," Bjornolf said. "Safer that way." Safer for the team, he wanted to say.

Hunter and Finn were gone for some time as they picked up breakfast burritos for everyone. When they returned, the men were still dawdling at getting dressed. Bjornolf hustled them to dress faster and hurry up and eat, suspecting that their snail-paced response had something to do with them trying to slow the team down. He wolfed down his own burrito, like Hunter and Finn did theirs.

Hunter was watching out the window when his cell rang, and he said, "Okay, I see you."

As two dusty black SUVs and a blue Ford Taurus pulled up in front of the cabanas, Bjornolf stayed with the Wentworths, watching Hunter's back as he went out to speak to the drivers.

Finn's cell rang. "Got it. Be right out." He turned to Bjornolf. "I'm going out to help Hunter. You stay with the Wentworths."

Bjornolf nodded.

Finn and Paul joined Hunter outside, and they began to inspect the SUVs while the men who had brought the vehicles drove off in the car. Anna and Allan remained with the woman and the kids inside the other cabana.

Bjornolf surveyed the area around them, looking for anyone suspicious, and saw a man speaking on a phone, watching the cabanas. Bjornolf got on *his* cell to let Hunter know. "Trouble might be coming. A man appears to be relaying our movements."

"Got it," Hunter said.

They couldn't do anything until someone made a move. Even then, they had to be careful not to create an international incident. Killing what appeared to be everyday, normal Colombian citizens wasn't an option.

"Vehicles are all clear," Hunter said to Bjornolf over the phone. "Bring the Wentworths out."

"Come on. Time to roll out," Bjornolf said to the brothers.

When he and the men vacated the cabana, he glanced in Anna's direction to see her herding the mother and kids outside. He gave her a curt good-morning nod.

Most of the team members were wearing jeans and T-shirts, vests featuring embroidered university emblems, and combat boots, and they looked like tourists. Paul was wearing that gaudy hot-pink palm-tree shirt. Bjornolf shook his head before he could catch himself, but he had to admit, Paul *did* look like he was on vacation.

Bjornolf's vest was camouflage, not quite touristy, but close enough.

Bjornolf couldn't help but stare at Anna's clothes. No matter what she wore, she wasn't just one of the guys. Her black T-shirt had a scoop neckline and stretched across her pert breasts. She wore a black vest over the shirt that hid her concealed gun. She was provocatively sexy and downright lethal. What better combination could an undercover operative like him want to watch his back?

Anna looked unsettled, her eyes flitting from him to Helen Wentworth. Something must have occurred last night.

Hunter said, "Bjornolf, you, Paul, and Anna ride with the kids and Mrs. Wentworth. The rest of us will go in the first vehicle."

Anna took Hunter aside and spoke softly to him, which had Bjornolf wondering if she had uncovered some new information. As the SUVs rolled out, Anna drew close to Bjornolf and whispered in his ear, "I questioned Helen about her involvement in the hostage situation last night."

Not entirely surprised, Bjornolf nodded and listened to her account. He glanced back over the seat. Kids had disappeared from view in the backseat. He assumed they'd fallen asleep. Mom had her eyes closed, her head against the seat back. She might not have been asleep, but with the rumble of the SUV's engine and the sound of the vehicles tires on the pavement as they made their way down the road, she wouldn't be able to hear Anna's whispered words.

"I couldn't get that much out of her." Anna let out

her breath. "She's no longer speaking to me so I figure I won't be able to get anything more out of her on this trip."

"Hunter will be checking into more of the story when we return. I let him know it looked like the word was going out to watch our vehicles. I'm sure we're going to have trouble up the road."

To his surprise, Anna wrapped her arm around his and nestled her head against his shoulder. "Good," she whispered. "The job was getting boring."

He liked a woman who could be ready for a moment's danger and would consider it boring when the situation was calm. A woman after his own heart.

But this certainly wasn't boring for him. Not with her hugging his arm like that, her hair and skin smelling of peaches and cream. He wanted to pull his arm free and put it around her protectively, but he didn't want to lose the contact they already had. He was also afraid she might move away from him altogether if she thought he was trying to be friendlier than she wanted him to be.

"Are you tired?" Bjornolf asked, still wanting to re-situate her so he was more in charge.

"Yeah, I'm tired," she admitted, snuggling her face against his chest. "I served extra guard duty to make up for last night. Aren't you?"

"Wide awake now," he said, referring to the way she'd aroused him so quickly.

She chuckled softly.

He listened to the way she breathed in and out against his chest, feeling the way her soft body pressed against his, her heart beating faster. His heart's pace matched hers, and his arousal was growing harder.

Trying to get his mind off what she was doing to his

libido, he glanced out the window at the winding road, cliff on one side, jungle closing in on the pavement on the other, having seen nothing for several miles except a couple of cars passing them.

"What… what if you're right," Helen said from the backseat, where she sat with the sleeping kids.

Both Bjornolf and Anna glanced back at her. She looked like she had barely slept last night—the skin dark under her eyes, her eyes puffy.

"About what?" Anna quickly asked.

Helen pursed her lips. "About… about…" She took in a deep breath and looked out the window.

"What is it, Mrs. Wentworth?"

Helen chewed on her bottom lip. "I think… I think maybe my husband has been having an affair."

Bjornolf frowned at her. "What makes you suspect that?"

"He had one fifteen years ago. Right after we were married. He would never say who it was, and when he said he'd made a big mistake and had given her up, I believed him. But somebody's been calling the house and hanging up when I answer. Unknown caller. I just figured it was someone who had the wrong number. After what happened out here, I just can't quit considering… what if… if this whole thing had been planned from the beginning?"

"What are you thinking?" Anna asked.

"William plotted to have me and the kids murdered," Helen blurted out.

Bjornolf felt Anna tense next to him. "Do you have anything to back that up? Anything that leads you to believe he wanted to get rid of you?" Bjornolf asked.

Her gaze on his, she quickly shook her head. Yet, he suspected she wasn't telling the truth. What the hell was going on?

"Has he ever acted in any manner that made you believe he's able to accomplish such a thing?" Anna asked.

Helen swallowed hard and hesitated too long to say, which made Bjornolf wonder just what William Wentworth III was capable of.

Helen looked out the window. "No one has to have done anything like that before… to want to do it now. If… if it meant he wouldn't have to pay out any money for a divorce settlement… stuff like that happens all the time. He never wanted the kids. They were… a mistake—for him, not for me. It would have been so easy to get rid of us if you guys hadn't shown up. And who would have thought he was lying?"

"Why tell us this now?" Anna asked. "Why not last night when I asked you if you knew he had other plans?"

"I had to think about what you said. I… was in denial that William could have wanted such a thing."

The spouse was always the last one to know, Bjornolf thought. "Are you certain he's having an affair?"

"I can't think of another reason he'd want to have us killed."

"Mrs. Wentworth, is there anything you can tell us that would prove any of this? Do you feel you need police protection?" Anna asked.

Helen continued to look out the window, then wiped away a tear and then a few more. "No. I can't prove anything. You're probably right. There's nothing to it."

"But if there is…" Anna said.

"We'll be fine."

"This isn't the kind of work we normally do," Bjornolf said. Hunter *would* have his people investigating because William had put the team's lives in danger, but he couldn't let her know they'd be checking into the kidnapping behind the scenes. "If you feel threatened in any way or learn anything further about this, let Hunter know. He'll give you his number so that you can reach him at any time."

"Thanks," Helen said dismissively, her back steeled as she avoided looking at Bjornolf.

He and Anna exchanged looks. Even if William wanted Helen dead, he might not try again. Not with the team knowing something about the case. But still, who knew what lengths someone would go to when they had loads of money and wanted to keep every penny of it?

Thankfully, the man making the calls in the jungle village, who seemed to have been monitoring their moves, either hadn't been or his cohorts missed stopping the team, because several hours later, the SUVs arrived in Bogota without further incident. The team and the Wentworths quickly made their way to the American Embassy. They dropped off the family so that embassy personnel could make arrangements to secure new passports for them and flights home. A sparkling Christmas tree sitting in the entryway of the embassy reminded Bjornolf of his next mission—with Anna.

Bjornolf towered in front of Elsie and smiled. "You be good and take care of your mother and brother."

She tugged on his hand. He leaned down and she whispered in his ear, although at this close range, anyone with wolf hearing could hear. "Can you spend Christmas with us?"

He smiled and gently pulled affectionately on a length of one of her curls. "I've got to rescue another kid. You be good and Santa will bring you lots of presents."

Paul patted Jimmy on the shoulder. "It's been good knowing you, son." He pointed to Bjornolf. "Like he said, be good. Santa should be coming real soon."

The mother profusely thanked them. Bjornolf couldn't figure her out. Did she really believe her husband wanted her and the kids dead, or had it been a case of an overactive imagination? Trauma like she'd been through could cause that. The two Wentworth brothers said nothing, looking glum.

Bjornolf noted that once Helen and William had left the vehicles, William made no effort to approach her, offer her a hug, or hold her hand. Nor had he done anything to show affection toward the kids. He hadn't before he retired to the other cabana last night, either. Hell, if the kids and wife had been Bjornolf's, he would have been hugging them to pieces and not letting go.

Finished with the job, Hunter and his team took one of the SUVs, leaving the other behind for Hunter's contact to pick up at the embassy. On the way to the airport, Bjornolf and Anna related the talk they'd had with Helen.

"You know what I think?" Paul asked.

"What's that?" Anna asked.

"The wife knows more than she's letting on."

"I thought the same," Anna said. "Like she knows William is capable of murder. And how would she know that?"

Hunter shook his head. "Hell, I thought it was a

simple case of blackmail, trying to steal money from his company, avoiding taxes, tax write-off. I'll have some men look into it."

Everyone was quiet after that, tired and ready to go home. Hunter didn't tell Anna all about the new mission, but she agreed to do it, whatever it was. Bjornolf hoped she would still be willing when she heard what it entailed. When they arrived at the airport, Hunter arranged for Anna to fly home with Bjornolf and him. They still had another two hours before their flight left for the States, so they dropped into one of the VIP lounges to drink a round of beers and sat in several lounge chairs circling a coffee table.

Bjornolf wondered what Anna was thinking as they all wound down from the mission. He was glad to be here with them, finishing the job like this.

Hunter turned to Anna. "I need to talk with you about another mission. You don't have a contract of your own anytime soon *after* Christmas, right? This might take a bit of time."

She shook her head, but she looked a little wary. "Bjornolf is working with you?"

"Yeah. But this assignment's close to home."

"Oregon coast," she said.

"Yeah. You'll need some winter clothes. When we arrive in Portland, we can take you shopping. Funds will come out of my budget. You'll actually need an assortment and Tessa can help you with it."

"An assortment?" she asked, looking puzzled.

"To blend in," Hunter said.

"And Bjornolf, too," she said.

Bjornolf dipped his head in agreement.

Looking intrigued, Allan and Paul shifted their gazes from Anna to Hunter.

Seeing their interest, Hunter asked, "Sure you guys don't want to come along for the ride?"

"Still got plans," Allan said.

Bjornolf was looking forward to this new mission. He smiled at Hunter and raised his beer to him. Hunter saluted him back. They both polished off their beers, and Hunter ordered another round.

This was one Christmas Bjornolf thought he might enjoy.

Anna gave him a pointed look.

Or not.

Chapter 6

AS THEY TOOK OFF ON THE FLIGHT FOR PORTLAND, Anna wondered what lay in store for her. She was always ready for a mission, but something about this one made her wary. Hunter was usually good about giving her detailed instructions, but this time he seemed reluctant to say anything.

Sitting in the middle of a row, Anna realized she'd fallen asleep against Bjornolf's shoulder, waking when the hostess offered drinks. Anna quickly sat up and looked at him to see if he'd noticed. He smiled down at her.

His sweet expression surprised her. That one smile undid her and her whole body warmed. Hunter, who was seated next to the aisle, passed two plastic cups of water over to Anna and Bjornolf and asked for the same.

She was dying to ask Hunter what the mission was, but she knew he wouldn't be able to say until they were in a private vehicle where he could talk freely.

She drank her water and felt revived. Ready for the next mission. *Bring it on.*

"So you didn't have any plans for the holidays?" Bjornolf said to her.

She looked at Bjornolf, whose gaze shifted behind her to Hunter. She suspected he was motioning to kill the subject. Christmas was not good for her.

"Me, neither," Bjornolf said, shrugging. "I have a

brother, but I haven't seen him in years. After the bear incident, life at home was never the same."

She was surprised to hear him speak about it again. Why had he confided in her? If she'd had such an experience, she wouldn't have told anyone.

He was watching her, not looking away, waiting as before for her response. She took a deep breath. "Your brother didn't go with you that day."

"Nah. He was always the good kid. Never did anything wrong. Never wild or adventurous. Sometimes I wish I had been more like him."

"A lot of people have depended on you, Bjornolf," she said softly. "I don't think anyone would have wanted you to be anything other than who you are."

He gave her one of his elusive smiles.

Her hormone levels rose. The problem with a guy like Bjornolf was that he intrigued her. But she wasn't going to tell him that.

"So… it happened at Christmastime?" she asked.

"Yeah. Shortly before then. You can't imagine what it was like to see the pack members for Christmas and know that one family had lost their son before the big day. I couldn't deal with it. Had nightmares about it forever."

She looked away before her own bad memories swamped her. "I don't do Christmas."

"None of it?"

"Unless I'm desperate. I don't mall shop if I can avoid it. I can't even imagine going to one this time of year. I don't need to see a rotund man with a fake snow-white beard and a bunch of squirmy kids waiting beside a faux candy-cane fence, with fluffy pretend snow all over the place. Or crowds of harried shoppers buying a bunch of junk that will be given away at white-elephant parties later. Even trying to find a parking place at such a time is a nightmare," she said.

He laughed.

She smiled, glad he didn't think she was a Scrooge. She wasn't. She just didn't have any need for Christmas.

"No Christmas trees, baking sugar cookies, viewing Christmas lights, watching sappy Christmas stories?"

She folded her arms, but she couldn't help smile at him. "Nope."

"No Christmas jingles?"

"Not a single one."

"I have to admit that while we were in the jungle and I was shadowing you with jungle noises all around us, I couldn't get the words to 'Jingle Bells' out of my head."

She laughed, the notion so funny that she couldn't help herself. "And when I saw you wearing all that camo paint, looking hot and tough, I thought you were so macho."

"I was. I am."

She heard Hunter chuckle beside her and smiled.

Bjornolf hadn't felt so relaxed in a long time. He enjoyed talking with Anna. He'd never told anyone beyond his wolf pack what had happened to his friend that day. He wasn't even sure why he had confided in her. To see if she looked at him with as much loathing as his own pack had done, maybe?

But she hadn't. She'd looked like she wanted to give him a hug. Both times. Except he knew that if she had, he would have responded with a lot more interest.

He wasn't into Christmas himself, but he kind of liked the idea of celebrating it with her as her pretend husband for the holidays, if only for Nathan's sake. He couldn't imagine what it would be like for the kid to have to face the holidays without his family. Maybe he and Anna could make a difference for Nathan this time.

He thought that if he could tough out the season, she should be able to. But she wouldn't tell him what she'd experienced, and he didn't know how to deal with it if he didn't know what deep-rooted difficulty had turned her off Christmas.

When they arrived at their destination, Tessa met them, red hair windswept, green eyes sparkling, white coat parted to reveal her expanded belly, covered in a pretty, pale blue maternity sweater. She quickly greeted Anna and Bjornolf, then gave Hunter such a heartwarming embrace and prolonged kiss that Anna felt embarrassed. Maybe because Bjornolf was there grinning at the exchange.

After loading the field packs into the silver SUV, Hunter took the wheel as Tessa sat up front with him.

What a contrast over a few days: from the hot, muggy Amazon jungle to snowy Oregon. And neither Anna nor Bjornolf was dressed for the change in weather.

"Okay, now what's the deal?" Anna asked as she and Bjornolf shared the middle bench seat in the SUV.

"Before we head home, we'll stop at the mall so you can both pick up some clothes to tide you over. On the way over there, I'll tell you about the mission. You heard Bjornolf brought home one of our teens who had run away, right?"

Thinking back to the last time she was on a mission on the Oregon coast, Anna chewed her bottom lip. "Yeah." This *couldn't* be about a runaway teen.

"Nathan is working at a Christmas tree farm and he smelled decaying bodies there."

Dead bodies. That sounded more like her type of business. Anna perked up.

"Tessa texted to update me on what happened while we were in the jungle. We've had several of our pack members check out the area, with the cover that they're looking for Christmas trees. The two dead men were *lupus garous*. But so far no one has identified their scent as anyone from our pack."

"Your police officers could investigate this," she said, sounding wary.

"They *have* as much as they can, unofficially as they picked up trees for their homes. There were no bodies. No one could prove anything. Not when all we have to go by is the faint odor of decomposing *lupus garous*."

"No chance the deaths could have been due to natural causes?" she asked.

"No. They smelled blood. And there have been no reports of any injuries or deaths in any records. So it appears to be a murder case."

"So you want me to work with Bjornolf to check it out and see if we can find some leads because we're not from around here?" She glanced at Bjornolf. He was watching out the window. She swore he was avoiding looking at her. But then again, maybe that was just her suspicious nature.

"Yes, but we've got another issue to deal with here." Hunter paused.

He *never* took this long to explain a mission to her.

Now *Tessa* was looking out the window. When Tessa did that, it meant she was hiding her expression. What the hell was going on?

"So what's the other issue?" Anna asked, bracing herself.

"Nathan needs protection."

Hunter's comment was so out of line with what she was thinking that Anna blinked. *Nathan?* She cast a surreptitious look in Bjornolf's direction. He was watching her now, waiting to see her reaction.

She frowned. "Okay, so Bjornolf is going to watch out for the kid," she said, but she already knew where this was headed. Or at least she had a sneaking suspicion or she wouldn't be needed for the mission.

"Nathan wants to continue working at the farm. I feel it's not safe for him to stay with another family who don't have your combat skills while the investigation is ongoing. You and Bjornolf will serve as newlyweds and will be an uncle and aunt to Nathan. He'll live with you in the meantime. That'll give you a cover while you're doing your research."

She closed her gaping mouth.

She could deal with investigating dead bodies. Taking out murderers, turning them over to the police if they were human—that she could handle. But babysitting a teenager?

When she didn't say anything, Hunter said, "You're perfectly suited to the job. You know how I select team members for a mission. That's why we have such a high success rate."

True, Hunter *normally* selected the right people to work on a mission. Most of their jobs *were* successes.

This time he was wrong. She opened her mouth to ask where on earth he got the notion she had any mothering instincts when it came to a teen, but he quickly added,

"Listen. You know what happens when a teen wolf runs away from a pack."

Did she ever.

"You've had firsthand experience."

"Yeah, well, I didn't have much of a choice. My dad and mom were murdered. I had no pack to turn to, and I had to fend for myself." As a teen, she'd dealt with life the only way she knew how. Wild and without any guidance from anyone.

"Which is just why I need you for this job. You know how badly that can turn out for one of our kind. Nathan's parents died in a car accident last year. He's run away twice, the second time nearly getting himself killed by hunters," Hunter said.

She sympathized with the teen. Truly she did. And she wished she'd had some kind of training in that sort of thing, but she hadn't.

"I'm not good with teens... I wouldn't have a clue what to do with one," she said in the gentlest manner she could manage.

Hunter shook his head. "You're perfect, no matter what you think about your own abilities. Besides, you've been there, Anna. You understand what he's going through." Hunter cleared his throat, glanced in the rearview mirror, and speared her with his indomitable gaze. "Bjornolf has volunteered to work with you."

This was such a bad idea. Working with Bjornolf in the field was one thing. Setting up housekeeping? The guy was totally hot, virile, and sexy, and pretending to be his mate had her thinking of just how far she'd be willing to *pretend*. And if she gave into her baser instincts? The teen could be scarred for life. Bjornolf, too.

What Bjornolf *wasn't* was some highly trained teen sitter. He was a loner, not a pack man and not a family man.

"I can't believe you talked Bjornolf into taking this mission," Anna said.

"Bjornolf convinced Nathan to return to the pack. He likes the kid. Bjornolf was the first one who seemed to have any real positive impact on him," Hunter said.

"I still don't understand why you need me. Bjornolf can bond with the teen. The two will be perfect for each other. All that overabundant macho testosterone flowing—who can beat whom at whatever games the two choose to play. The situation should be perfect for the two of them," she said.

Bjornolf chuckled under his breath.

She'd almost forgotten he was sitting near her. "I could work separately from him during the investigation."

"The whole situation is part of your cover for the murder investigation you're conducting. Besides, you've done this very thing before," Hunter added.

"Just because I hooked up with one of your SEAL team members some years ago, pretending to be his mate… that was different."

"How?" Hunter waved his hand, dismissing her concern. "It's no different. Bjornolf is just as dedicated to the mission."

She felt her face, her whole body, flush with annoying heat. Paul had been the other SEAL and had been completely professional with her. Nothing physical had ever come between them. Twin beds, even. Except for pretending to be together, everything had been… separate.

Working with Bjornolf would be an entirely different story.

"If you're concerned that wolves like us have been murdered, Nathan shouldn't be involved," Anna said.

"He *is* involved. He's the one who discovered the dead bodies' scents. He's got his foot in the door already."

Hunter pulled into the crowded mall parking lot. He cut the engine and looked over his shoulder at her. "You can do it," Hunter said. "You don't give yourself enough credit."

She realized what she was feeling was total panic. "All right."

"You're undercover, Anna. Just like always. You can fake being Bjornolf's wife."

She glanced at Bjornolf.

His teeth shown in a wolfish grin. "We can practice nearly lethal sparring whenever we're not celebrating the holidays or investigating the trouble at the Christmas tree farm."

He had the most devilish gleam in his eye, making her think he could be more dangerous than any other part of the mission.

Chapter 7

WHILE TESSA HELPED ANNA PICK OUT CLOTHES AT ONE of the department stores, Hunter went with Bjornolf while he found what he needed.

Grabbing up briefs, three pair of jeans, some shirts, and sweaters, Bjornolf listened to Hunter telling him some of the details he needed to know about the cottage and other important information. But what Bjornolf really wanted to hear was why Anna was so against Christmas. As soon as he had started talking to Anna on the plane about it, Hunter had given him the universal kill order, slicing his hand across his throat.

"About Anna and Christmas…" Bjornolf needed to know because it could be important to the mission. Not only that, but he wanted to help her get through it in the worst way. If he knew what her basis was for not liking the holiday, he'd be better able to cope with her feelings.

Hunter shook his head.

"You know, though."

"I know. I learned about her during the thorough investigation I do on anyone I want to recruit to work with us."

Bjornolf seized several pair of socks. "Does Tessa know?"

"No," Hunter said a little more vehemently than Bjornolf thought necessary. The message was clear: leave Tessa out of this.

"The rest of the team?"

Hunter folded his arms and said nothing.

"What if it impacts the mission? I should know the details."

"It happened long ago. It's never affected anything she's done with the team."

"With others, then? Has she ever worked an operation like this? During Christmas?"

"Drop it, Bjornolf. If she wants to tell you about it, she will. Otherwise, it's a closed topic."

It wasn't closed for him.

Hunter paid for Bjornolf's purchases, then they went to locate the ladies. He saw Tessa looking red-faced, as if she were on the verge of shifting so she could take care of a customer she was fighting with over a sweater.

"Does Tessa have issues with Christmas, too?" Bjornolf asked, smiling.

Anna wished she'd brought her own clothes with her. Anything to avoid the worst shopping experience ever.

The only thing that made it better was that poor Tessa, who had to be horribly uncomfortable with twins due soon, was such an angel in helping Anna to choose the right clothes. Anna couldn't remember a time when she had ever shopped with another woman. She had certainly never been with one who was excited about helping her look her best.

Bjornolf had been carrying his own purchases, but he stepped in to carry several of Anna's bags. Hunter ended up having to carry a few of Anna's also. It was Tessa's fault, really.

Anna wouldn't have bought more than a couple of things, and she didn't mind washing them out for the next day. But Hunter didn't seem to mind the expense. In fact, he almost seemed in high spirits over the whole business.

Which made her suspicious.

When they arrived in the pack's territory, they picked up a rental Land Rover. Anna insisted on getting a second vehicle, though she fully intended to pay for it herself, but Hunter shook his head and used his credit card on the second car, too.

"Nathan's working at the farm until closing tonight," Hunter said.

"Okay, we'll leave our stuff at our new home. After we get settled in, we'll drop by the farm and pick out a Christmas tree," Bjornolf said.

"We don't have to get a tree." Anna grabbed the keys for her rental car and headed to the vehicle. No wonder Hunter had been so secretive about what she was to do on this mission.

"If you two need anything at all, just call me or Tessa," Hunter said, smiling just a little.

"Will do." Bjornolf followed after her. "We can use the Christmas tree for our cover. We're not going to be the only couple without a tree for the open-house tour of homes scheduled in a couple of days."

"Open house? When did this happen?"

"While you and Tessa were shopping, and I was picking out a few things, Hunter filled me in on some of the details."

"Fine," Anna said, but her tone of voice said otherwise. "You pick out a tree, and I'll search the farm for the odor of dead bodies and any other clues." She glanced back at Bjornolf as she reached her car. "What do you know about it, anyway?"

"The men hadn't been dead for long. Only a wolf could have smelled how long it had been."

"What about the owners of the tree farm? Are they wolf?"

"Human—husband, wife, teenaged daughter."

Anna rested her hand on the car door handle. "Teen... girl? Human? And Nathan is working there because?"

"He needed a job to occupy his thoughts after his parents died, to keep him from running away. He loves the forest, so the tree farm is the next best thing for now. He cuts the trees for customers, loads them up, and delivers them when they need him to. We'll pick one out. He'll bring it home tonight. It's part of our cover."

After getting directions to the beach home, Anna drove the fifteen miles up the road, then pulled into the driveway. Bjornolf parked beside her. Like the other cottages Hunter and Tessa owned, this one was nestled among pine trees, a long way from the next cottage, and sat overlooking a rocky beach below. The setting was perfect for a wolf. Plenty of woods to run in, the Pacific Ocean to swim in, and a private beach.

A wraparound porch furnished with a porch swing and four rocking chairs made the place appear homey. The house was a pretty pale blue with the shutters and trim all painted white, making it appear like a recreational retreat for a family reunion.

Right now, the cottage was dark, just like she liked it. No Christmas lights. No warm fire glowing in the fireplace. Perfect for someone undercover and not wanting to pretend to be newly married or to celebrate the holidays in any fashion. A single someone not raising a teen boy.

The wind whipped through the evergreen-needled tree branches with a whooshing noise, and the waves crashed along the rocky beach below the cliffs as sea birds squawked out at sea, the fragrance of salt, fish, and pine filling the air.

Even though the assignment wasn't what she wanted, she couldn't help but take another deep breath of the chilly air that was all woods, water, and wilderness—a wolf's ideal home.

She grabbed some of her bags while Bjornolf hauled his and the rest of hers up the stone path to the front door. She spied mistletoe hanging atop the door frame— probably Nathan's idea of a cute joke.

Bjornolf opened the door and walked in, turning to see what she was looking at. He glanced up at the mistletoe. "Since Nathan works at the Christmas tree farm, he probably got a sprig of it and placed it there in case a girl came over to the house to see him."

"No way am I dealing with teen hormones gone amok," Anna said, pushing the door shut with her hip.

Bjornolf was studying her, but she couldn't read what he was thinking. He shrugged. "It's tradition." He didn't say anything further but motioned for her to take her bags down the hallway. "Two bedrooms. Bunk beds in one. A king-sized bed in the master bedroom."

"How do you know that?"

"Last mission when I was here, Meara put me up in this cottage. While you were trying on some clothes, Hunter told me your guns are in the right-hand dresser drawer. Mine are in the left. Nathan will stay here, and you and I will share the big bed."

"You thought wrong." She attempted to smile sweetly

at him, but it was more of a wolf-got-the-prize kind of look.

His expression was a lot more wolfish—like he had every intention of changing her mind.

She glanced at the large terra-cotta and stone fireplace filling one wall, its warm golden-oak mantel begging for some kind of decoration. An ivory sofa, pale-blue-and-green plaid chairs, and an oak coffee table the same color as the mantel took center stage in front of a large-screen TV. Now why would anyone want to watch television when they had so much outdoor beauty to enjoy?

Floor-to-ceiling windows showcased the pine trees framing the ocean. She stared at it for a moment, lost in its beauty. Then she realized that Bjornolf was probably observing her, and she had a job to do. She wasn't here for fun or relaxation.

She hurried down the hallway and entered the master bedroom. The huge, king-sized bed was covered with a pale blue quilted coverlet. A white armoire and dresser, a hand-hooked blue-and-white floral rug, and paintings of blue and white flowers on the walls finished the decor. She looked at the bed again and figured she'd get lost in it, then left her bags next to the closet. She turned. He was looming in the doorway, watching her.

"You and the other male wolf can share a room and bathroom," she said matter-of-factly, as if she was in charge, ensuring he understood she was serious about this. She felt that Hunter and Bjornolf had decided all of this for her. So it was time for the she-wolf to show she had some say in the whole setup.

Looking down at her with a superior expression, he

handed her the remainder of her bags and folded his arms. "How will *anyone* believe we are mated wolves if we sleep apart?"

Bags in hand, she motioned to the hallway. "Your side." She waved at the bedroom. "My side. Now, if you don't mind, I'm going to change before we go to the farm." She paused, thinking she didn't need to explain a prior situation to him, but just in case he'd gotten the wrong impression concerning the mission when she served as Paul's wife, she wanted to set Bjornolf straight about the living arrangements. "For your information, when I pretended to be Paul's wife, we slept on separate beds."

Bjornolf grinned at her. "Good to know. That way when I see him again, I don't have to kill him."

Bjornolf thought that the more he saw of Anna, the less he'd be hooked on her. That he'd get tired of her, rub her the wrong way, and she would do the same to him. But it wasn't happening. The more he saw of her, the more he wanted to see of her.

He was determined to help Nathan deal with his parents' deaths over the holiday and look into the murders. Even though he knew that he and Anna would have plenty of trouble to deal with, he was damned glad she was here and hadn't insisted on working alone or refused to do the mission.

He headed outside to the back patio, then climbed down the wooden steps to the beach below and called Nathan on his cell. "We're here and it's a go."

"Hot damn!" Nathan said.

That's how Bjornolf felt about Anna being here. "We'll be by the tree farm shortly. She's just changing clothes, but expect a reluctant aunt."

Nathan said, "I'll make her glad she agreed to the mission."

Bjornolf had no idea what Nathan had in mind, but he was pleased the boy seemed in such high spirits. "We might need to work at it. Got to get back to her. See you in a bit."

Before he left the beach to join Anna, he called a friend. "I need you to check into something for me. An Anna Johnson. I need you to dig deep and see what you can learn about any traumatic experience she might have had around Christmastime."

"She's a wolf?" Reid asked.

"Yeah."

"How far back?"

"No clue."

"You always give me the hard cases."

"That's because I know you'll always come through for me."

"Okay, I'll look into it and see what I can find."

"Thanks, I owe you several." Bjornolf headed up the steps to the cottage, hoping his friend wouldn't find something concerning Anna that would be better left buried.

Once Bjornolf and Anna were settled in the Land Rover and on their way to the tree farm, he cast another glance her way, loving the charcoal-gray pants she wore, along with sexy, heeled, dark gray boots, a white fleece jacket, and a pale gray turtleneck. She looked so soft and cuddly in the fleece that he wanted to wrap her in his arms. He reminded himself she was also packing a weapon somewhere beneath that jacket.

To get his mind off how huggable she looked, he asked, "Have you ever been to a Christmas tree farm?"

"No." She folded her arms across her chest.

"Never?" He was unable to hide the surprise in his voice. What was it with her and Christmas?

"No."

"Then you bought them in a parking lot?"

"No." This time she sounded annoyed.

He sighed. "Artificial tree, then." He was surprised. Most wolves he knew bought a real tree. It was the one time during the year when they could bring the outdoors inside.

"No. You?" she finally asked, as if she was tired of the conversation and didn't want to speak of it any further.

He couldn't believe she'd never had a tree. "Trees in the woods to begin with. Much later… tree farms. One year we bought one from a parking lot, but it wasn't half as fun seeing the trees lying there, dying. That was the year before my parents… died."

"I'm sorry about your parents," she murmured.

"I'm sorry that yours are gone, too. That's probably why neither of us has bothered with the holidays for some time. No family to share them with."

She glanced at him. He gave her a small smile. He was attempting to dig for information. She gave him just as small a smile back. She wasn't taking the bait.

"Hunter told Nathan he wanted him off the job. *Immediately*. Nathan insisted that he stay because it was the only way he'd consider staying with the pack. He wants to feel useful. I suspect the owner's daughter has something to do with his wanting to work there as well," Bjornolf said.

Anna shook her head. "She's human. I can just imagine the mess he could get into with a human girl if he thought he was falling in love."

"Right. Hunter didn't mention it to you, but Nathan wanted you and me to protect him while we learned about the tree-farm deaths."

"Why would Nathan want me to help? I understand him wanting you—but with me, he doesn't even know me."

"He's heard of your exploits on the last mission here."

"What exploits?"

Bjornolf shrugged. "I have no idea what rumors were spread in the pack about your mission when you were protecting Meara."

"Nathan better not have heard about you tying me up in the hotel room and think he'll get to see a repeat performance firsthand." She closed her eyes and groaned. "That's probably exactly what he'd heard about."

Bjornolf chuckled. "Hell, if I have to have a mate, I want someone like you who can take anyone down."

She fought smiling at him, but she wasn't successful.

"You really never had a tree?" he asked, not liking that she'd missed out.

She shrugged and looked out the window. "First time for everything, I guess." Then she considered him again. "*Don't* expect me to do anything with it."

"You mean decorate it? Nathan and I'll set it in water and all." He hadn't thought a whole lot about what went on the tree. He hadn't helped decorate one in years.

Anna didn't say anything.

"We'll figure out something. We don't have any stored ornaments from last year like we would if this had been for real. We'll have to go shopping for some."

"Actually, you should take Tessa. If you have a fight over an ornament with another customer, Tessa will win the confrontation with a growl."

"She nearly gave Hunter heart failure. He thought she was ready to strip and shift. I'd rather go with you. You're a known commodity."

She cocked a brow at that.

"As far as the shifting part goes. The rest of you I'm still trying to figure out."

"Shopping is not my thing."

"Now there's a woman after my own heart."

———⁂———

When they arrived at the tree farm, Bjornolf drove into the parking lot next to a building all lit up with white twinkling lights and a green and red sign that said "Everton's Christmas Tree Farm and Gift Shop." Five other vehicles were parked out front, making it look like business was fairly good.

Nathan shoved the gift-shop door open and hurried out to greet them. Bjornolf swore the teen had grown another inch or two since the last time he'd seen him, his hair blond and naturally curly. He wore a heavy navy wool sweater, blue jeans, and hiking boots. Bjornolf got out of the car while Anna hesitated.

Nathan was watching Anna, looking hopeful. She pushed open her car door and Nathan rushed forward. She'd barely stood before the tall, lanky kid enveloped her in a heart-warming bear hug and said, "Aunt Anna, I'm so glad you're here."

Bjornolf closed his gaping mouth and waited for the explosion. Instead, Anna gave Nathan a hug back and whispered, "Are we being watched?"

Nathan grinned, and that wasn't faked at all. Neither was his exuberant hug, Bjornolf noted, and he wondered if the kid had a crush on Anna.

"Uncle Bjornolf." Nathan shook his hand, then took hold of Anna's hand as if he was afraid she was ready to flee. From the expression on her face, she looked like that's what she had in mind. "Let's go inside and we can have a cup of hot chocolate first. All the customers are treated to that. I made you both some ham sandwiches so you could eat out in the woods when you go to pick out our tree."

Bjornolf thought Nathan was going to hand Anna over to him, but instead he walked between them, keeping a firm grip on Anna's hand. Her cheeks actually turned a little rosy.

He smiled at Nathan, following along with the game for now. He decided the kid was sure good at playing people.

"Did you want me to cut the tree down for you? Or do you want to do it?" Nathan asked.

Anna was looking over her shoulder at the tree farm, taking a deep breath. Bjornolf was also trying to smell any odor of decay.

"Maybe you can show us where the best trees are," she suggested.

"Oh absolutely! I hope you want a big tree. They're the coolest."

Anna cleared her throat.

Bjornolf figured she wanted one that was as little as possible. Something small enough that it wouldn't take long to decorate, take up too much room, or be noticeable. "As tall as we can fit into the cottage, Nathan," he said. "We have to make sure we can put a star on top."

"Angel," Anna said, contradicting him.

Bjornolf stared at her, then smiled a little. "Yeah, an angel."

"Angel. I like that." Nathan led them inside the shop where the smell of coffee and hot chocolate, cinnamon and spices scented the air and a fire burned in a cheery fireplace. Christmas wreaths were hung up all over the gift shop.

"You can see red deer, elk, red-tailed hawks, squirrels, and tons of birds in the trees out there," Nathan said, pouring Anna a mug of hot chocolate.

Anna sipped the chocolate slowly, and Bjornolf indicated that he wanted a mug, too.

"If you'll show us where the best trees are," Bjornolf said, drinking the chocolate, then putting the empty mug down on the table, "we'll be good to go."

Nathan took Anna's hand again, and she glanced at Bjornolf. He raised his brows, not sure what to do.

Nathan seemed to miss the interaction—either that or he was ignoring the looks they'd given each other—and started giving his sales pitch as they walked outside. "We've got noble fir, Nordmann's fir, grand fir, Fraser fir, Scotch pine, white pine, and blue spruce trees either left wild or moderately trimmed."

"What do you think, honey?" Bjornolf asked, drawing close to her free side and wrapping his arm around her shoulders.

Nathan grinned at Bjornolf but did not release Anna's hand.

"It's up to the two of you," Anna said. "How many acres of trees do they have here?"

"Five hundred," Nathan said.

"How did you find… what you found?" Anna asked, being careful since customers were shopping for trees somewhere in the vicinity.

"I was looking over the tree farm with Jessica—she's the owners' daughter. We were working way out there, and we smelled a hint of something dead."

"Hunter told me she's human," Anna said.

"Yeah, but anyone can smell dead stuff when the odor is so strong. It's just that only we can tell what died if there's no sign of a body."

Anna and Bjornolf kept smelling the air, but all he could get were strong whiffs of the pine and fir trees.

"So you smelled a human…" Anna said.

"Wolf," Nathan corrected.

"And?" Anna prompted.

"I called Tessa and told her what I'd smelled—I pretended she's my aunt."

"So are any of the men who work for the owner wolves?"

Nathan shook his head.

"Any other scents in the area where you smelled the dead wolf?" she asked.

"No. You know how strongly the smell of dead things lingers. If anyone had moved the body, and someone had to have, their smells were washed away."

"How far out had you gone?" Anna asked. "I feel as though we've already walked a mile or two."

"Don't listen to her," Bjornolf said, squeezing her shoulder. "She just navigated miles of dense jungle, fought kidnappers, you name it, so this is a walk in the park for her."

Nathan grinned at her.

"Yeah, but it's a lot colder out here. Why were you so far away from the gift shop, Nathan?" she asked.

Nathan flushed a little and squared his shoulders. "I was just taking Jessica for a walk."

To make out, Bjornolf suspected. The smell of a dead body had to have put a real damper on things.

"She's human," Anna said, as if she was playing the role of Nathan's mother.

He nodded and Bjornolf thought he looked a little sad.

"Aren't there any girls in the pack you're interested in?" Bjornolf asked.

He shook his head. "Too young or too old."

"You can't turn her," Anna said. Bjornolf glanced at her and saw her fierce expression.

Nathan frowned. "Hunter turned Rourke and… and Tessa even."

"Rourke by *accident*," Anna said. "Not on purpose. With Tessa, it was a different story. Neither had family, so it wasn't an astronomical problem. But this girl has parents. You can't do it."

"Tessa had a brother and…"

Anna said, "No. Hunter's the pack leader. He had to take care of the *consequences*."

Hell, Bjornolf hadn't even realized the boy was thinking along those lines. More than ever, Bjornolf knew Anna was perfect for this job.

For a long time, they walked in silence. Bjornolf

knew Anna was right. He knew too that Nathan understood, even if he didn't want to accept it. The knowledge that Hunter had changed three humans would muddy the water a bit as to what was acceptable *lupus garou* behavior. Some turned humans ended up being a real liability to a pack. Hunter was more than fortunate everything had worked out all right—for the most part.

"If you are calling Hunter your uncle, why didn't you stay with him and Tessa?" Anna asked.

"Are you kidding?" Nathan said, his voice full of disbelief. "They're newlyweds!"

Not exactly, though they still acted like it. But they were about to be new parents.

Anna shot back, "Bjornolf and I are, too! And lots newer, like as of today, I might add!"

Nathan and Bjornolf stared at her for a moment, then Nathan grinned and Bjornolf couldn't help but smile, really wanting to get into this role.

"Yeah, well, I'll try to give you two as much privacy as I can," Nathan said, still smirking.

Anna rolled her eyes.

"Besides, I couldn't stay with our pack leaders. They'd watch every move I made."

"*We'll* watch every move you make," Anna promised, as if that was payback for his helping to set up this arrangement in the first place.

She suddenly stopped and sniffed the air. "Was this where you'd smelled one of the dead wolves?"

Chapter 8

"This was where the body had to have been." Nathan waved his hands in the general area between two rows of Douglas firs as he explained to Bjornolf and Anna what he'd found. "The odor of decay was here. As soon as I smelled it, I got hold of Tessa and she contacted one of our police officers in the pack. He and several of our pack members came by to purchase trees for Christmas. Nobody recognized the scents."

Still firmly holding Anna's hand, he headed in another direction. "Over here is where I smelled a second body." Nathan pointed to an area between rows of Colorado spruce. "Right in here."

Bjornolf frowned, recognizing the odor and not liking this scenario. "It smells like Montoya Sanchez, a SEAL I knew about six or seven years ago."

"A SEAL?" Anna asked, looking up at him with inquisitive, worried eyes. "What about the other man?"

Bjornolf shook his head. "I don't recognize the other."

"How well did you know him?" Anna asked.

"About as well as I do anyone I'm serving with during only one mission. He was a good guy. Family man. Kept talking about housebreaking a puppy. I can't imagine how he could have gotten himself killed here."

"I'm sorry," Anna said with real regret.

"A SEAL." Nathan shuddered. "Damn, if someone could kill one of *you* guys…" He glanced back in the direction of the gift shop, though they couldn't see it for the trees. "I should be heading back to work. Any of these trees look all right for our house?"

"Do you have a favorite?" Anna asked.

Nathan's amber eyes lit up. "Yeah." He hurried them back in the direction of the gift shop.

Bjornolf admired Anna for thinking so quickly on her feet. He would never have thought to ask the boy if he'd already made a selection.

"This one," Nathan said, pointing with his free hand. "A blue spruce. Isn't it beautiful? I kept hoping no one would buy it—not that there aren't a million trees out here. But all its sides are perfect, and we don't have to hide a bad spot against a wall. It's still short enough to fit in the house, isn't it?" Nathan looked at Bjornolf for his take on it.

He opened his mouth to agree but Anna said, "Sold. Deliver it after you get off work, and tomorrow the two of you can decorate it."

Nathan looked at Bjornolf.

"She never had a Christmas tree before," he explained. "She doesn't know the first thing about decorating one."

"We'll show you how," Nathan said undeterred, tugging at her hand. "It's easy. I'm off tomorrow until later in the afternoon. We can go to the store and buy decorations."

"Is Hunter paying expenses?" she asked Bjornolf.

"*I'm* paying for it," Bjornolf said. "This is my first Christmas in years, and I'm going to enjoy it."

Anna looked like she wasn't sure if he was teasing or telling the truth. Then she sighed and looked as though she was finally willing to play along. A little.

After Bjornolf paid for the tree, Nathan slapped his forehead. "I forgot to give you the ham sandwiches to eat while you were walking through the woods."

"That's okay," Bjornolf said. "You bring them home and we'll have them for dinner tonight, if you'd like."

Nathan glanced at Anna, wondering if she was going to fix home-cooked meals the way his mother used to. Anna was looking back in the direction of the trees where they had smelled the scent of the dead men.

"See you later," Nathan said and gave Anna a hug before he headed back into the gift shop.

"It's going to snow," Anna said as she and Bjornolf got into the Land Rover, and he drove out of the parking lot.

"Lightly, maybe an inch or two." He glanced over at her, meaning to ask if she had gotten anything out of the situation with the dead bodies, but she had closed her eyes, her head leaning against the window.

Ten miles down the road, he pulled into the drive-through of a fast-food restaurant, ordered burgers, fries, and bottled waters, and they continued on their way. Anna hadn't stirred.

Light snow was falling by the time Bjornolf drove into the driveway of the cottage, and everything was dusted in white powder. Anna had napped all the way back. He guessed she hadn't had that much time to recuperate from their jungle mission.

"Are you hungry?" Bjornolf asked as he parked the Land Rover.

She lifted her head and sniffed the air in the car. "You picked up hamburgers and french fries?" She sat up a little taller.

"And bottled water. Before we arrived, Hunter said Tessa and Meara bought some groceries for us and stocked the pantry and fridge. For now, I figured we'd just grab some fast food so we wouldn't have to wait to cook a meal."

"Sounds good." She seized the bag of food.

Bjornolf got the front door. "Nathan's hurting, you know."

"I know." She sighed, then changed the subject as Bjornolf closed the front door. "Nathan wasn't trying to make you jealous, by the way."

Bjornolf followed her into the kitchen and pulled blue-and-white floral plates out of the cupboard. "You mean when he held your hand and wouldn't let go?"

She placed the foil-wrapped hamburgers on the plates. "Yeah. You didn't need to put your arm around me to show ownership."

He dumped the fries onto the plates, pulled a bottle of ketchup out of the fridge, and poured some on his plate. After taking a seat, he dipped a fry into the ketchup and met her darkened gaze. "He was afraid you wanted to run away. He was trying to make you feel needed."

She shook her head. "*He* was feeling needy. You didn't have to act so possessive."

He laughed. "Part of the honeymoon, Anna. You didn't think I was going to let our nephew hold your hand while I stood in the wings watching, did you?"

She shook her head as if she couldn't believe he'd say that. She took a bite of her hamburger and made the sexiest sound. "Hmm, you know just how I like it."

"I know a lot about you," he said with a smirk. In

fact, he knew practically everything about her. Well, nearly everything.

"Really? You know which movies that I love to watch?"

"Yeah, when you were sleeping on the plane, I asked if Hunter knew. Adventure, historical, epic, lots of fighting, swords, martial arts, that sort of thing."

"Did you get us some movies?"

"I asked if he'd drop a few by the cottage. He was going to have someone do that when they filled up the fridge and pantry. We'll need to get ready for the pack open house."

She didn't say anything, her expression saying she stubbornly resisted the idea.

"Anna, Nathan's putting on a show, pretending that everything's all right. That he's happy to take part in Christmas. That everything's normal. But it isn't. I imagine he'd like nothing better than to run away."

Having finished her meal, Anna stood up, trying to look as though what he said didn't bother her. But his words hit her like an iron fist to the jaw. "I know. All right, Bjornolf? I've been there, okay?"

Bjornolf stared at her, saw the same wounded look in her eyes that he'd seen in Nathan's, and felt horrible for not recognizing she had some real issues. He skirted the kitchen table, pulled her into his arms, and kissed her like he had at the jungle-village cabana. Just like he knew she had wanted him to.

At first she stiffened at his brushing kiss, his mouth sweeping gently over hers, willing her to give in, just a bit.

Enough, her body language said as she started to pull away.

"No," he whispered against her lips. "Let me in, Anna. Don't push me away."

Her eyes were bright with tears as she looked up at him, confused and unsure.

"Hell," he said and clasped her to his chest, holding her tight. He wanted to destroy every chink in her armor and give her whatever solace she needed. He tried kissing her again, and this time she lifted her face to his, cupped the back of his head, and pulled him closer.

That about undid him—made him forget who he was, who she was, what they were doing here.

Their tongues tangled as he pressed his body against hers, his cock instantly springing to life. He pressed his knee between her legs, wanting to get inside her, to feel every inch of her against his body. She slid her hand up his shirt and ran her warm fingers over his abdomen. "Hard," she whispered.

Hell, yeah. All over.

That's when he heard the truck pull into the drive, and before he could disengage from Anna, the front door opened. Wishing they could have prolonged the intimacy, he fought scowling at the intrusion.

Anna jumped away from him. She wiped tears away and quickly said, "I've got to unpack." Then she hurried off down the hall.

Nathan stood in the doorway, shifted his shocked gaze from Anna to Bjornolf, then glowered at him. "Why was she crying?"

After setting up the tree and settling on the couch to watch one of the movies, Nathan set the plate of ham sandwiches on the coffee table. He had already found Bjornolf's bags in the guest room, so he knew something was up between Bjornolf and Anna.

Bjornolf had started a movie, but Nathan still wanted to know what was going on. "I thought you said you were both going to be sharing the master bedroom."

"I changed my mind for the time being."

Nathan lifted his can of soda off the table. "You mean *she* changed your mind for you."

The kid was too bright for his own good.

"Did she fight you for it?" Nathan asked, sitting a little taller.

Unable to contain his amusement, Bjornolf shook his head. "Some battles are not worth fighting… right away."

"Wait until I'm around when you decide to change her mind. You said you'd teach me everything you knew about fighting."

That wasn't exactly what Bjornolf had in mind.

While Nathan ate both of the sandwiches, Bjornolf drank a cup of coffee.

"Anna is… kind of upset," Bjornolf said quietly.

"Yeah," Nathan said, folding his arms over his chest. "I could see that much."

Bjornolf let out his breath in exasperation. "Not because of me."

Nathan turned his attention to focus on Bjornolf and waited to hear the truth of the matter.

"Christmas isn't her thing."

Nathan's eyes widened. "Who doesn't like Christmas?"

Bjornolf shrugged. "Anna, apparently. Maybe something happened when she was a kid. I don't know. Sometimes adults lose the spirit of Christmas."

"Anna's alone," Nathan said, finally getting the picture. "So she never celebrates Christmas." He frowned at Bjornolf. "What about you?"

"Sometimes. When you get older, sometimes it's just not as important as it used to be. If there's no one to share it with…" He shrugged.

Nathan was frowning at him again. "I'm not going to give it up, ever."

Bjornolf managed a smile. "Good."

Nathan ran his hand over his pant leg. "We're still going to have Christmas, aren't we? I don't want Anna to be sad. Can we… help her somehow?"

"We can't fix others." As much as Bjornolf would like to make Anna feel wonderful, he knew he couldn't. She would have to reach within herself to find that which would make her whole. "But I sure as hell want to do anything I can to make her feel better about the holidays."

Nathan looked skeptical. "Then don't kiss her anymore. You made her cry." He turned his attention back to the movie, and that was the end of the discussion.

———

Anna tried, but was damned if she couldn't sleep. She flopped this way, then that. She'd napped too much during the day. She tried not to think of the kiss. Or how she'd encouraged it. Or how she would have liked to take it further if Nathan hadn't arrived when he did.

The fighting in the movie had been so loud that she couldn't hear what Nathan and Bjornolf were saying, but she guessed it had been about her.

Nathan had looked so shocked to see her crying that she was certain he would be angry with Bjornolf for making her cry. Yet he hadn't. She wasn't even sure why she was in such a funk.

After the guys went to bed and the house had been quiet for a while, she got up, slipped on a pair of black jeans with same color turtleneck, socks, and boots. She grabbed her weapons belt, a black ski hat, and a jacket.

She intended to check out the Christmas tree farm while everyone was gone, and she wanted to be alone, with no distraction in the form of one sexy SEAL.

While walking quietly toward the living room, she saw the blue spruce. It was beautiful, even without decorations, making her feel as though some of the woods had made a home here. She breathed in the smell of it and couldn't help but love it. She felt bad that she might ruin Nathan's Christmas after he had just lost his parents, so she dropped her gear on the couch and walked into the kitchen. After rummaging through the cabinets, she found packages of microwaveable popcorn. She returned to the bedroom where she found a sewing kit, and with it in hand, she walked back to the kitchen.

After popping two bags—no way could she smell the mouthwatering popcorn aroma and not eat some of it—she sat down on the couch. She began stringing the popcorn together, inserting the needle and thread in the center of one kernel and then the next. When she'd finished the last of the popcorn in the bowl, she tied off the string, got up from the couch, and went over to the tree. She began to wind the garland around the fragrant branches. Once she was done, she stepped back and admired her handiwork. Perfect, she thought, a smile curving her mouth. Her part in decorating the tree. It hadn't even killed her.

Now it was time to do some murder investigation work and put aside all thoughts of the holidays.

Gun tucked in her holster, she closed the door behind her, locked it, then hurried to her vehicle, hoping Bjornolf wouldn't hear her leave. He'd follow her in short order if he did.

Like she often did on the job, she wanted to concentrate on this part of the work *alone*.

Chapter 9

BJORNOLF DIDN'T INTEND TO INTRUDE ON WHATEVER Anna was up to. As long as she stayed in the cottage, he was satisfied with listening to her move about the house. He thought of pretending to need something to drink and seeing what she was up to. It was killing him not knowing. Besides, he still wanted to settle things between them.

He was wearing out the plush beige carpeting with his pacing. Then, making a decision, he threw on his clothes and headed for the bedroom door. That's when he heard the front door open and click shut. *Hell*.

She had to be on her way back to the tree farm to investigate the crime scene, but she wasn't doing it alone. No matter how often she might have done such a thing in the past, they were together in this. A team. She'd quickly learn that one way or another.

He was hurrying straight for the front door, when he spied a bowl of half-eaten popcorn and another that was empty. Then the tree caught his attention. His jaw dropped. Well, he'd be damned. A warm glow worked its way through his chest as he stared at the sight of the festive-looking country popcorn garland wrapped around the tree. The work had taken her time, energy, and patience, and yet she had done it.

Breaking away from his surprise and the admiration he had for her all over again, he hurried to the Land

Rover and took off for the Christmas tree farm, hoping he could catch up to her before she began working alone.

Bjornolf still hadn't caught up to Anna when he eased up on the gas and began to analyze the situation further. She was a professional. He knew from studying her profile that she did a good job investigating situations alone. Just as she did a good job working with a team. If she felt the need to investigate this on her own for now, he'd let her.

Except she wouldn't exactly be on her own. He had every intention of watching her back like the ghost he could be.

Anna thought Bjornolf was following her, but then figured she had assumed wrong when he never caught up to her. She was almost disappointed, but there was no way she would have woken him to ask him go with her, just because *she* couldn't sleep.

Driving the speed limit while on a mission was important as she did not want to get stopped for a ticket. A cop would remember her if something went wrong during her investigation. She hadn't seen any headlights behind her for the past half hour. Nathan and Bjornolf were probably snoring in happy unison.

Patches of ice made her tires slip a little as ghostly snowflakes drifted from the heavens in the dark night. By the time she arrived at the tree farm, the light snow had covered everything in a sheet of pristine white. She drove past the gift shop and parking lot. The shop's sign was still lit and a few security lights illuminated the ghostly mist of snow in the chilly air, but the store windows were dark.

She parked off to the side of the road alongside a chain link fence. In the dark, she supposed she was safe enough from discovery. She climbed over the fence, hating the way the metal rattled. To her wolf's hearing it sounded as loud as an ear-piercing alarm signal.

With barely a sound, she landed on the other side in a soft snowdrift, then headed toward the area where she had smelled the dead bodies. Half an hour later, as she was poking around the pine-needle-covered ground with the toe of her boot, using a small flashlight to aid her, she discovered something. She swept away the light layer of snow and found a small piece of half-buried metal. When she tugged, it pulled free of the matted pine needles, and she found it was attached to a long chain. *Dog tags*.

She gave a little involuntary shudder. Had the other man been a SEAL, too? Or just another former service member?

Her heart quickening, she shoved the dog tags in her pocket, anxious to get this information back to Bjornolf and Hunter. She wondered why the dog tags had been left there. They wouldn't have fallen off the man. The killer wouldn't have tugged them off and discarded them, leaving evidence behind. The pine needles wouldn't have buried the tags from seasons past since the deaths had occurred very recently unless the mulch was applied lately. In the dead of winter? She didn't think so.

Had the man struggled with his murderer here? Was he able to remove his dog tags and bury them with the hope that someone might discover the truth?

She would discover the truth. The murderer would pay dearly for the wolves' deaths.

The crunch of footsteps coming toward her instantly caught her attention. Her skin prickled with awareness and her body chilled even further.

She turned off her flashlight and quickly headed down a lane of trees. She moved away from the footsteps, her own steps light and soundless, like a wolf's.

Without warning, a stout, black-haired man stepped in front of her, towering over her, his fleshy fat cheeks red. Her heart did a flip. Flashlight in his gloved hand, he pointed the beam of light into her eyes.

Blinded, she squinted, her heart still racing.

"Stealing a tree in the middle of the night, are we?" he asked gruffly. He was wearing gray pants, a brown coat smudged with dirt, muddy work boots, and a black knit ski cap. He looked like someone who might work on the farm.

Her spine tingling from surprise, she felt a lot more rattled than she liked. She took a deep breath to smell him and couldn't detect that he was a wolf. Once he lowered the flashlight and gave her a really good look, she saw his eyes were blue. Not a wolf then.

She might look like a cat burglar ready to steal the family jewels. A tree thief? Hardly.

"Stealing a tree? No. Nathan, my nephew who works here, called and said he'd lost his watch out here. He said he was getting ready for bed when he realized it," Anna smoothly said. "I told him I'd come and help him look for it. You know his parents died last year, right? His father gave it to him on his sixteenth birthday and he's really torn up about it."

"So where is he?" The man didn't take his cold eyes off her.

"I don't know. I couldn't find him, so I thought I'd
hunt for it myself since I was here already." She looked
down at the ground again as if she might still be searching for the watch. "He said he lost it out here where
he'd taken us to look at the trees earlier today." She
flipped on her flashlight and waved it around the area.
"He dropped off the tree we bought at our house. We
weren't home at the time. Then he came back to look
for it, and when he couldn't find it, he called me to help.
I thought he'd still be here."

"In the dark." It wasn't a question.

"We were afraid one of your sleds would run over it
during the day and ruin it. And it's supposed to snow
more. It's not waterproof. I figured I'd check since I was
here already, and I might just see it. You know how kids
are. They can never find anything on their own."

The man narrowed his beady eyes at her. "I've never
seen him wearing a watch."

He was bluffing, watching her for a reaction. How
would he know whether Nathan wore a watch or not?
Not that Nathan did. *Lupus garous* didn't wear watches
or other jewelry because it was too much of a nuisance
if they had to shift quickly.

"Why are you out here alone tonight?" he asked, taking a step closer.

Her heartbeat sped up. If he grabbed her, he'd find
himself flat on his back, but she didn't want to get physical with him and make him even more suspicious.

Footsteps from behind her sounded. Expecting another guard on duty protecting Christmas trees, Anna
turned and saw Bjornolf headed in her direction, his
steely dark eyes focused on the man questioning her.

He looked like he was still on the jungle mission, ready to protect her and kill any man who threatened her.

She took a breath in relief. In the jungle, they took down the enemies. No problem. In a case like this, the man was harmless. She couldn't do anything but try to provide a cover for herself and not look like *she* was a thief.

The man took a couple of steps back. A bit of warmth seeped into her bones as Bjornolf drew nearer.

"My wife isn't alone." Bjornolf slipped his left arm around Anna's shoulders and she leaned into him a little, savoring his protectiveness and warmth. He extended his right hand to the man for a handshake in greeting. "Bjorn and Anna Jorgenson."

The man hesitated, looking as though he doubted that they were just Nathan's relatives. He didn't take Bjornolf's hand but instead said, "Lemme see some ID."

Bjornolf released Anna and dragged out a wallet, then pulled out a driver's license and gave it to him. The man flashed the light over it, then nodded and handed it back. "Yours?" he said to Anna.

"Former cop?" she asked, caustically. She knew he wasn't, knew he was taking the proper precautions after having come across trespassers in the dark, but she didn't have to like it. She didn't have any ID that showed she was Anna "Jorgenson," either.

She passed over her driver's license, waited for the man to say something, and was prepared with an answer about her last name being different from Bjornolf's.

He cocked a brow, looked at her, and said, "Says here your name is Anna Johnson."

Bjornolf grinned. "We're newlyweds." He gave Anna

a squeeze, either for show or reminding her that she was supposed to remember the role she was playing.

She instantly said, "I'm not changing my name." She smiled up at Bjornolf. "Woman's prerogative. It's too much of a hassle. What if the honeymoon doesn't last?"

"Oh, *honey*, it'll last." Bjornolf gave her a look like he would show her just how much so, once they were back at the cottage. She swore he wasn't playacting, either. And she had to admit his comment made her wish he wasn't just playing a role. "Come on. I know Nathan's upset about this, but we can return at daybreak and see if we can locate it then."

She gave him another smile that said, "Right." Then she looked at the man. "Your name is…?"

"Everton. The owner. Tell Nathan if he wants to make arrangements to have his kinfolk come look for something of his in the middle of the night to get permission first."

"So… can we have permission?" she asked, trying to sound sweet and innocent.

"No. Come back in the morning when we're *open*."

She looked up at Bjornolf, slipped her arm around his waist, and said, "Guess we ought to go home to bed, then."

"Exactly what I had in mind, honey."

They turned to leave and had taken a couple of steps, when the man said in a surly, commanding way, "Wait!"

Bjornolf stiffened beside her, his eyes narrowing as they faced the man.

"I didn't hear you calling Nathan's name. If you were looking for him," Everton said.

"She was. She has a soft voice," Bjornolf growled as

if he didn't like that the man was questioning Anna's story, and if they needed to take this to a physical level, he was game.

Anna loved him for it. She expected the man to ask why he didn't hear Bjornolf calling out Nathan's name and she stiffened a little.

"Anything else?" Bjornolf asked the question as though the man had better not pose another one.

Everton slid his gaze from Bjornolf to Anna, his expression irritated. He looked like he didn't believe them. "Nah. Just don't come back here again when we're closed."

Anna was dying to ask Everton why *he* was wandering around the property in the middle of the night. Bjornolf quickly said good night and escorted her off the farm.

She had to admit Bjornolf was good for a rescue. She was also glad they had their own vehicles at the Christmas tree farm. That way she didn't have to hear his guff the whole drive back to the cottage about why she shouldn't have gone alone tonight.

What she didn't expect was for him to escort her through the parking lot, walk her all the way to her car, pull her into a hard embrace, and kiss her like they were newlyweds. Long and penetrating, hard and gentle, and every kind of delicious kiss in between. He finally released her and dragged in a breath of cold air. His heart was pounding furiously, his breath short, puffs of white vapor floating between them.

The kiss was nothing short of miraculous, full of feeling, and she wondered if he'd been worried that a bad guy might have taken her out. Any team member wouldn't want to lose their partner, but his concern for her seemed like it was much more than that.

"Damn but you taste good, Anna," he said softly, his eyes dark with feral need as he rubbed her arms. The heat sizzled through her blood beneath the jacket and sweater she wore.

"He better be watching us," Anna warned in a whisper, but she didn't mean it. She loved the way he kissed.

Bjornolf gave her a devilish smile and a quick kiss on her cold nose, his mouth hot against her skin. "Follow you home, honey." He pulled her door open, and once she climbed in, he closed it for her. She waited for him to enter his own vehicle and start the engine before she drove off.

She hadn't needed to wait for him, but something in the back of her mind nagged at her. Bjornolf had come to watch over her. What if someone tried to take him out and the only one who could save him was her? Not that they were in a jungle environment fighting drug-running terrorists here. But who knew what they were really up against?

Her lingering there had nothing to do with his kissing her, or pretending to be newlyweds if Everton was watching. Her duty as part of this new team was making sure Bjornolf had backup if he needed it, she told herself.

As his Land Rover followed her, she thought of the night she'd led him to the hotel where he'd finally tracked her down and gotten the best of her. She couldn't help but look in her rearview mirror, watching his headlights and feeling a sense of déjà vu. Except that time, she'd thought he was an assassin. This time, he was on her team. Only it seemed as if he was looking for more than a temporary arrangement.

Yeah right, she scoffed. How much of that was her interest in him rather than his interest in her, and she was projecting what she wanted rather than what he truly desired?

Anna assumed that they'd talk as soon as she parked and Bjornolf followed her into the house. What she didn't expect was that she'd wait for him to walk her to the door, even allowing him to take her hand as if they were wolves on a date.

What was wrong with her? With him?

They didn't need to pretend to anyone here.

Bjornolf didn't say a word, just held her hand possessively and escorted her to the porch. Then he unlocked the door and closed and locked it behind them.

"Did you want some cocoa?" he asked, as if he didn't want the night to end.

She shook her head. "You have to go with Nathan to buy Christmas ornaments tomorrow."

She saw a flash of disappointment cross his face. She was surprised he hadn't said a word about her investigating the crime scene on her own.

She remembered the dog tags in her pocket and pulled them out. "I found these right before Everton came across me." She glanced down at them and read the inscription. "Thomas Cremer. The other dead man, maybe?"

Bjornolf wasn't looking at the dog tags when his gaze met hers. He'd been observing her face with a mixture of respect and astonishment. "Now I know why Hunter recommended you for this job."

She gave Bjornolf a slight smile, appreciating his comment more than a little.

He took the tags and examined them, sniffing them. "The second dead body we smelled."

"Yes," she said solemnly. "The man had also been in the service."

"I'll let Hunter know in the morning. Guess we ought to turn in." He looked hopeful that she'd say he could join her in her bed.

She gave him a quick smile and headed down the hall before she changed her mind. "'Night, Bjorn." As a humorous touch, she'd called him by the shortened version of his name that he'd given the man at the tree farm.

"Night, honey," Bjornolf said as if they truly were newlyweds and he'd be joining her in bed shortly.

She looked back over her shoulder and saw the wicked gleam in his eye, a challenge that said he wasn't leaving the situation as it was for long. She gave him a sassy smile back, daring him to make her change her mind.

She walked into the room and was about to close the master bedroom door when she heard Bjornolf curse as he stalked out of the guest room. He began yanking off his shirt as he headed for the back door.

"What's wrong?" she asked, framed by the doorway into the master bedroom.

"Nathan's gone."

Chapter 10

Nathan had left the house as a wolf and headed through the forest. For wolves like Bjornolf and Anna, Nathan's trail wasn't hard to find. He left paw prints in the half-frozen snow, and scruffs of his black fur snagged on tree branches. He wasn't trying to hide his trail, which made Bjornolf suspect that the boy wanted to be followed.

He hoped that Nathan hadn't gotten some clue concerning the murders and charged off to investigate on his own.

Bjornolf should have wanted Anna to stay back at the house so she would be safe from hunters and so he could work alone like he normally did. But he found he didn't want to work alone and realized he was making up a hell of a lot more reasons why she should be with him. And that was a real change for him. He'd never needed anyone.

Having never seen Anna in her wolf form, Bjornolf took his fill of her as they paused to catch the trail again. Even as a wolf, she was petite, almost like a red wolf. Her face was more beige than gray, with a little white under her chin and a golden color framing her face. A small amount of gray dusted her cheeks, giving her a distinctive appearance.

Her ears were perked, listening for any sounds as the breeze stirred the pine branches. Peering into the woods, her amber eyes were soft with concern, but her tail was straight out behind her in alpha mode. Her slight body tense, she was ready to spring into action as soon as she caught Nathan's scent again.

She suddenly lifted her chin and howled for Nathan. Bjornolf knew she was howling for the boy, but he envisioned her howling for him—calling him to her in the snowy woods.

Bjornolf also let loose a howl. His howl was deeper, not as musical as Anna's, a command to come home. Their howls were a way to communicate with other wolves, to declare this was their territory, to gather the pack, or to locate a mate.

They waited for a moment, but when Nathan didn't respond, Anna dashed off and Bjornolf raced after her. Glad to be running with Anna, panting, zigzagging across the snow-powdered earth, he tried to pick up Nathan's scent as they moved farther away from the cottage.

Where was the kid off to? Bjornolf thought Nathan might have gone to the Christmas tree farm, but he hadn't run in that direction.

Worse, it was one in the morning when they started out after him, and they'd been trailing him for two hours. It would be dark for several more hours, but if Nathan continued to run, eventually it would be too late for any of them to return home before it was light out. Anna and Bjornolf would end up having to hide in the surrounding woods or risk the long trek back home in daylight in their wolf skins.

They took a drink at an icy cold stream and then crossed it. The mossy rocks were topped with an inch of snow, and the bare-branch deciduous trees and ever-greens were also coated with snow.

Bjornolf glanced at Anna. She was looking in the direction of Portland, her ears twitching back and forth.

A red wolf pack resided in Portland and the surrounding territory, led by a wolf named Leidolf. The city was still a long way off and Bjornolf was certain Hunter had never talked to Leidolf about SEAL business, the team, Anna, or himself. Leidolf would consider them encroaching on his pack's territory and wouldn't like it.

The day was gray, with clouds covering every square inch of sky. Dawn was creeping over the landscape, silent, exposing them to danger—hunter danger.

It had been light out for a couple of hours when they reached the relative safety of Forest Park, over five thousand acres of woods within Portland, stretching for more than eight miles over hilly terrain overlooking the Willamette River. Nathan's scent was getting stronger. Bjornolf smelled the odors from the nearby zoo butted up against the park, heard a lion roar, and wondered if wolves that weren't shifters were also penned up in there. Anna sniffed the air, her posture alert and eager as she knew they were getting close to their quarry.

The park was already open. Any number of people could be running, hiking, biking, or horseback riding through here so they weren't without risk.

Anna turned her head, listened for a moment, and then took off running. She was determined to locate the teen before he came to harm, which meant a lot to Bjornolf. As much as she'd intimated that she wasn't into kid stuff, she wasn't letting this go.

He took off after her, not liking the path they were

moving on… toward a group of stately homes backed
up against the park, mostly hidden by huge evergreens.
One of them in particular made him frown and sniff
the ground.

The scent of wolves was heavy here along the entrance to the path. Male, female, young, old. Bjornolf
suspected it was a safe house for wolves who belonged
to the pack but lived in the outlying areas and were visiting Portland for the day.

Anna loped down the winding path through the woods,
eagerly sniffing the ground. Nathan had been here.

When Bjornolf followed her, he found her standing at
a beige stone wall topped with snow. She was studying
the wolf door in the redwood gate, calculating the risk
of entering another wolf's backyard. He was going to
nudge her face, to let her know that he wanted her to stay
here while he investigated the backyard and she watched
for Nathan.

But she had already made up her mind.

Nearly making his heart stop, she dashed for the gate,
pushed the wolf door open with her nose, then barged in.

Bjornolf shoved his nose through the door, raced
around a wall of evergreens, and found Anna stopped
at a patio filled with ornate wrought-iron café tables
and chairs. The backyard featured a copper statue of
two wolves standing together and a fountain displaying
a group of wolves frolicking at the base while playing
with butterflies in flight. The scents in the yard further
indicated that this was a wolf-owned house.

Icicle Christmas lights dangled from the gutters
around the house, while a Douglas fir tree inside
filled the picture window, showcasing mostly red,

green, and white Christmas ornaments and colorful sparkling lights.

He smelled Nathan's scent and a she-wolf's scent—both had been here recently. But there was no sign of either of them, unless they were in the house…

Bjornolf spied an auburn-haired man standing at a window, his eyes growing large when he saw Bjornolf join Anna. The man looked angry and was speaking into a cell phone as he stared at them. He was tall and wearing a midnight blue T-shirt, his muscular arms showing that he'd have some power behind his moves. Bjornolf was sizing up his competition, not wanting to fight him, but if it meant protecting Nathan, he would.

The man's amber eyes darkened. His gaze shifted from Anna, discounting her as a threat (a foolish thing to do in Bjornolf's estimation), and focused again on Bjornolf.

A teenage girl joined him at the kitchen window, her long curly hair just as auburn, her eyes widening when she saw the two wolves. She quickly spoke to the man. Bjornolf didn't think that Nathan was in the house, or the man would have greeted them already.

Was he calling Leidolf to warn him that gray wolves were invading their territory?

Chapter 11

LEIDOLF KISSED A SLEEPING CASSIE ON THE SHOULDER, her copper curls spread out over her naked ivory skin. She'd just fallen asleep after having nursed their twin boys a few minutes ago, and he didn't want to disturb her. His second-in-command, Elgin, was already gathering men from their ranch jobs. A gray teen wolf was spotted in Forest Park, having kidnapped a teen she-wolf from her house. There would be hell to pay for it if the girl's father had any hand in it.

Leidolf only hoped he could get Carver to stand down until he got there and determined what was going on. He was grateful the father had sense enough to call him before he took action, which had to mean something else had happened that stopped Carver from going totally ballistic.

Leidolf glanced at his sons sleeping in the bassinet near the bed, the white eyelet ruffles reaching the carpeted floor. Up above, a white lace-trimmed canopy decorated in bows of red and green plaid etched with sparkling gold thread had been added for the holidays. His sons' hands were curled into fists, their mouths making sucking motions while their backs were touching as if they were still in the womb, listening to each other's heart beating, feeling the warmth of the other. He wondered how he could have ever gotten so lucky.

Leidolf had joined his men outside when he got the

second warning call from Carver. A couple of adult gray wolves had showed up in Carver's backyard, undoubtedly searching for their wayward teen.

"More bad news," Leidolf alerted his men as they pulled on coats and hats. "Not only has a gray teen wolf taken Carver's daughter, Sarah, from her home, but now it appears the parents have just arrived in their wolf forms, trying to track him down."

Fergus and Elgin, Leidolf's pack sub-leaders; and Quincy and Pierce, twin brothers; and four other reds had gathered to help with finding the teens. Ogden, a gray from Hunter's pack who had mated one of Leidolf's reds, also offered to locate the kids.

Rubbing sleep from his eyes, seventeen-year-old Evan walked out of the bunkhouse, his brown hair uncombed, strands dangling over his dark eyebrows. Despite the cold, his flannel shirt was unbuttoned and hanging open, revealing a well-muscled chest from all the work he did on the ranch—some of it extra duty for all the shenanigans he'd pulled. "What's going on?"

"Trouble with a teen," his father, Fergus, said, his amber eyes pinning his son with accusation. "You know how much difficulty they can be." His father folded his arms across his broad chest, peeved with his own son for all the problems he'd caused this past year. "And you know how Carver is about his girls."

The mention of Carver's girls got the boy's attention. Immediately, Evan's eyes grew wide, and he hastily buttoned his shirt. "I'm going."

"You're staying," his father countered, both of their gazes locked in confrontation. "Carver is angry enough about you and his daughter Alice. An uneasy truce exists between the two of you right now, and I want to keep it that way."

"I'm going," Evan said again, this time looking at Leidolf for his approval.

Despite not wanting to go against the father's decision, Leidolf slapped Fergus on the back. "Your son could be a help this time."

Fergus was a good sub-leader, but he had been thinking of his son's welfare, not how the boy could aid the pack. He studied his son, then seemed to come to the same conclusion as Leidolf had and nodded. "Maybe you could talk some sense into the kid before Carver kills him, Evan."

Evan headed for his father's black pickup truck. "If the guy's laid a hand on Alice, *I'll* kill him."

The boy took off with Alice's twin sister, Sarah. He doesn't seem to be interested in Alice. Leidolf shook his head, got into the Suburban with Elgin, who was driving, and called Hunter Greymere, the only gray-wolf pack leader he knew of in Oregon. If the teen didn't belong to him, Leidolf wasn't sure where he'd come from. He might have thought the teen was a runaway, but not once the female and male adult wolves had come looking for him.

"Yeah," Hunter answered on the first ring, sounding grumpy.

Leidolf smiled. "This is Leidolf. Sorry to disturb you. I'd ask if your mate has had the babies yet, but it's probably a little too early. Bad night?"

Hunter grunted. Leidolf heard the sound of a coffee mug being set on a surface with a ceramic *clunk*, and then liquid, probably coffee, pouring into it.

"I have a situation."

Hunter grew quiet and listened to Leidolf.

Hating to bring it up when they'd made a friendship of sorts, Leidolf took a deep breath. "Three gray wolves are here stirring up trouble."

"Three gray wolves," Hunter murmured, as if he was trying to figure out which members of his pack would be traipsing through Leidolf's territory.

Leidolf quickly added, "It's a teen and his parents."

"A teen and..." Hunter paused, then said, "Hell. I'll call you right back. Wait... let me explain who I think they are. I have a teen who has run away a couple of times since his parents died last year. He's been working at a Christmas tree farm near here and suspects a couple of wolves died there."

"Gray or red?" Leidolf asked, frowning.

"Gray. Not from my pack, either. I've got a SEAL, Bjornolf Jorgenson, and Anna Johnson, one of my covert operatives, helping to uncover the mystery while taking care of the teen. If they're the ones in your territory, they've tried to track Nathan down. He's been having trouble coping with his parents' recent deaths."

"I'll let my people know," Leidolf said, sympathizing with the teen and with what Hunter had to deal with. "We're headed to the safe house that borders Forest Park. No need to send any of your pack members here. I've got it under control."

"I don't understand why he'd venture into your territory," Hunter said, sounding genuinely perplexed.

"Teen hormones," Leidolf guessed. "I don't know how they met, but apparently he knew one of our teen she-wolves from somewhere. I hope we get to him before her father does. If she's compromised..."

Hunter swore.

Knowing Hunter was ready to go to Portland in protective alpha-leader mode, Leidolf assured him, "I'll take care of it, Hunter. I'm sure between your SEAL, Anna, and me, we'll get the boy where he needs to be— home with your pack. Stay with Tessa. She needs you close at hand for now. Believe me. I've been there. Got to go. Keep you updated."

"Make sure your people know what they're up against," Hunter warned.

"Yeah, I sure will."

Nathan running off with a girl was exactly what Anna *didn't* want to be involved in. How many girls was he chasing after at the same time?

She'd never run off with a boy... well, once, but that was different. No one knew or cared. Was Anna's lecture the reason Nathan had run off to see the teen she-wolf?

She groaned. Why did Hunter believe she could be a good influence on the kid?

Nathan had to have met the girl before. She couldn't blame the dad for the way he was reacting, but she didn't want Carver to hurt Nathan. She felt sick to her stomach.

Anna didn't shift from the wolf. Carver's wife directed Bjornolf to a bedroom where he could get some clothes. When he returned, he was dressed and carefully explained the situation to Carver: Nathan's background, his parents' recent deaths, and his first holiday without them. Carver's expression said he didn't give a damn what Nathan's situation was, only that he'd stolen his daughter and could be putting her in harm's way.

Taking the situation in stride, Bjornolf mentioned that the girl had left willingly with Nathan, which hadn't helped a whole lot. He was trying to say that it wasn't a coerced situation. If Nathan had forced the girl from her home, the scenario would have been *much* worse.

"Nathan's hurting," Bjornolf said, and for a moment, Anna saw real pain in Carver's dark eyes. She knew then that Bjornolf had touched some deep-seated chord of sympathy for the boy.

Nathan didn't have anyone.

Carver had told them that Leidolf and several of his men were on their way to help search for the missing teen. Anna hoped that no one else would find the teens before she and Bjornolf could protect Nathan from his own folly.

———

Henry Thompson sipped a cup of coffee in his living room as his wife, Chrissie, hurried the kids out to their biological dad's waiting car. Thompson was a self-made millionaire, one of the lucky ones who knew how to play the stock market and didn't need to work a regular job. Instead, he spent his time with Chrissie and the kids while taking care of situations that arose concerning wild animals as a zoologist for the Oregon Zoo.

The phone rang, and he looked at the ID, noting it was a call from his hunting buddy. "Thompson here."

"This is just up your alley," Joe said, his voice eager

with excitement. "We've got more sightings of wolves running through Forest Park."

"You're… kidding," Thompson said. He knew his friend wouldn't be, but he just couldn't believe it. Last time he had to deal with wolves, he'd had an ordeal with a man named Leidolf. Were they the same wolves? Leidolf and his wife had sworn they were taking the wolves to a red-wolf reserve back east.

"There are three adults," Joe said. "Two male, one female."

"Red, right?"

"No, that's the odd part. One male and female are gray. The other is a male red."

Leaving the half-finished mug of java on the coffee table, Thompson crossed the living room to his den, grabbed his coat, and retrieved his hunting rifle from the locked gun cabinet.

"I'll meet you at the park," Joe said.

Tranquilizer darts at the ready, Thompson was headed out, determined to save the wolves, when he saw Chrissie returning. "Hold on a sec," he said to Joe.

"What's wrong?" she asked, as she joined him, her brow furrowed.

"Got to go. Wolves sighted in Forest Park." He pulled Chrissie into a hot hug. "Keep the bed warm. I'll be back before you know it."

She shook her head and tugged on his coat button. "You'll be running around the woods for hours looking for them." Then she turned her face up and kissed him. "But I know you mean to protect them. I couldn't love you more for it."

He kissed her back, vowing that he'd return before

the kids got home from school, then headed for his pickup. "Where exactly were they sighted, Joe?" he asked over the phone.

"They're headed toward one of the exclusive residential areas."

"Great." He shook his head. "Whoever spotted them had to be wrong. Wolves no longer wander through Forest Park. Haven't for years."

Joe gave a short laugh of disbelief. "Yeah, that's what we said the last time. And you know what happened then."

Thompson paused, hand on his door handle, his eyes on the wolves painted on the side of his truck. Could they be werewolves?

Nah…

———•———

Anna, Bjornolf, and Carver returned to his house when they were unable to track his daughter's scent. That meant the teens must have shifted, dressed, and left the area.

As Carver headed for his bedroom, his mate, Aimée, directed Bjornolf and Anna to the guest bedroom and said to Anna, "We have several changes of clothes in the closet and dressers for wolves who need them on occasion. Feel free to borrow anything you'd like. Sarah must have given Nathan a change of clothes. I checked out front and her car is gone." She shut the door for them.

Anna shifted into her human form and was completely naked. She was in too much of a hurry to worry about Bjornolf being in the same room as her. If he was as much of a professional as he was supposed to be, he would be shifting and putting on the same clothes that he'd thrown on earlier to have the talk with Carver.

He *wouldn't* be eyeing her naked body.

She frowned as she pulled the first drawer open and discovered only men's boxers. She went to the next drawer and found bras and panties.

Rifling through them, she looked for anything in black when Bjornolf leaned over to peer into the drawer, naked as they come, and pointed at one of the bras. "Get the red one and the matching panties."

She turned slightly and saw him taking his fill—of *her*, not the underwear in the drawer, and the internal meter that measured her embarrassment went through the ceiling.

Chapter 12

ANNA COULDN'T HAVE BEEN MORE SURPRISED THAT Bjornolf had been watching her search for the right undergarments. She jerked out black panties and a bra, feeling her body heat so much she was certain it was already red enough for him.

Anna pulled on the black panties—she couldn't find anything but sexy lace—wishing they were much more utilitarian.

"Then again, those look great," Bjornolf said, his voice rough and his gaze heated as he slipped on a pair of ivory boxers, not hiding a full-blown erection fast enough before she glanced at him.

"You're supposed to be a professional," she chided, fastening the bra over her breasts.

What kind of wolves wore these things? Not only was it low cut, but it squeezed her breasts together and pushed them up, making her feel as though she could be on display in one of those girly calendars.

"Nice," he said, his voice even more gravelly with lust as he considered her breasts.

She snorted, but before she could pass by him to get to the closet, he seized her arm and pulled her gently to him. His action was both possessive and guarded. Possessive in that she could tell he desired her from his darkened expression, his scent changing from keen interest to rabid arousal. Guarded in that she assumed he

wanted to ensure she craved him in the same way, and
so he hesitated to take this further.

She didn't pull away from him like she should have.
They had a job to do, and fulfilling some crazy sexual
fantasy wasn't going to get it done. They were standing
in a guest room of a red wolf pack's house in borrowed
underwear while a teen under their care was running
loose with a teen from this household. They certainly
didn't have time for *this*.

"They'll be all right, Anna. I promise you."

If they were running around as humans, they'd be
safe enough together for now. She assumed.

That was all the time Bjornolf gave her to think about
Nathan and the girl. He cupped her breasts, his thumbs
skimming over the flesh mounded together in the sexy
bra, his eyes focused on them. Then he dipped his head
to kiss her.

She gave in to the madness and kissed him back, his
hands shifting to her ass and pulling her against his rigid
arousal, the boxers doing nothing to hide the fact he was
hot for her.

All Anna's frustration and worry melted away in
that one passionate, prolonged, soul-startling kiss, as
Bjornolf's hands slipped down her panties and cupped
her flesh. She moaned into his mouth as he kissed and
licked and nipped and growled.

They needed a room. They had a room. Not here.
What was she thinking? They needed to find Nathan.
Jeez, what was she doing?

Bjornolf's mouth moved in compelling kisses over
her jaw, down her throat, to the swell of her breasts. She
wanted his mouth on her nipples, licking and suckling.

She wanted him between her spread legs, and God, she was already wet for him.

Again.

"We… can't," she said with the greatest regret.

He let her slip away then, yet there was no regret in *his* expression. Only hunger—feral and predatory. She knew to the marrow of her bones there was no stopping what he felt for her: pure lust. He had it bad.

She also had it bad for him, but at least she had her priorities straight. Well, she was trying to keep them straight.

He was staring at her, his eyes dark as midnight, his whole body tense as if he might just follow her into the closet and start kissing her all over again.

The sound of someone's hurried footsteps headed in their direction in the carpeted hallway didn't break their eye contact.

"This isn't over, Anna," he said softly, the hardness and tension in his posture so at odds with his spoken words. His comment was a promise, not a threat.

She knew then that she didn't want this hot, passionate swirl of emotions that existed between them to be over.

Aimée called through the door, "They're okay. The kids are at the mall. Carver told Leidolf they're fine, so he and his men are returning to their ranch. He wishes you both good luck with your mission."

Anna let out the breath she had been holding, relieved beyond measure that both teens were fine.

"Sarah texted me," Aimée continued. "They're shopping for Christmas ornaments for your tree—but I imagine there's something more to it than that with Nathan coming all the way here to see her in his wolf coat. Nathan wanted to surprise you. They said they were still looking for the perfect angel for the treetop for Anna."

Anna couldn't help it. All of a sudden, tears just sprang forth and were dribbling down her cheeks as fast as she could furiously wipe them away. Between the angel comment and knowing he was all right, that both kids were okay, the worry, the stress… she just… lost it.

Bjornolf's heated expression quickly changed to surprise, then worry. He said to Aimée, "Thanks for the good news. We'll be out in a minute."

"Carver's pacing out in the backyard. He said he needed to cool his heels a bit. He's thinking of letting them come home in their own good time. That's going to be a first."

"Good. I think it's for the best," Bjornolf said, pulling Anna into his arms.

Aimée said, "Take your time. I'm cooking lunch, and we all want you to stay."

"Thanks," Bjornolf said. "We'd like that."

Anna never cried. Well, occasionally over a sad movie, but generally speaking, she did not cry. Twice in front of Bjornolf now? What was her problem? He had to think she was some kind of basket case.

"I'm okay," she whispered, hating that she was soaking his chest with her tears.

He stroked her back with one hand while keeping his arm planted around her waist, holding her tight. He had no intention of letting her go until he was sure she felt better.

He kissed the top of her head as she snuffled, finally getting her emotions under control.

"I'm sorry," she said. "I'm not normally like this."

"At least I wasn't kissing you this time."

She saw he was smiling down at her with the warmest, most tender expression. She chuckled and he kissed her wet cheek.

—⁓—

With her auburn hair in a braid hanging down her back, Sarah walked beside Nathan in the crowded mall, hand in hand. He hadn't seen her in three months and had been avoiding her, thinking that it would be better to stay away because of her father. And… for other reasons. The human girl, Jessica Everton, daughter of the owner of the Christmas tree farm, topped the list.

Sarah had been thrilled to see him when they had first met at her house, but she'd also been scared. Afraid that her father would kill him if he learned that she'd already met Nathan and hadn't told her father about him.

He really did like her, maybe because she could relate to him since she'd lost her mom like he'd lost both his mom and dad. But more as a friend. He thought she wanted more from him than he was willing to give.

"You haven't texted me in months, Nathan," Sarah said.

"I'm sorry. You said your father would kill you if he knew you were seeing me. I thought…" Nathan shrugged.

He'd had enough to deal with already. He hadn't been happy with any of the families he'd lived with so far. He hadn't known how staying with Bjornolf and Anna would be, even if it was only short-term. Though, if they got along well enough, he hoped it might turn out more permanent. He thought living with a couple of undercover operatives would be cool.

"It was easier not to see me," Sarah finally said, hurt

in her voice, drawing him back to the shopping expedition and the problem at hand.

Yeah, it was easier not to see her. The issues of her father not wanting her to see a wolf of another pack, of Nathan's not having a real home but being bounced from one family in the pack to another—and then just dealing with a girlfriend who was a wolf from a different pack—all complicated the issue. Especially when she learned he'd been seeing a human girl.

"I'm working now," he said.

"You could've texted."

"I'm sorry." He didn't know what else to say. He *did* like Sarah. As a *friend*.

They walked in silence. They'd already bought several boxes of colorful ornaments, but they still hadn't found the angel Nathan thought Anna might like.

"I wish I had the money for the ornaments on me. Kind of hard traveling as a wolf to bring anything with me."

"Just send it to me when you have a chance." Sarah sighed. "So… what's Anna like? You said she works undercover. Is she really tough looking?"

"She's really cool," Nathan said. "*Tomb Raider* kind of woman. Only she's never had a Christmas tree before. Can you imagine? Bjornolf says she's sad about the holidays."

Sarah stopped him and looked up into his face, her brows pinched together. "Why did you really run here as a wolf, Nathan? You know everyone's going to be upset about it. Your pack, mine. My dad and his new mate. My sister, even. Why didn't you just drive up here?"

He let out a deep breath. "I don't know. Sometimes…

I just have to run. Bjornolf and Anna had gone out to investigate the tree farm. I thought of joining them, but they need to do their work without me underfoot."

"You felt unneeded?"

"Yeah, I guess. I caught them kissing last night, and she was crying."

Sarah frowned at Nathan.

"I think she really likes him," he said, "and I know he likes her. But something's upsetting her. I think it's the holidays. She didn't want to decorate the tree. But you know what she did? She made a popcorn garland. She worked for an hour stringing it all by herself in the living room. I would've helped her, only I thought she was just eating popcorn. He shook his head. "I thought... if I did something, like bring home the ornaments, maybe she'd feel better. I had to get the urge to run out of my system first. And... I wanted to see you."

He had wanted to see her to settle things in his mind because he couldn't get Jessica Everton, the human girl he *wasn't* supposed to be falling for, out of his thoughts. He knew Anna was right when she said he couldn't get involved with a human girl.

Yet he couldn't help it. Maybe it had to do with the fact she was a human who smelled like a she-wolf.

—∿∿—

Dressed in blue jeans and a gray sweatshirt, Bjornolf used Carver's phone to call Hunter and let him know that the teens were fine. "We'll be home later this afternoon. I didn't even think about Nathan's job, though..."

"I already called them and told them he was sick with the flu. If he wants to go to work tomorrow, that's fine. If he needs to stay with the two of you for the next couple of days to sort out things, that'll work also."

"Okay. About the murder case—I haven't had a chance to tell you what happened. Last night, Anna found some dog tags where Nathan had smelled a dead body. The name is Thomas Cremer."

"Cremer. I'll share this second name with Finn."

"Did you learn anything more about the Wentworths from our last mission?" Bjornolf asked.

"Not yet. I have Rourke, our investigative reporter in the pack, looking into things. He's got a lot of connections, and he's good at ferreting out information. Maybe he'll unearth some clues for us."

Bjornolf let out his breath, wanting to mention how upset Anna had been. He wanted to see if Hunter knew what was distressing her so much, but decided it would be best not to share that bit of news. Hunter might want to take her off the case, worrying about her safety in the frame of mind she seemed to be in. Bjornolf knew that neither Nathan nor he could get through the holidays without her, and he wasn't about to give up his pursuit of something deeper with her. He had no intention of putting it off any longer.

"Talk to you later, Hunter."

Anna was outside in the backyard with Alice, Sarah's twin sister. Alice was showing Anna the gardens. He smiled as he watched Anna move about in the light sprinkle of snowflakes as if she was a snow sprite, thinking how much he'd love wrapping her in his arms.

Nearby, a "thwack, thwack" rent the air. Carver was chopping wood with such vigor that Bjornolf figured he was trying to let out some of his pent-up frustration over Nathan and his daughter.

Carrying a couple of logs, Carver came inside, acknowledged Bjornolf with a nod, glanced back at the window to see what he'd been watching—Anna and Alice—then tossed one of the logs on the fire and set the other in a copper wood box. "Sarah said she and Nathan will be here in about twenty minutes. Are you and Anna mated?"

Bjornolf turned his attention from Anna as she swept her hair into a ponytail to Carver, who looked more than curious. "We only first met several months ago."

Was he mated to her? Bjornolf was definitely thinking along those lines. They'd make one hell of an undercover team.

Aimée frowned at Carver as she set out the silverware on the table in the formal dining room. Carver's mate was a pretty woman with red gold hair curling about her shoulders and a light smattering of freckles bridging her nose. She looked more sweet than seductive, like his Anna did.

His Anna. That's the way Bjornolf was already feeling about her.

"You shouldn't ask such a thing," Aimée scolded. "That's personal."

Carver rubbed his chin as he looked from his mate to Bjornolf, pondering the situation. "What's holding you back, son?"

Bjornolf couldn't remember the last time his own father had called him that. He was amused the man was so curious.

"It's complicated," Bjornolf answered as he looked

out the back window and saw Anna brushing the snow off the nose of a wolf statue while smiling at Alice. He wondered what Anna would be like in a backyard of their own with a teen of their own.

"That's exactly what I said when I met Aimée. It's complicated. I wanted her, no doubt about it. She was feeling the same about me." Carver winked at her and Aimée blushed furiously. "I had two twin daughters and I didn't want to mate with just any old she-wolf who might treat my girls poorly."

"The wicked, old she-wolf stepmother syndrome," Aimée said.

"So what's *your* reasoning for holding back? You don't already have a mate, do you?" Carver asked.

The wily wolf had to know the answer to that, just from the way Bjornolf had such a time keeping his eyes off Anna, as if he was afraid she'd vanish in the blink of an eye.

"No," Bjornolf said with a half smile.

"Been mated and have offspring already that you're worried about?"

Bjornolf shook his head.

"Then what? It's sure as hell not because you don't want her. And I can tell the woman's as interested in you. While I was chopping wood, I overheard Alice asking Anna if she was planning to mate you, and when I cast a glance in their direction, the she-wolf was blushing to high heaven. She didn't laugh at the suggestion or deny it. You're as good as mated, to my way of thinking. So what are you waiting for?" Carver shook his head and washed his hands at the sink, not giving Bjornolf time to answer. "Seize the moment. You never know when another wolf might come along and snatch your woman right up. Then where will you be?"

Killing the male wolf, Bjornolf thought darkly. The back door shut with a *clunk*.

The doorbell rang, and from the hurried footsteps moving in that direction, he assumed Alice and Anna were headed for the front door. Bjornolf and Carver hesitated. Both were annoyed with Nathan for running off. They also knew they had to handle the teens carefully or chance having them run off again.

He and Carver went into the living room to greet Nathan and Sarah, but instead they saw Alice and Anna standing at the front door talking to a big blond-haired, bearded man wearing camouflage hunter's gear. His blue eyes were challenging Anna as he said, "Hi, I'm Henry Thompson and I work in a special capacity with the zoo. Eyewitnesses said they saw wolves enter your backyard."

Alice turned to her father, looking for his help. Confronting the threat, Carver immediately approached the door, his whole posture stating he was in charge.

"I'm sorry," Carver said gruffly, not sounding sorry in the least—more like *get the hell off my property*. "We don't even own a dog."

"Are you friends with Leidolf Wildhaven?" Thompson asked, as if he knew something more about the wolves than he should.

Carver narrowed his eyes. His hesitation spoke volumes. Carver finally said, "He's a wealthy rancher." Like everyone in Oregon should know that.

"Yeah, but are you friends of his?" Thompson persisted.

"Did you say you're a police officer?" Carver asked.

Thompson smiled, but the look was *not* friendly. "Not exactly. I help police wild animals running loose in the area that might come to harm."

"Okay, so I said we don't have any dogs here. Or wolves."

"May I have a look around your backyard? Your neighbors said you have a dog door in your back gate."

Because of the woodland setting, the neighbors were a long way from each other and a mini-forest surrounded each of the homes in the development. The neighbors couldn't have *seen* the dog door in the gate unless they'd come onto Carver's property.

Carver smiled, his expression dark and threatening. "No, you don't have permission to traipse around my backyard."

Thompson turned his attention to Anna and Bjornolf. "Do you know Leidolf?"

Bjornolf thought Thompson would have made a good alpha wolf with his tenacity.

Both he and Anna shook their heads. Bjornolf had never met the red wolf leader.

"I'll find the wolves. I always do." Thompson's threat was a promise. Then he turned to leave, paused, and said over his shoulder as an afterthought, "You can tell Leidolf I said hi." Then he headed for his pickup truck as Carver shut the door a little too forcefully.

"Lock the back gate, Alice, just in case Thompson decides to snoop around back there and sees wolf prints," her father said.

"We can sweep the snow," she said eagerly.

Carver watched out the window. "It's too late. He's headed to the cul-de-sac, and then he'll go through the vacant woods and around the back of the property. He'll see the tracks leading up to our gate even if he doesn't try to enter the backyard. Dogged damned bloodhound."

"I'll lock it." Alice grabbed a broom out of a closet and flew toward the back door and outside to sweep the snow anyway.

Thankfully, Leidolf and his men weren't coming to search for the teens. If Thompson had found them here, what would he have concluded?

A blue sedan pulled up out front, and Carver muttered under his breath, "Finally."

Nathan and Sarah. Now how would he handle *this*?

Chapter 13

AIMÉE JOINED CARVER—ALONG WITH BJORNOLF AND Anna—in the living room and took hold of Carver's arm as if to calm him. Before Nathan and Sarah reached the front door, Aimée said to Bjornolf and Anna, "Thompson's the one who put Leidolf and Cassie in the zoo when they were running as wolves."

"Thompson and Leidolf sound like they have a history, and not a good one at that." Bjornolf wanted to put his arm around Anna, but she was already headed for the door and opened it as Sarah raised her hand to twist the doorknob from outside.

Anna stretched out her hand. "Hi. You must be Sarah. I'm Anna Johnson."

If Nathan had been in his wolf's coat, he would have appeared as bowed as he did in human form, and his tail would have been between his legs. He glanced at Anna, avoiding Bjornolf and Carver's gazes, and looked as though he wanted to be swallowed up by the terra-cotta tile floor in the entryway.

"We were so worried about you." Anna pulled Nathan into a hug.

<hr />

Bjornolf had no idea how they managed to get through lunch. Carver was furious. Bjornolf was upset with Nathan for putting everyone in danger. Bjornolf was even more concerned about Anna's state of mind. She barely ate more than a couple of bites of food, withdrew from the small talk, and avoided looking at anyone.

Nathan and Bjornolf couldn't help glancing in her direction, both wanting desperately to make her feel better.

Nathan cleared his throat and rushed through his words to Carver. "I want to date Sarah." His eyes were dark with challenge as he met Carver's.

Bjornolf swore the older man was fighting a smile as he paused in the process of cutting a slice of roast on his plate.

"When and where?" he asked.

Nathan's mouth dropped open a little, then he clamped it shut.

On the trip home, no one said a word for several miles as Bjornolf drove a rental car with Anna up front with him. Nathan was in the backseat behind her.

"You really like Sarah? She seemed like a nice girl," Bjornolf said finally.

"Yeah. Um, I like her. A lot."

Anna swore Nathan wasn't telling them the whole truth.

Nathan cleared his throat. "I'm so sorry that I ran like I... I did." His voice broke on the last word. "I thought maybe if I saw Sarah again, I'd realize she was more suited to me than Jessica. Because Sarah's a wolf. It didn't work. I like Sarah, but she's not... Jessica." Nathan let his breath out on a heavy sigh. "Sarah will want to kill me."

Anna reached over her seat back, took Nathan's hand, and squeezed it. "You don't really want to date Sarah, do you?"

"No. I mean, she's a friend. Sure. But… I think she wants me to be more than that."

Anna's own teen years had been such a muddled mess; how could she offer advice? But she was worried about him.

"Was it because of me that you ran off?" Anna asked.

"No… well, and yes. You didn't make me do it. But I got to thinking about what you said about Jessica being human and you were right. Seeing Sarah didn't change the way I see Jessica, though."

Anna took a deep breath and nodded. She couldn't think of anything to say that would help, so she turned around to watch out the windshield, glad he was safe.

"I'm sorry I ran away. I promise I won't again."

Anna sighed heavily. "I felt the same way when I was your age. I think sometimes I'm still running away. We're here for you now. I mean that. You've got a pack who cares about you. I didn't have any of that. It's really tough out there living without a pack. Believe me. You don't want to lose what you have."

"She's right, Nathan. I was about your age when I lost my parents. They were missionaries killed while doing what they were called to do. When that happened, I was as wild as could be, no rules, no curfews, no family, nothing. I would have given up all that freedom just to have my family back."

"I thought you were fine with not having anyone," Nathan said. "I heard some of the pack members called you a ghost. That you never worked with a team. That you were your own man."

"I worked with several different teams over the years. Lots of good men. The last twenty years or so, I've been alone. But you know what? If I needed someone to watch my back, I didn't have it. No one knew I even existed. If I got wounded, I was on my own. When everyone else left the mission behind, I had to find my own way out."

"You were ghosting different SEAL teams for a long time, weren't you?" Nathan asked.

"I was."

"Then you started to follow Hunter's team. Why?"

"They were gray wolves. Not humans."

"And they had Anna working with them," Nathan said.

Bjornolf glanced in her direction. She was watching him, curiosity in her expression.

Bjornolf chuckled. He'd developed an affinity for Hunter's team—the camaraderie, the closeness, their successes—and he'd wanted to help them keep it going. He had to admit adding Anna to the mix sure livened things up.

Anna frowned and then said to Nathan, "He began to see them as his family."

"And you, Anna," Nathan insisted. "I loved the popcorn garland you made for the tree. Why didn't you come get me? I would've helped."

"You were asleep."

Nathan let out a snort. "Not with Bjornolf pacing back and forth across the room. I couldn't sneak past him. He wanted to be the one with you. He wouldn't have wanted me to spend the time with you instead."

Anna smiled. "I could have sworn you were both snoring away in your bunk beds."

That was something Bjornolf wanted to change tonight. He wanted Anna in bed, in the master bedroom where they should have been together all along.

—⁓—

When they arrived at the cottage, the sun had already set. Nathan stirred in the backseat and sat up. "Can I help you take the rental car back?"

"Hunter said one of his people will take it back. Thanks for offering," Bjornolf added, realizing the kid was trying to make amends and take some responsibility for his actions. He glanced at Anna. Her eyes were closed, her head was pressed against the window, and she had appeared to be sleeping for the short ride home.

Nathan whispered, "Oh, yeah, I gotcha."

Bjornolf glanced into the rearview mirror and raised his brows, questioning Nathan's remark.

Nathan tilted his head in Anna's direction. Then he said in a hushed voice, "I won't be any more trouble. I swear it. You can sleep with her, and I'll stay put. You don't have to babysit me. Honest."

Bjornolf considered Anna, saw the hint of a smile on her lips, and shook his head. He was trying to come up with a way to change the subject before Nathan said too much more about the sleeping arrangements and got them both into hot water, when Nathan said, "You like Anna. A lot."

Bjornolf sighed. Yeah, he did. He hadn't realized just how much the she-wolf had gotten under his skin. He'd thought he could resist her charms on this last mission, just stay in the background watching the team's backs. But he couldn't, not when he kept wanting to dash out and save Anna from the threats all around her.

He wanted much more than that. Her. For his own. They could work together. Live at her place in New

Jersey, or even find a new place. They could keep track of Hunter's missions and ghost the team together, or just sign up as part of the crew.

"We're here," he said to Anna. In a way, he wished she was still sleeping so he could carry her to bed. It was better that she wasn't because they had to decide the sleeping arrangements *together*.

She stretched and said, "Good. Time for bed."

"You slept already," Nathan said. "Did you want to decorate the tree now?"

"Tomorrow," she said, sounding really dragged out. After the run they'd had all night, they were exhausted.

She reached for her car door, but Nathan bolted out of the car to get it for her.

She smiled at him as Bjornolf grabbed the bags of Christmas ornaments. He'd go along with whatever Anna decided as far as decorating the tree went. Then he was taking her to bed.

She patted Nathan on the shoulder. "We'll do it tomorrow after we've had a good night's sleep. I'll enjoy it more then," she said.

Nathan's expression brightened.

"I bought eggnog just for the occasion," Bjornolf said.

"With rum," Nathan said, grinning.

"Only for the adults." Bjornolf got the front door for Anna.

Somehow Nathan shot through the door ahead of them and headed for the bedroom. Before Bjornolf had shut and locked the front door, Nathan had grabbed Bjornolf's bags and was hauling them toward the master bedroom.

"Guess it's decided." Bjornolf slipped his hand around Anna's.

She snorted. "When a teen makes decisions of that magnitude for the adults, we've got a problem."

"I see no problem at all."

Anna looked at him. "I don't even know which side of the bed you sleep on."

"There's only one side of the bed for me to sleep on. Your side."

She shook her head. "You think you are one hot stud of a SEAL."

"I am—where you're concerned. But *only* where you're concerned."

"Night," Nathan quickly said, not even looking at them as he dashed into the guest bedroom and shut his door with a *thunk*. The lock *snicked* home.

And that decided that.

—◈—

Anna led Bjornolf into the kitchen, asking, "Have you got any brandy?" She wasn't sure what he had in mind, despite his sexy innuendos. But she couldn't just go to bed with him. Not yet.

She'd tried to sleep in the car on the brief ride home. Despite being tired from running all through the night and part of the day as a wolf, she wasn't able to sleep. She couldn't quit thinking about the way Bjornolf had slid his large hands down her panties and cupped her naked ass. How he kissed the swell of her breasts, and the way he pressed his erection against her belly, taunting her with just how much he wanted her.

The thing of it was, wolves didn't show this kind of interest in one another unless they were *really* interested in something permanent. They were genetically engineered that way—mating for life with life spans that outlasted humans.

She tried to ignore the growing craving she had for him. At the back of her mind, the thought plagued her that he was just teasing and not really wanting her. She also worried that if she ever had a mate and had children, she would be as rotten a mother to them as her own had been with her.

Bjornolf poured them both glasses of peach brandy, handed her one, then carried his and the bottle to the living room as he followed her.

"First, we have to have a fire." He reached for a matchbox, and she realized tinder and wood were already stacked on the hearth and ready to go.

"We're going to bed," she reminded him, "or I'm bound to fall asleep on the couch."

"I'll carry you to bed. Fire first."

"You were sure I'd agree with this plan of Hunter's? That I'd stay with you and Nathan?"

Bjornolf lit the tinder and turned to face her. He had the most devilish look in his expression. "He knows how to pick the right people for a mission. You couldn't have been more perfect, Anna."

Perfect for the mission? Or for Bjornolf?

"Nathan and I will put out the outdoor lights together tomorrow. He has the next couple of days free from work, Hunter said."

"Yes!" Nathan said from the bedroom, and she could envision him pumping his fist in victory. She also realized he was listening to every word they said. Reminder to self—don't let things get too heated.

"*Go… to… sleep, Nathan,*" Bjornolf said, his words a strict command.

"Nearly there," Nathan said, trying to sound like he was drifting off.

Bjornolf smiled at Anna. His sexy I-want-you expression, with his brows raised and his darkened eyes, told her that the bedroom wasn't going to be used just for sleeping tonight.

She frowned at him and said in a hushed voice, "We can't do this with him in the house."

His smile broadened and he looked like one satisfied wolf—just by getting her agreement, in part. "Yeah we can. Parents do it all the time."

Her mouth dropped open, then she clamped it shut. She wanted to say they weren't his parents, that she'd never been around a teen in a situation like this, but she held her tongue.

They decided to get down to business and put the lights on the tree. A warm fire glowed in the fireplace as Bjornolf helped Anna spread out the strands of lights, then began draping them around the spruce like she'd done with the garland.

When they finished and stepped back to see if they covered the tree fairly uniformly, he plugged the lights in and they admired the sparkly blue spruce.

"It's beautiful," she said, her arms wrapped around her chest, the lights sparkling off her dark eyes.

"Even more so when we put the ornaments on it tomorrow," Bjornolf said, but he was thinking how beautiful Anna looked standing before the tree, picture perfect for Christmas. Feeling tired all of a sudden, he wanted to take her to bed now, but he didn't want to push her too fast. "Do you want to watch a movie?"

She turned to look at him, studying his sincerity.

"I'd fall asleep. Besides, I'm afraid we'll keep Nathan up."

They both looked back at the guest room door, expecting Nathan to say something, figuring he was dying to but was feigning sleep.

"I agree. He's got to get his sleep."

"We do, too," Anna remarked as Bjornolf banked the fire. She turned off the Christmas tree lights, plunging them into darkness.

Bjornolf grasped her hand and moved her toward the hall. "We will." He had no intention of sleeping with her. Certainly not right away.

Unless Anna had other notions. Her unpredictability was one of the things that drew him to her. He envisioned she'd start ripping off his clothes as soon as they shut the door to the master bedroom.

Now that scenario he could deal with in a heartbeat.

Chapter 14

ANNA COULDN'T HELP BEING NERVOUS ABOUT WHAT she and Bjornolf were going to do next. She thought he was the right one for her, but was she the right one for him? He didn't know what he was getting into when he took her on. She was always trying to prove herself with the guys. Maybe because she'd tried so hard to prove her worth to her parents, and they never had seemed to think her worthy of their attention. Ever.

He closed the door to the bedroom and watched her as she took a seat on the end of the bed.

"We're not going to just sleep, are we?" she asked.

He shook his head, but he didn't take a step closer, as if letting her get her bearings first. "We're going to do it, Anna," he said matter-of-factly. "Tonight, tomorrow, sometime soon. Sooner, I hope, than later. But we're going to do it."

"Because?" she asked.

He moved across the floor like a stealthy wolf, and her heartbeat quickened. She didn't feel the fight-or-flight feeling she had the last time he was with her in a room like this. She wondered how she was going to prove to him that her moves were just as hot and sexy as his.

"Are you sure you want to do this?" she asked.

"Yeah. I am." Bjornolf pulled Anna from the bed. "We'll make one helluva killer team."

A killer team. She smiled. That decided it.

Bjornolf saw the sudden change in her mood. She was shifting from being unsure of where this was going… to—"Damn the torpedoes! Full speed ahead!"

Once it was decided, there was no going back. He'd planned to talk with her first, but screw that. They'd talk to each other for the rest of their very long mated lives. Now was the time for action.

Neither of them were willing to go slowly. As she tried to pull off his gray sweatshirt, he was sliding his hands under the soft sweater she wore, wanting to feel her breasts confined in that sexy, black, lacy push-up bra. Then he wanted to free them. She was hampering his progress as she pulled the sweatshirt up his chest, exposing him, but he wasn't letting go of her sumptuous breasts.

She growled at him—actually growled! Then she leaned over and licked his nipple and pulled on it with a tender nibble. He should have known she'd try to take charge of the situation. He released her breasts, yanked the sweatshirt over his head, and tossed it to the floor.

He had planned to pull off her sweater next, but she slipped her leg behind his. Before he realized what she was up to, she grabbed his shoulders and pushed. The oldest trick in the book and he'd fallen for it—literally. He fell flat on his back with an oof, landing on top of his field pack full of clothes, which softened the drop.

She didn't miss a moment to straddle his hips, yanking off her ponytail holder, then her sweater, and tossing them both aside. The gleam in her wickedly happy expression said she loved being on top. Not just for sexual play, but that she needed this because of their last encounter where he'd gotten the best of her.

He slid his hands over her thighs, knowing he could easily flip her onto her back and straddle her, but he wanted this to be her show. Unless she needed more sparring to make her feel like a worthy opponent. Whatever Anna wanted, Bjornolf had every intention of giving it to her.

He smiled at her, letting her know he was ready to play some more.

She leaned down and licked his other nipple, her lace-covered breasts rubbing his chest, as she moved her jeans-clad mons over his hard-as-steel erection. To think they'd delayed consummating their relationship for this long… What a waste of precious time. They'd have to make up for it.

Her hands slid up his chest, her silky hair draped over his skin as she tugged on his nipple with a gentle pull of her teeth. She had the most amazing mouth, and everything she did whetted his appetite for more.

He reached behind her back to unfasten her bra. He wanted her breasts rubbing against him, skin to skin, her mons brushing against his arousal, her scent mixing with his, claiming him, ensuring other wolves knew they belonged together.

Too much fabric still separated them, but he couldn't find the fastener on the back of her bra. He took hold of her shoulders and pushed her back so he could examine the garment, her breasts nearly falling out as she leaned over. He groaned at the mouthwatering sight of them. He reached for the fastener in front, but she pulled away from him and grabbed the buckle of his belt.

That's when he flipped her on her back. No Mister Nice Wolf any longer. He wouldn't last.

She grinned at him, then scrambled to get away. He grabbed her leg, diving for her, pinning her to the floor, his chest to her back. Not exactly what he had in mind. He'd wanted her breasts topside so he could unfasten the bra.

This way could work also, he decided. He slid his hands between the carpet and her breasts, unfastening the bra as she arched her butt up. Now *that* was an interesting maneuver. It didn't get her anywhere, but it definitely got him hot.

Now that he was on top, he rubbed his arousal against her cleft, wishing they had already dispensed with their clothes.

He could feel the tension in her body, feel her need to outmaneuver him again. She seemed to be warring with herself to let him have his way with her or spar with him as he caressed her luscious breasts, one in each hand, squeezing the hot, swollen flesh and feeling her nipples harden.

She moaned in pure delight, her buttocks rubbing against his arousal until he was so pumped that he feared he'd come in his jeans. Definitely not the way he wanted to start their mated relationship.

He slid his hands down her belly and felt for the button at the waist of her jeans, unfastened it, and unzipped the zipper. He was concentrating on that when she tried to flip him over, but only managed to nearly knock him off, turning so she was face up. *Perfect*. He re-situated himself firmly below her hips.

She was flushed, her breathing wild, her heart pumping fast, her breasts bared for his pleasure, as he yanked the jeans down her hips. With a quick thrust, she lifted her hips, pushing with her feet against the floor, and tried to unseat him again.

"Won't work, Anna," he cautioned, seeing the smile spring to her face again. She was having fun. He raised up to pull her pants lower. He jerked his own belt free and unbuttoned his jeans, then pulled down the zipper. She licked her lips, her dark eyes fastened on his zipper.

"On the bed or here?" he asked, his voice hushed.

"Here," she said, patting the floor. "In case the bed squeaks."

"Right." He'd forgotten about Nathan.

Bjornolf pulled off her jeans and tossed them aside. He stood to remove his jeans, while he took in her sweet, sexy body, naked except for the lacy bikini panties. He'd dropped the pants to his ankles and was about to step out of them and kick them aside when he saw her expression change.

In an instant, he knew she was going to attack. She jumped up from the floor, and before he could react, she slammed her hot, soft body into his, tackling him to the bed with a thump, the jeans still around his ankles like a noose.

Her hands went straight to his package, caressing his cock through the boxers as she hummed in delight.

He groaned as he kicked off his jeans and wrapped his legs around hers, capturing her. He combed his fingers through her hair, his erection throbbing with need against her pelvis, rubbing him with wicked purpose. She felt so good.

She moved against his body, her breasts pressing against his chest, her mouth meeting his, their kisses greedy, hot, passionate. He couldn't get enough of her.

Tongues connected, tasting the peach brandy they'd shared. *Sweet*.

He slid his hands down her panties, cupping her soft cheeks, squeezing. She let out a little sigh of delight that pleased him. Then she slipped his cock out of his boxers and touched the broad head, eagerly stroking him. God, that felt good. "You're wet," she whispered.

He dipped his fingers between her legs and plunged one in between her folds. "You are, too."

"Not just wet," she whispered, as she rubbed her body against his.

He felt the ripples of climax inside her then, realized that with Anna a little sparring was good for foreplay, and vowed they'd have a room just for that—to keep in great shape and combat-ready—wherever they ended up living.

"I'm ready," she gasped, breathless, her eyes dark with arousal. "If you are."

He opened his legs to release her, and she pulled off his boxers. He quickly dispensed with her panties and dragged her under him. He entered her gently at first but quickly picked up the pace. Her heady scent mixed with his, the two of them smelling of the outdoors, of snow and firs and pine, of peach brandy and of her sweet peach-scented shampoo. Their hot, delicious sexy and overactive pheromones had him driving into her over and over again until he muffled her cry with a penetrating kiss. He exploded inside her, having never felt this complete.

He rolled off her and saw the expression on her face. She was one sleepy, well-satisfied she-wolf with a tired smile on her face. He tugged aside the covers. Then he moved her to their side of the bed and curled up beside her, spooning her, pulling the covers over them. He hoped they could solve the murder mystery quickly and painlessly so he and Anna could make some plans for their honeymoon.

———～～～———

Bjornolf's cell phone rang the next morning, and he realized the last time he had used it was before he and Anna went after Nathan the night before last.

Before he could throw on some boxers and retrieve the phone from down the hall, he heard Nathan say, "Hi, Hunter. No, it's me, Nathan. They were making a ruckus in the bedroom for most of the night. It's quiet in there now, so I think they're still sleeping. I'll tell him as soon as he gets up."

Bjornolf groaned and looked down at Anna. She was smiling up at him.

"I don't think Hunter had this in mind when he hired us for this job," Anna whispered, touching Bjornolf's chest.

A fresh shiver of need rocketed straight to his groin.

Bjornolf leaned down and kissed her forehead. "I'm not too sure about that. I'll go see what Hunter wants. It's time to put up the outdoor Christmas lights anyway. You just rest." After the wild night they'd had, they both needed a daytime nap.

She nodded and closed her eyes.

He took a quick, *cold* shower, then grabbed a pair of fresh boxers, noting that Anna was tucked under the covers and sound asleep. She looked beautiful, her hair tousled and spread out across the white pillowcases, her face angelic in sleep. His undercover operative. His sexy she-wolf.

He finished dressing and headed for the kitchen to get a cup of hot coffee.

Nathan had laid strings of lights all over the couches, getting them ready to put up outside. Bjornolf smiled at him, glad the kid was ready to help. He noticed Nathan had already had eggnog for breakfast, the filmy glass sitting in the kitchen sink. Bjornolf eyed it for a second.

"I didn't drink any rum in it. Honest," Nathan said. "You would have smelled it. That's the problem with living with wolf chaperones."

"You're right." Bjornolf noticed the coffee percolating, but Nathan hadn't had any. "You having some?"

Nathan shook his head.

"Thanks for fixing it." Bjornolf poured himself a mug, then said, "Who called? Hunter?"

Nathan's face turned a light shade of red. "Uh, yeah. You… heard?"

"Yep. Another disadvantage of having wolf chaperones."

Nathan nodded. "Or teen wolves who can hear all the noise being made down the hall."

Bjornolf fought a grin. "We were sparring."

Nathan's face fell, then the smile returned. "Yeah, right." When Bjornolf didn't confirm Nathan's suspicions one way or another, he asked pointedly, "You're mated, right?"

Normally, Bjornolf wouldn't have said. But this wasn't a normal situation.

"Yeah, we're hitched, wolf-style." Meaning mated, no marriage necessary. It was a done deal for life.

Nathan nodded, trying to look serious, but he couldn't hide a full-fledged grin.

That worried Bjornolf a bit. He hadn't considered living with Nathan beyond this mission.

"Okay," Bjornolf said, not willing to ponder the situation further. "Let me talk to Hunter, and then let's get those lights up. Open house is tomorrow, and we've got a lot of work ahead of us."

Bjornolf walked outside into the crisp, cold winter day. He had the phone to his ear as he carried several strands of lights draped over his arm. Nathan had already brought out several more and a ladder, plus plastic hooks to hang the lights to the gutters.

Bjornolf was impressed.

"Is this the right way?" Nathan asked. "I've never hung lights up on a house before."

"That's it." Bjornolf heard Hunter's voice and said, "Bjornolf here. You called?"

"Yeah, you first."

Bjornolf was watching Nathan as he hung the lights meticulously, making sure the hooks were evenly spaced. The kid was doing a good job, and Bjornolf couldn't help but be proud of him. His father must have been just as pleased with him.

"I don't know anything new on the case," Bjornolf told Hunter.

Nathan looked down at him, all ears.

"That's not what I meant," Hunter said.

Bjornolf frowned. "Anna?" he guessed.

"Yeah. Well, what of it?" Hunter sounded growly and protective of *his* teammate.

Nathan looked like he might be in trouble for having

said anything about hearing Anna and Bjornolf last night. Bjornolf raised his brows at Nathan and smiled, reassuring him that *he* was fine with what Nathan had said to Hunter.

"Sparring practice," Bjornolf told Hunter.

Nathan grinned and continued hanging more lights.

"Sparring practice," Hunter said. He didn't say anything more for a moment.

Bjornolf stepped forward to hand Nathan a new strand of lights. "Yeah."

"Who won this time?" Hunter finally asked.

"Depends on who's telling the story."

Hunter laughed. "I can believe that. How's Nathan doing?"

"Nathan's great. He made us coffee. Didn't drink rum in his eggnog, and he's hanging Christmas lights on the house. Couldn't ask for a better kid."

Nathan's ears tinged red, but he smiled, and Bjornolf was glad that Nathan heard him praise him. Especially after what had occurred yesterday over the running-to-Portland situation.

"What about the two of you? Can you handle it?"

"He might have to stay at your house at night if he wants to get some sleep," Bjornolf said.

Nathan quickly shook his head, frowning.

"Forget it. He says no. We'll get him some earplugs."

Hunter laughed. Then he got serious again. "Finn discovered that both of the dead men had been working with the DEA. I'm wondering if these agents were investigating someone at the tree farm. What if they learned that the guy was dealing, but before they could report it, the agents were murdered?"

"Or," Bjornolf said, not liking a different scenario, "what if they couldn't report it?"

"Meaning the drug dealers were wolves?"

"Yeah. Only they didn't know you had a pack here and could have helped them out."

"Sounds like a possibility. It's not like there's a map of where *lupus garou* settlements exist in the States and beyond."

"What about the Wentworths? Any lead on them?"

"They've returned home. Rourke's headed to their one-and-a-half-million-dollar estate located next to Forest Park in Portland to do an interview on their harrowing adventure. We're hoping he might learn something."

"Wentworth?" Nathan asked, climbing down the ladder to move it again.

Bjornolf looked up at him as he climbed back up the ladder. "You know a Wentworth?"

"Everton, the guy who owns the tree farm, has a half brother named William Wentworth."

"He wouldn't happen to be 'the Third,' would he?" Bjornolf asked.

"Uh, yeah. Everton says it in a sarcastic way as if the dude thinks he's really cool cuz he's the Third. I don't think he likes his half brother at all. Not that I'm really surprised. When Everton was off delivering some trees to customers a couple of days ago, William dropped by to see Jessica's mom, Dottie. He acted really friendly. Gave her a big hug and kissed her.

"They didn't realize I was in the back of the shop hanging some fresh Christmas wreaths. When he saw me, he quickly moved away from her and gave me a look that could kill. I just figured the guy was being nice to her because they were related—by marriage. But after the look he gave me, I wondered if something more was going on."

Bjornolf relayed the message to Hunter.

"We'll check into it," Hunter said. "Anything else?"

"Yeah, one other thing struck me as odd. When Anna and I were out investigating the tree farm the night before last, a man named Everton caught us and asked for our ID. I just thought it strange that anyone would be on guard duty watching over a tree farm late at night."

"Everton?" Nathan asked, pausing to hook up the next section of lights.

Bjornolf was getting a bad feeling about this as he studied Nathan's frown.

Nathan said, "He never guards the place. At night, he's always watching sports on TV in the basement. I know because I've sneaked in to see Jessica and her dad never knew it."

Chapter 15

WHAT WAS EVERTON DOING WANDERING AROUND THE tree farm at night if he didn't normally do so?

"So what happened at the tree farm, exactly?" Nathan asked, sounding alarmed.

Bjornolf told him about the man who had caught Anna trespassing and how she'd used Nathan and his faux watch as an alibi.

"Where were *you* when Jessica's father was hassling Anna?" Nathan sounded like he was about to take Bjornolf on for not protecting her.

Bjornolf fought smiling. The kid was cute. "I was there." Not that Bjornolf had to explain himself to Nathan, but he wanted to. "He asked for an ID and Anna said she wasn't changing her name to mine."

Nathan's eyes widened. "Will she now?"

Bjornolf snorted. "We don't actually get married on paper."

"Oh. Yeah." Nathan hung up another section of lights, then climbed down the ladder to move it again. He climbed back up and then turned to Bjornolf. "When was the first time you had sex with a human girl?"

Hell. Bjornolf stopped unraveling strands of lights and looked up at Nathan. "This isn't about that Jessica Everton girl, is it?"

Nathan frowned, turned, and continued to hang lights off the house.

Not good. "How old is she?" Bjornolf asked. He hadn't expected to have *these* kinds of talks with the kid.

"She's seventeen. Like me. But we can do it with human girls because as wolves we can't get them pregnant."

Bjornolf frowned at him. "Most of the time, no."

Nathan's jaw dropped.

"It happens occasionally. Haven't you ever heard Tessa's story?"

"She was mated to Hunter before she got pregnant."

"Her mother was the byproduct of her human grandmother and her werewolf grandfather's union."

Nathan stared at Bjornolf for a moment. "Oh." Then he began hanging the lights again.

"It's rare, but still risky."

Nathan turned. "But Tessa wasn't one of us. Hunter had to bite her."

"Yes, but that's not the point, is it? Her mother's mother became pregnant. *That's* the point. Further, we usually have multiple births so all of a sudden you wouldn't have one child but possibly several."

Nathan was quiet for a long time. Then he said meekly, as if he was afraid that Bjornolf would tell him that his thoughts on that subject were also urban legend, "We can't get STDs from humans."

"You're right. Still, Jessica's underage and jailbait."

Nathan sighed. "You're not going to tell me about the first time you had sex with a human?"

"You know how long we live, Nathan." Bjornolf was sure Nathan's father hadn't talked to him about his own sex life before he mated Nathan's mother. He wasn't sure what the protocol was here. Bjornolf's father certainly never talked to him about the birds and the bees.

"Yeah, I know once you reach puberty, you age only one in thirty years."

"So it's been a very long time."

Nathan's eyes widened. "You don't remember?"

Bjornolf frowned at him. "Of course I remember."

"Well?"

"She was sixteen."

"Sixteen? That's worse than me."

"You've already done it with Jessica?" Bjornolf shouldn't have sounded so astounded, but he had guessed the kid was trying to sound him out, to see if Bjornolf thought it was acceptable. *Before* he did it.

Nathan turned and hung another strand of the lights. "I shouldn't have. I guess. Do you think Anna knows?"

Bjornolf was surprised Nathan would worry about what Anna thought. Then he recalled how she'd lectured him about not getting involved with a human girl. Which made him wonder when Anna had been involved with a human boy for the first time. That thought made his gut clench. It shouldn't matter what she'd done so long ago, now that she was his.

Bjornolf shook his head. "I don't know if Anna guessed or not."

"She didn't like it that I was seeing Jessica," Nathan said morosely.

"If we have sex with a wolf-shifter, it's for life," Bjornolf warned, thinking that's maybe why Nathan tore off to see Sarah. "So for years we seek… companionship with humans until we find a worthwhile mate. Don't go having sex with Sarah unless she's truly the one you want to be with forever, or you'll both be stuck with each other for a very long time. No divorce for mated wolves."

"Which means it's okay to be with Jessica for now."

"No," Anna said, shoving the door open with her hip. She walked across the snow-covered grass, carrying a tray of hot, buttery crescent rolls and mugs of cocoa topped with mounds of whipped cream.

Nathan turned a little red as he eyed her.

"I brought you some breakfast. Not much, just something quick to snack on while you work."

"You cook?" Nathan said, sounding surprised and at the same time glad as he climbed down the ladder to snatch a roll and a mug of cocoa.

"Don't *ever* let Hunter and the SEAL team know. They think a woman should do all the cooking on missions. They tease me about it, but it's not all bantering. I let them know otherwise."

"Your secret's safe with me." Nathan scarfed down two more rolls.

"Thanks, Anna." Bjornolf grabbed a couple before Nathan ate them all and helped himself to the other mug of cocoa. He'd fixed cocoa and rolls tons of times for himself before, but something about Anna preparing them made the food and drink taste even better.

"Yeah, thanks," Nathan managed to say before he took another bite of his roll, concentrating on devouring them.

"Don't worry," she said to Nathan in a teasing tone. "I'll feed you again." She glanced up at the house, and her expression softened as she spied the lights hanging near the roof. "The lights are nearly done. They look *great*. I can't wait to see them tonight when it's dark."

"Yeah, it'll look great," Nathan said. "We'll be going inside to work on the tree next. Okay?"

"Sounds good." Anna smiled at them warmly, then headed back inside. She shut the door.

Nathan stared at the door and calculated when she might be well out of earshot. "I think she heard us talking. I mean, about most of it. Don't you?"

"Yeah, I think she did." Bjornolf could just imagine her questioning *him* about his encounter with the sixteen-year-old human girl next time they were alone. Or maybe not. She might not want to touch the subject because he was liable to ask her about *her* past misadventures.

"Jessica's adopted," Nathan finally said.

"She's still human." Bjornolf was finally getting that Nathan was *really* hung up on the human girl.

"She…" Nathan paused. "She smells like a wolf."

Bjornolf didn't say anything for a moment, trying to process that bit of information, then asked, "What do you mean exactly?"

Nathan shrugged. "She smells like a wolf. Like all of us do—part wolf, part human. I asked if she owned a pet wolf. She laughed at me. Of course she smells more human because her parents hug on her all of the time. Probably because she's adopted."

Bjornolf stared hard at the boy, not believing this.

Nathan sighed. "Tessa was the granddaughter of a wolf. Maybe Jessica is also."

"She can't shift then. If this is true."

"She told me she believes in the paranormal. I thought she was hinting that she was a *lupus garou* but that she was afraid to come out and say so."

"You didn't tell her about us, did you?" Bjornolf growled. Not that a human would believe Nathan, but still, they didn't tell humans what they were. *Period*. Not unless they had to turn them.

"No. Of course not. Sure, I was hoping she was one of us. But why would humans have adopted and raised her? Why wouldn't a wolf pack have taken her in?"

Maybe because her parents didn't belong to a wolf pack. Bjornolf still couldn't believe it. "Is she from here?"

Nathan shook his head. "She's from Santa Fe, New Mexico, but she doesn't know who her parents were. She's searched, too."

"So when she said she believed in the paranormal, what did she mean?"

Nathan sighed. "She meant ghosts. I wasn't going to talk about *lupus garous* until she did first. When she spoke of ghosts, I couldn't hide my disappointment. Of course she thought I believed she was crazy for thinking they were real."

"What did you say?" Bjornolf asked carefully.

Nathan frowned at him. "I didn't say, 'Hey, I'm a werewolf. Imagine that.' I just said, 'Wouldn't it be cool if other paranormal beings existed? Like werewolves.'"

"And?" Bjornolf prompted, not believing Nathan would risk saying anything.

"She told me that werewolves do exist. She said it so cheerily I thought she meant for real." Nathan frowned. "'In books,' she said. Then I wondered if she was seeing some guy who was a wolf." His hands tightened into fists. "Maybe he'd had his hands all over her. Maybe that's why she smelled like a wolf."

"You would have smelled the male wolf, Nathan," Bjornolf said, seeing just how upset he was becoming. "You would have recognized his scent and known him.

You didn't, did you? Only smelled wolf on her? Like she was a wolf?"

"Yeah."

"Okay. When was she adopted? What age?" Bjornolf still couldn't believe it without checking the situation out himself.

"When she was a baby, she said. Before she even knew her birth parents."

"You don't know her birth name?"

"No. She doesn't know it. Her parents don't know it, either, or are keeping what it was from her, afraid she might try to find her birth parents."

Bjornolf let out his breath. "Anna and I are going to need to meet this friend of yours as soon as we can."

Hell, if Nathan had sex with her and she turned out to be one of them, he was essentially mated to her for life.

Anna had been stunned to hear Nathan speaking to Bjornolf about sex and human girls. But Nathan obviously needed a parental sounding board, so she didn't want to stifle him. She cleaned up the kitchen, unable to quit thinking about the trouble Nathan could be in.

She went out back and cut some lower branches off a few fir trees to use on the mantel, taking in great breaths of the chilly air, thinking about how Tessa and Hunter had met each other in these very same cabins.

Bjornolf was right about Tessa. It was really rare that a *lupus garou* could get a human pregnant, but all it took was one mistake like that. From what she'd seen of Nathan, he was responsible at working a job and had been great about decorating for Christmas, but raising multiple babies at once? She was sure he wasn't ready for *that*.

Why hadn't the boy's father discussed the subject with him?

Not that her parents had ever done so with her. Which had gotten her into a lot of trouble.

After a short while, Nathan and Bjornolf came inside where the cabin was fragrant and warm. Anna loved the piney smell of the greenery she'd used to trim the mantel.

Nathan touched Anna's arm, breaking into her thoughts as he delighted in showing her all the decorations he'd bought. He demonstrated how to put them on the tree to make sure that the silver, gold, blue, and purple balls were placed evenly around it. "You can get the branches lower on the tree while Bjornolf and I can get the ones higher."

She shook her head. "I'm not *that* short. Besides, the bottom of the tree needs more ornaments than the top."

Nathan took the hint. "Uh, yeah, right. I'll help you with the lower branches."

"I'm impressed with your selection of decorations," she said, genuinely feeling so, though she was having a really difficult time not worrying about Jessica now that they suspected she might be a wolf. Jessica needed to be with their wolf kind, if she was one of them. She needed to learn how to live like they did. The problem was that they couldn't just take her away from her adoptive parents.

Then a new worry plagued her. How long ago and how many times had Nathan had sex with Jessica? Was she pregnant? As a human, that was one thing. But as a werewolf?

What a nightmare.

"I'm impressed, too," Bjornolf said, kissing Anna on the cheek, but being careful not to be overly affectionate with her in front of Nathan. Bjornolf hooked a silver ball near the top.

"Nathan said that the man who owns the tree farm, Everton, is a half brother of William Wentworth III."

Her jaw dropping, Anna stared at Bjornolf. "That's too much of a coincidence."

"I agree. Hunter said the two murdered men were DEA."

"DEA." She thought about that for a moment, pausing to place a purple ball midway up the tree. "Remember, Wentworth has a big pharmaceutical company. Twenty-five percent of drugs come from tropical plants and trees in the Amazon. When we were given the assignment to extract him and his family, I wondered if there was a connection. I did a little research. His company discovered one of the anti-cancer drugs that was extracted from periwinkle and other rainforest plants. One of the drugs has greatly increased the survival rate for acute leukemia patients. So his company is doing a good job.

"But what if legal drugs are only part of his business?" she continued. "The legit side. What if he hooked up with one of the Colombian cartels to access the illegal kind, too? Or to distribute them here, using his cover of making legitimate drugs? Making lots more money at it. No expensive research. Just grow the stuff and distribute it and collect the dough, tax-free. Because of his other connection, no one would even suspect he'd have other kinds of dealings down there."

Bjornolf nodded. "Very possible. No one would ever

know, except for maybe two wolf agents with the DEA who suspected the truth."

"Why would they have been at the Christmas tree farm, then?"

She knew Nathan was listening to them. Normally, she wouldn't have talked shop in front of someone who wasn't on the investigative team. In Nathan's case, he seemed to have inside knowledge. The only drawback was if Everton was involved, Nathan might feel a need to warn Jessica.

He didn't say anything about what was being said, but she was certain he was trying to think of anything that might help them with piecing the puzzle together.

"Wentworth might have tried to set Everton up if the two don't care for each other," Bjornolf said.

"What if Everton is in on this?"

Nathan was in the process of moving an ornament already on the tree to another spot when he paused to look at Anna, but he didn't offer anything.

Anna sighed and folded her arms across her chest. "We have to look at every possible reason why Wentworth would tell his brother, Jeff, that we shouldn't have killed their kidnappers in the Amazon, and why DEA agents were murdered at the Christmas tree farm. It's possible that Everton is involved up to his eyeballs. He may know about his half brothers' involvement and have blackmailed them even, wanting a share of the money. Maybe he got rid of the DEA agents for Wentworth." She paused. "Remember when William and Jeff were talking, and the one said they had led trouble to someone's doorstep, but they weren't there to take care of the mess this time?"

"Yeah, I remember."

"I wonder if the agents disappeared around the same time." Anna shook her head. "Without more to go on, it's a guessing game."

Nathan went to the sack to get one last ornament out. "Are you ready?" Nathan pulled out the angel. "See it's gold, copper, and silver with a gray wolf standing beside her long skirt."

Warmed to the marrow of her bones, Anna smiled. "It's beautiful, Nathan. The prettiest angel I've ever seen." It had been killing her not to take a peek before the guys came in from outside.

"I was afraid you might want something else. That you envisioned a different kind of angel. Something softer, maybe."

"She's perfect." Anna went to hug him, and he quickly looked at Bjornolf, as if seeking his approval.

Bjornolf gave him a nod and a smile, but Anna had already moved to embrace Nathan. "You're so sweet, Nathan. I've never celebrated the holiday. You've helped to make this one so special to me, and I'll never forget it."

He hugged her back, then he said to Bjornolf, "My dad always put the star on the tree. Did you want to do the honors?"

Nathan was fighting back tears, just like she was. Bjornolf gave her a small smile and squeezed her hand, and she noted his eyes were misty, too. "I'd love to."

She realized then she'd never think of the holidays again as one of those hassles in life, involving crowded shopping centers and annoying Christmas jingles played over and over again. She put her arm around Nathan's shoulders and watched as Bjornolf put the angel and wolf ornament on top of the Colorado blue spruce tree.

"We'll have the most beautiful tree of any of the open houses, guaranteed," she said proudly.

"Yeah, it's pretty cool, isn't it?"

Bjornolf cleared his throat. They both looked over at him. "Anna, you said you knew how to cook?"

In short order, they had baked chicken thighs, asparagus, and baked potatoes on a big serving dish sitting in the center of the cherrywood dining table.

Bjornolf and Nathan looked at the table, then at Anna. "We need holiday decorations for the table for the open house," Bjornolf said.

"Yeah," Nathan said.

They both studied Anna, waiting for her response. She wanted to say she didn't "do" shopping. But after all that Nathan had done, she couldn't say no. She sighed. "After lunch, all right?"

Nathan gave Bjornolf a high five.

She was doomed.

After lunch, Bjornolf and Nathan put away the dishes. She could really get used to this, but she figured when...

She paused as she wiped down the table. She hadn't even considered what might happen beyond the mission—what would become of Nathan, or where she and Bjornolf would end up.

"I need to make a quick call. Be right back." She headed into the bedroom and shut the door, then fished out her phone and called Hunter. "I need you to look into something for me."

"About the murders?" Hunter asked.

"No. About a Jessica Everton, adopted daughter of

the owners of the Christmas tree farm. She was born in Santa Fe, New Mexico."

"What are we looking for?" he asked.

"To learn if her real parents were wolves."

Chapter 16

SHORTLY THEREAFTER, ANNA GOT A CALL FROM Hunter letting her know that Rourke, their investigative reporter, had just called to tell Hunter that once he'd interviewed Helen Wentworth and after investigating some leads, he suspected Jessica Everton might be a wolf. First, according to Mrs. Wentworth, there was the case of a mysterious adoption—no evidence of papers, the Evertons' own loss of a baby daughter, Jessica's behavioral problems, no birth record for her that he could locate—and the scent of wolf when he'd dropped by to see the girl at the tree farm.

Anna shared the news with Bjornolf and Nathan. "We'll finish decorating for the open house after we go shopping. Then Nathan, you arrange for Jessica to come over for dinner tonight."

They couldn't put this off any longer than that.

He looked skeptical.

Anna sighed and took his hand. "Nathan, if she's truly a wolf, and if you two had sex, then you've mated with her. If you've mated with her, you could very well have gotten her pregnant. We *have* to learn the truth and deal with it."

He frowned. "*You* shouldn't have to do anything. Hunter took care of his mistakes all on his own."

Anna nodded. "True. But he's the pack leader. He had to. You're not even legally an adult yet. We'll help you in any way we can. Okay? Hunter and the rest of the pack will, too. That's what a wolf pack is all about, Nathan. We take care of each other through the good stuff and the bad. You don't have to do this alone."

He bit his lip, then said, "She thinks she's pregnant."

Anna quickly closed her mouth, not wanting to look so astonished.

"I got angry with her because I knew I couldn't have made her that way. That was one of the reasons I left to see Sarah." Nathan glanced at Bjornolf. "Until he mentioned that in rare cases our kind could get a human pregnant." He took a deep breath. "Jessica's too afraid to get a pregnancy test and see what it shows. She swore I was the only one she'd been seeing."

Anna didn't say anything for a moment, shocked at the newest revelation, then nodded. "Call her, Nathan. Tell her you'll pick her up for dinner tonight. That your aunt and uncle want to meet her. Then we'll go shopping."

Now, if only Jessica's parents were all right with it, and Jessica was, too.

Anna suspected nothing would go as planned. When did it ever?

Bjornolf hoped they could learn the truth about Jessica tonight at dinner and then work on how they would handle it after that. For now, they were at a shopping mall for last-minute decorations to finish off the house for the pack parade of homes.

Anna had changed into a pair of cobalt blue jeans, the back pockets decorated with sequined hearts to catch the eye. She wore high-heeled boots and a white crocheted sweater that dipped low in front, showing off a hint of cleavage. She looked like a million bucks, and he couldn't help staring at the ensemble, nearly running into a number of different customers in the crowded department store.

Casting Bjornolf a small smile, she said, "You like it?"

He and Nathan both were looking at her lacy sweater and they said in unison, "Yeah."

She pointed to the decorations sitting on a table. They switched their gazes to the table set up with holiday trimmings, place mats, plates featuring reindeer, shiny gold silverware, and linen napkins bound in crystal and gold ties.

"Oh yeah," Nathan said.

Bjornolf's gaze drifted to the hint of the swell of her breasts. "Oh yeah."

Nathan chuckled when he saw what Bjornolf was talking about.

Christmas music played overhead as shoppers seemed to fill every aisle of the department store. Some shoppers were in a rush, while others were carefully considering merchandise, poking at clothes, lifting china to examine it, and sifting through bath towels. Where Anna was concerned, Bjornolf had never seen a woman shop so quickly in his life.

Once she saw the Christmas settings displayed on the table, she said to Bjornolf and Nathan, "How about that? Isn't it perfect?"

She didn't really ask for their opinion, he wryly thought. Before they could answer, she gathered the eight placemats she had been eyeing on a shelf, and they helped her find matching linen napkins, and crystal and gold napkin holders. She took the whole centerpiece and shoved it into Bjornolf's hands, grabbed the runner off the display table, and said, "Done."

Bjornolf looked at Nathan to see his take on it. He raised his brows and smiled.

As if considering her choices, she folded her arms and looked at the table again. "Maybe we're not done. We could use a set of red Christmas plates. They'd be perfect for Valentine's Day, too. We can add blue and white decorations when it comes to Memorial Day, Flag Day, and Fourth of July celebrations."

Bjornolf suspected Anna had never celebrated any of those holidays. Her enthusiasm was contagious and he was doubly glad she was a quick shopper. He looked forward to sharing every one of those holidays with her next year, and making up some of their own.

They were out of there in no time.

"Can we stop at a drugstore on the way back to the cottage?" Anna asked.

"Sure," Bjornolf said.

When they pulled into the strip mall, both Bjornolf and Nathan were going to join her, but she said she'd be just a minute. Nathan sank against the car seat, looking relieved.

They parked in front of the drugstore situated at the end of a small strip mall of four shops: a card shop, a dress store, and a bookstore, in addition to the drugstore. In silence, Bjornolf and Nathan studied the drugstore display windows filled with Christmas decorations and a clutter of advertisements as the door closed behind Anna, and she disappeared from view.

Nathan cleared his throat. "She's getting a pregnancy test for Jessica. Isn't she?"

"I suspect so. Jessica needs to know if she is pregnant as soon as possible. She has to realize she's got us for backup. She has to have a support system *now*."

"I really screwed up, didn't I?"

Bjornolf had been there. His own messes had seemed insurmountable at the time, but somehow he'd managed to muddle through.

"Some lessons are harder to learn than others. You really do care for her, don't you?" Bjornolf didn't mean to sound so judgmental, but he hoped Nathan truly loved her because they'd be together for a very long time, and there was no undoing what they had done.

Nathan nodded. "Yeah. I do. Ever lie awake at night thinking of the day you spent with someone special, and you want to repeat the day over and over again?"

Yeah, he did. Anna had stolen his thoughts more times than he wanted to admit.

Nathan glanced at Bjornolf. "Like with you and Anna?"

Bjornolf fought a smile. No one ever questioned him about his relationships with women. He assumed Nathan needed confirmation more than anything. "Hell, yeah. You know you have it bad when you're thinking about nothing at all, doing something, and suddenly out of the blue you're thinking of her. Like driving the car, then there she is taking up space in my brain again. Bright as day."

Nathan shook his head. "That's just like me. I'll be cutting a tree for a customer, and all of a sudden, I'll think of the way she smiled at me earlier in the day and offered me a cup of hot chocolate. I mean, it's more than that. I can't wait to see her, to be with her again."

"So you ran because...?"

"I was confused. She was raised by humans. I thought she was human. What Anna said was right. We can't turn people just because we want to. I was using Hunter's situation as a crutch to fall back on. He did it and it turned out okay, so I could, too. Except he's not a teen. And he's the pack leader. I thought… I thought if I saw Sarah, I would change my mind about wanting Jessica."

Concerned, Bjornolf frowned. "With Sarah, you didn't…"

"No." Nathan gave him a get-real look. "I knew *she* was a wolf."

Bjornolf breathed in a sigh of relief. Sarah's father would have killed Nathan. Bjornolf tapped his thumbs on the steering wheel.

Nathan sat morosely staring out the windshield. Soft, white snowflakes began to flutter down from the heavens.

"If she's a wolf *and* pregnant *and* your mate, she should come to our open house tomorrow. It's a pack gathering. Everyone should get to know her. It would be the perfect time to make her feel welcome. Give her a network of wolf families to fall back on," Bjornolf said.

"If she wants. She might be too overwhelmed with the whole thing." Nathan paused. "What are we going to do when you and Anna leave?"

Bjornolf took a deep breath. "Anna and I haven't even decided where we're going to be living beyond this mission."

Nathan studied him carefully, then quietly said, "I hope you both decide to stay here."

Bjornolf smiled at him. "I don't think anyone has ever told me that before."

Nathan looked skeptical for a moment, then seeing Bjornolf was serious, he grinned. "Well, I have."

"I'll have to talk with Anna. But we'll see." Bjornolf looked back at the drugstore.

"You're worried about her." Nathan looked from the windshield to Bjornolf.

"Yeah," he said. "She's taking too long. Not her style. Let's go."

The two of them headed for the drugstore as an elderly lady and man using walkers tried to get through the door. Barely able to suppress the urgent need to dash into the store and ignore the older couple's troubles, Bjornolf held the door open for them.

Once the elderly couple had made it outside, Bjornolf and Nathan rushed inside, following Anna's scent. They found she'd lingered in front of a display of boxes of dark chocolate thin mints. Not what he'd expected. They headed for the aisle where the pregnancy tests were shelved.

"She was here," Nathan said, anxious. "But then she moved right on past as if she didn't linger."

"It's okay. We would have seen her leave the store. She must have thought of something else we needed for dinner tonight or decorations or something."

"I'll go that way," Nathan said, motioning to the right, "and you take the other half of the store."

Bjornolf didn't argue about who was in charge, just nodded, seeing something of himself in the kid and approving. With his long stride, Bjornolf ate up the drugstore's linoleum tiles, avoiding the aisles she hadn't walked down. He soon spied Nathan headed in the same direction he was. The employees' back-door entrance.

Shit. Not only must she have left the building this way, but she'd been with one hulking brute of a man named Everton. From the scent she'd left behind, Bjornolf could tell she had been angry, and so was Everton. Bjornolf's heart was pounding furiously. He and Nathan burst outside, letting the door slam behind them. They quickly surveyed the parking lot for any sign of movement.

"What would Roger Everton want with Anna?" Nathan said, hurrying with Bjornolf to search the employee parking lot to the strip mall.

There was no sign of Anna or any vehicle that Nathan recognized as belonging to the Everton family or any of their staff work trucks. No movement at all.

"He thought she discovered something at the tree farm?" Bjornolf said, racing with Nathan around the strip mall because the employee door was locked and they couldn't get back in without a key. How had Everton gotten the upper hand with Anna? Bjornolf knew she'd be armed. She had tons of tricks to use on a man who tried to take her hostage.

His blood cold with worry, Bjornolf was already on his cell phone to Hunter before they reached the Land Rover. "Roger Everton abducted Anna at Riley's Drugstore. We're not sure where they've gone, but we're heading to the Christmas tree farm. He's the same man that said he was Everton when he caught us investigating the farm."

"I'll send the troops, Bjornolf. We'll get her back."

Yeah, but alive and in one piece? Or dead like the wolf DEA agents? Bjornolf floored the Land Rover.

When Bjornolf got off the phone with Hunter, he

heard what he assumed was Nathan talking to Jessica on his phone.

"I don't know what's going on with your dad, but he just abducted my aunt." Nathan sounded both worried and hot with anger.

Bjornolf had nearly forgotten their cover in all of this madness.

"Let me know if you see your dad return home. My uncle and I are headed for the tree farm. Some friends of his are also. Okay, Jessica?"

There was silence for a moment, then Nathan said, "I love you, too." He sounded almost embarrassed to declare such a thing in front of Bjornolf, and when he ended the conversation, he quickly looked at Bjornolf to see if he'd been listening.

Nathan laid the phone on his lap and stared out the windshield.

"Is everything all right with Jessica?" Bjornolf asked. He was full of worry for Anna, but he was also concerned about Jessica, should Everton turn on her.

"It's all my fault," Nathan said.

"No. It isn't," Bjornolf said sternly. "We're here because we're trying to uncover a couple of murders. It appears Everton is involved in this murder business, and it doesn't have anything to do with you."

Nathan shook his head. "Not about that. Jessica texted me when we were shopping earlier. She'd spoken to her father about coming to our place for dinner. He wanted to know where we were so he could talk to you. She said she could tell he was angry, but he was trying to hide how he was feeling from her. She asked which store we were at, hoping that you and Anna would convince him it was fine that she had dinner with us. He must have gone to the store, saw us leave in the Land Rover, and followed us to the drugstore."

What the hell was going on with Everton? Bjornolf wondered if he suspected they were not Nathan's relatives, that they were there to investigate the murders. *Hell*.

"Where's Jessica and her mom?" Bjornolf asked, attempting to sound in control of his emotions when he was about to have a meltdown. He thought it best that both of the women be away from the farm, immediately.

Nathan studied him. "Her mom was in Portland for the day. Jessica's by herself."

"Is Jessica's home near the Christmas tree farm?"

"On the property. Behind the gift shop. There's a road that skirts around to the back of the shop. The house is set back, surrounded by pine trees that tower over the place."

Bjornolf ground his teeth. He wanted Jessica to stay put until they arrived, reporting to them if Everton and Anna showed up. On the other hand, she would be safer with one of the wolf-pack families until they could sort the situation out. He didn't trust that Everton would not harm her if he knew she'd learned what he was up to.

"We could have a wolf pick her up and take her to his home, but it would take longer. Or we could tell her to drive to one of the family's homes, but she might not feel comfortable doing that. Her father might catch her trying to leave," Bjornolf said.

"We're half an hour from there," Nathan said. "Everton's got at least ten to fifteen minutes head start on us. But we don't know if he's really going to the tree farm or not."

Nathan called Jessica back. "We've got friends on the way, but it will take some time for them to get there."

"He was angry, Nathan. I've never heard him so mad." Tears choked Jessica's voice.

"Okay... okay, um..." That was one thing Nathan couldn't handle. Women's tears. Worse, he couldn't think of what to tell her to do to stay safe.

"He said that your aunt and uncle weren't really your aunt and uncle. He thinks they're trying to steal me away."

"What? That's crazy! You don't believe that, do you?" Nathan meant about the stealing part. He'd have to explain that they weren't really related, though.

"He said... he said he caught them sneaking around the property like they were trying to find a way to break into the house. He told me he didn't call the police on them because he knew they were friends of yours, and I care for you."

"Do you believe him? That they were trying to break into your house?"

"No. He lied. No one was anywhere near the house but my mother and father and me. Well, and you when they weren't around."

Nathan took a settling breath. "Okay. Bjornolf and Anna aren't dangerous, alright? They're like my god-parents. They—"

"He's back," she said in a strangled whisper, sounding scared to death.

"Anna? Is Anna with him? Jessica, answer me!"

"He's... he's opening the trunk." Her words shook.

Nathan barely breathed.

Bjornolf's heart was racing so hard that Nathan could hear it. Bjornolf couldn't drive any faster without getting himself and Nathan killed on the road, but he was pushing it as hard as he could. Nathan knew Bjornolf was straining to hear what Jessica was saying. He didn't want him to hear the truth if Anna was no longer alive.

"Oh my God. He's carrying something in an old army blanket," Jessica said.

"Like a body, Jessica?"

"He's putting the… the… oh God, I see a hand. A woman's hand. He's tossing her body into the bucket of the backhoe."

"Jessica, listen to me." Nathan's blood pounded so hard that he could hear it throbbing in his ears. "Jessica, I want you to leave. *Now*."

"He's taken the keys to my car. I looked. They're gone."

"Open the back door to your house. Remove your clothes and shift into a wolf." He felt Bjornolf glance in his direction, but he didn't say anything.

"Jessica, *listen to me*. I *know* you've done it before." Nathan suspected she must have shifted a few times since she'd reached puberty. He spoke forcefully, urging her to break through her fear and take care of herself in a wolf way. "We can't see it because of the clouds, but the moon's full. You must feel it. You can shift again. I can also. Bjornolf and Anna are just like us. Get *out* of the house. Hide in the woods until help arrives."

He heard a door squeak open and his heart plunged. Was it her father, returning after disposing of Anna?

"Jessica?"

"All right. All right. Promise me you'll come for me." She stifled a sob. "I love you. I have to go," she whispered.

He listened into the phone. He heard the rustling

of clothes, and then the scrambling of wolf claws on the tile floor before the sound of the backhoe's engine growled in the distance, moving away from the house and into the woods.

Nathan gripped the phone so hard that he was surprised he hadn't crushed it. He couldn't look at Bjornolf, couldn't tell him that they could be too late for Anna. Her first Christmas… and her last. Hot tears filled his eyes.

"Turn wolf as soon as we get there," Bjornolf suddenly said.

Breaking free of his thoughts, Nathan glanced at him. "What?"

"You'll run faster. Howl for the pack. One of us needs to remain in human form. I'm trained to take down the enemy as a human. You aren't. You'll do better protecting Jessica with your wolf teeth."

"We go after Anna first, right?" Nathan asked.

He wanted to protect Jessica, but he knew she could hide from her father, while Anna was the one who needed rescuing pronto. He yanked off his sweater, then began tugging at the buttons on his shirt.

"Yeah. But you can't bite Everton unless we have no other option. Then you find Jessica. Keep her safe until the troops arrive."

He prayed that Anna wouldn't need the troops. That he and Bjornolf would save her before it was too late.

Chapter 17

SHIT.

Anna hated shopping, but as soon as she'd spied her favorite dark chocolate mints—the sole thing that made her take notice of the holidays—she felt a gun poke her ribs.

With a quick twist of her head, she'd looked up into the mottled red face of one very angry Everton.

She couldn't register why he had targeted her in the drugstore. Why he had a gun. Why he acted like he wanted to kill her.

"You're one of them, aren't you?" he growled softly in her ear.

"One of whom?" she asked, honestly not knowing what he meant. Her first thought was that he knew she was a wolf. He couldn't know *that* unless he was also a *lupus garou*, but he wasn't.

Did he think she was DEA? *Hell.* That's probably what he thought. That she was investigating the other agents' murders and also was one. Which meant? A death sentence for her. It also had to mean he was involved in the men's killings or the cover-up, or both.

She wanted to use her martial arts on him. But because she was in such close proximity to two ladies picking out vitamins and four elderly customers looking at other kinds of health remedies, she was certain his gun would go off, and he'd hit somebody. If not her.

She couldn't risk it.

With a gloved hand shackled to her arm, he pulled her through the store and into a short hallway that housed an employee bathroom. His target was the employees' back door. She quickly noted the fire exit sign and the statement that opening the door would set off the alarm, which gave her hope. With their enhanced wolf hearing, Bjornolf and Nathan would be alerted.

Apparently the warning sign was just for show because when he opened the door, nothing could be heard except the creaking sound of rusty hinges. She was on her own.

Once she was outside, she went all ninja she-wolf warrior on him for a few seconds. She slammed her fist into the bridge of his nose, using the bottom part of her hand like a hammer, breaking the cartilage. It twisted and made a loud *crunch*. Blood gushed forth, and he howled in pain.

In the next instant, she kneed him in the thigh with a sharp jab, missing the more vital groin area because he jerked to the side when she broke his nose. He cursed and clamped something over her face.

She struggled, kicking his shins, and scratching a gloved hand that held a damp cloth over her nose and mouth. The odor from the cloth was pleasant, nonirritating, and sweet smelling. *Chloroform*, her brain instantly registered. Trying to fight harder, to break loose, she felt herself drifting like a footloose cloud away from all the others bunched together in the sky. Snowflakes collected on her eyelashes as she stared up at the blood gushing from Everton's crooked nose.

The red blood, his red splotchy face, the black ski

cap stretched across his big head, and even the white snowflakes faded to gray, and then to black.

The next thing she was aware of was bouncing around in the trunk of a vehicle. She was wrapped up in a scratchy wool blanket, standard army issue. Every bump in the road bruised her as the roar of the tires rolling over the snowy pavement filled her ears. Icy cold air circulated around the top of her head. The uninsulated space was freezing. Worse, she couldn't recall how she had gotten into the trunk of a vehicle or why.

Car fumes and the smell of the old musty, moldy blanket and a rubber tire nearly asphyxiated her.

Then bits and pieces of memories floated into her sluggish brain—she was looking for pregnancy tests in the drugstore. No, the dark chocolate thin mints had caught her attention first, and she hadn't even made it to the aisle where the pregnancy tests were shelved. Then Everton had grabbed her.

For a moment, she focused on an image in her mind's eye of Nathan and Bjornolf, waiting patiently while she ran into the store. No way was she going to admit to them—if she got out of this mess alive—that she'd been thwarted by a display of her favorite chocolate mints.

Her cell phone vibrated against her hip. She moved her hand to reach her jacket pocket and realized her wrists weren't bound. Thank God for small miracles! She tried to move her hand to her jacket pocket but couldn't concentrate enough to get her fingers into it. Ready to scream with frustration, she tried again, missing the pocket over and over.

The phone stopped pulsating. *No!*

The vehicle continued driving, and she wondered

where Everton intended to finish her off. The tree farm? Somewhere else? Woods abounded in the area so it would be easy to dump her anywhere, and she might be lost forever.

She still kept trying to reach her phone. Why couldn't her brain make her hand do what it was supposed to do?

Her heart lurched when the annoying buzzing from her phone started up again.

She shoved at her pocket and this time managed to get her hand inside and grasped her phone. *Don't stop buzzing.* By the time she got her cell out, the call had ended. She barely had time to be frustrated and upset before the phone started vibrating again as if the caller wasn't quitting until he got through to her. God, she loved whoever it was.

She peered at the caller ID, having difficulty fixing on the name as it blurred. *Hunter.*

"Yeah." Anna held the phone against her ear, straining to be heard. She thought she sounded as though she'd just woken from a hundred-year nap.

"Anna, thank God. Where are you?" Hunter's voice was frantic.

"Trunk… car… driving," Anna said. Her words were slurred and annoyingly took their time to come out of her mouth.

"Anna," Hunter said, his voice gruff, commanding, as if he was going to tell her to get her act together.

"I'm… here." She tried to sound as forceful as Hunter, more… in charge of her situation, but her voice was whispery soft without any real body or bite.

"Drugged?" Hunter asked.

"Chlor—form."

"Okay, listen up. The whole pack is searching for every vehicle that the Everton family and their workers drive."

"Everton," she breathed out, trying to reveal his name so they wouldn't be looking for the wrong man.

"Yeah, Roger Everton. Actually, Everton is just the name of the business. He changed his name to that when his father didn't leave him anything in his will."

"Great." So Everton probably thought she and Bjornolf were DEA and trying to get his adopted daughter away from him by inviting her over to dinner that night. Then they'd interrogate Jessica for all she knew about her dad's involvement in the murders.

"Bjornolf and Nathan are going to the tree farm. They suspect he might be headed there," Hunter said.

She didn't say anything as she wondered how the other men had been killed. She was almost certain Everton had buried them somewhere on the five hundred acres of the tree farm. He probably intended to bury her somewhere nearby, if not in the same spot.

"Anna?" Hunter said.

When she didn't say anything, Hunter ordered, "Don't go to sleep! And don't hang up on me! Keep talking."

"Tri… angu… lating?" she asked, attempting to shake free of the grogginess, but the harder she tried, the more she felt like she was going to pass out again. Then she realized her mistake. She had a phone with GPS. "Ping… ing?" she got out before Hunter responded.

"You bet. Finn's on it."

"Tell… him…to…" A rough bump in the road shook her, and she nearly lost the phone.

"Tell him what, Anna?"

"Put… a… rush…"

"A rush on it. You got that, Finn?"

She could almost see the two men smiling at each other as if they didn't know that she was in kind of a hurry here. She smiled, too. Then they'd be serious again and so was she.

After that last thought, she blacked out until she felt her body draped over a hard shoulder that dug into her ribs. She heard the impatient footsteps of her kidnapper as he headed somewhere, his boots crunching on the crusted-over snow. She realized then that the army blanket didn't smell just musty and like wool and the great outdoors, but like the two DEA agents who had died.

That meant her senses were returning little by little. The fog still cloaked her brain in a numbing sort of way, but she was coming to the conclusion that she might have a little fight left in her—if she could remain awake long enough.

Then he tossed her and she felt for a moment like she was sailing through the air. She landed hard on something metal. Despite the blanket padding her head, it banged against the heavy steel, and at impact, a sharp pain shot through her skull. Not enough to knock her out. Instead, it shook her from her drugged stupor a little.

Her heart began skipping beats when she thought she was in a coffin. An engine roared to life, and whatever she was in vibrated. She guessed the vehicle was some kind of earth-moving machine. She wondered if he intended to bury her alive.

Her blood turned to ice. She fumbled under her jacket for her holster. Why hadn't she thought of the gun before now? Her fingers touched the metal, and she let out a tentative sigh of relief. He hadn't checked her for weapons.

Thank God the vehicle he was driving was slow moving. She hoped he was going to go a long way before he dumped her body. Maybe she could wake up enough to aim the gun accurately before he attempted to kill her.

She tried to reach her phone to tell Hunter where she was and realized it had been in her hand when she passed out the last time.

Now… it wasn't.

Chapter 18

THEY WERE NEARLY AT THE TREE FARM WHEN Bjornolf got a call from Hunter.

"She's alive, Bjornolf," Hunter assured him. "She's groggy from the effects of chloroform, but she was speaking on her phone with us only moments earlier."

Guardedly relieved, Bjornolf couldn't say anything for a minute as he wheeled into the farm's snow-covered gravel parking lot. His emotions were so raw that he couldn't believe he—who was always in control of them on any mission, no matter the circumstances—could be so full of anger and, at the same time, so terrified he might lose Anna.

"According to Everton's daughter, Jessica, he just drove up in a car and parked it outside his home," Bjornolf said, trying to keep his breathing steady when he felt sick to his stomach. "He's taken Anna in a backhoe somewhere on the farm. The girl has shifted and hidden in the woods, proving she's one of us."

Hunter let out his breath. "Finn has just confirmed that Anna is at the farm. Her digital cell phone was pinged, and he's determined its latitude and longitude via GPS, so we've got our police officers headed in that direction. They should be there in a couple of minutes."

Bjornolf screeched the Land Rover to a halt. "We just arrived," he told Hunter.

He opened his door but before he could bolt in the

direction that he heard the backhoe moving, Nathan, in wolf form, squeezed between the steering wheel and Bjornolf's chest and leaped out.

Bjornolf with gun in hand—and Nathan with canines readied—raced after the backhoe.

Somewhere in the distance in the woods, the backhoe stopped.

So did Bjornolf's heart. He wasn't close enough yet. If Everton dumped her in an open hole, he could have her buried before Bjornolf reached her.

Gunshots rang out. He prayed the man was a lousy shot.

Vehicles started to pull into the gravel parking lot behind him. The army had arrived. Were they already too late?

No more shots rang out. The vehicle wasn't moving, though. The engine was running, but the backhoe was standing still.

Bjornolf raced through the trees and didn't think he'd ever make it in time. The stillness was what killed him the most. No sounds of a woman crying out in pain. No more gunshots exploding. Just the sound of birds twittering in the trees and the backhoe engine rumbling.

He bolted out of a stand of blue spruce and saw a new section where seedlings were being planted. The backhoe rested at the edge of a huge pit. Nathan was bounding around the backhoe, smelling the scents on the vehicle and tracing them to the pit.

There was no sign of Everton. Or Anna. *Hell.* Had Everton heard Bjornolf coming and run?

Where was Anna? Everton couldn't have run off with her, not in the drugged state she was in. What about the shots? She had to be wounded, if not dead.

Bjornolf bolted for the backhoe, believing then he might see Anna rolled up in the blanket in the digger. Shot.

She wasn't there. Dirt and chipped yellow paint. The digger was empty. He stared at it as if thinking that if he looked long enough, she'd materialize.

A groan from the pit had him pivoting and shifting his attention down into the hole. Nathan barked and dug at the edge of the pit.

"Anna!" She was standing in the mud in the middle of the eight-foot-deep hole, which was covered by an undisturbed light layer of snow in patches. She held a gun in her hand, pointed at a body nearby, a blanket on the muddy earth beside her feet.

Everton was lying on his back, clutching his blood-ied chest. Blood was also leaking down his crooked, swollen, and discolored nose. His eyes closed as he groaned again.

"Anna!" Bjornolf said again, not believing she wasn't even wounded as he fell to his knees and reached down for her.

Nathan bounced around him, whimpering and not helping in the least, his tail wagging, just as grateful to see her alive. Then he lifted his muzzle and howled. A she-wolf howled back.

"Jessica," Anna whispered.

"Go to Jessica," Bjornolf said to Nathan.

Anna pocketed the gun, then reached up to Bjornolf. "You're not rescuing me," she said, sounding incredibly tired. Still, she was forceful enough in the pronounce-ment, and he had to smile. "You're *not*," she reiterated vehemently. "You're just giving me a hand up."

"For the second time," he said, reminded of having

to help her in the jungle not all that long ago. "That's
your gun." He was surprised as he pulled her up against
the muddy wall, her white jacket and sweater and jeans
soaking up the wet earth. He couldn't believe Everton
hadn't disarmed her first.

She sighed, leaning against Bjornolf as if the last bit
of energy she'd mustered had been to stand and shoot
Everton. "We're a mess and we have a dinner party to
throw shortly for Jessica and Nathan," she whispered
against Bjornolf's chest.

As if *that* was happening. She had to be distraught
about everything that had happened, yet she was concerned about the dinner with Jessica. He loved Anna.

He remembered Hunter then. He yanked out his
phone, hit autodial, and said, "She's alive, Hunter.
Everton's in a pit, bullet in the chest."

"Thank God," Hunter said and Bjornolf knew he
wasn't just relieved that they'd caught Everton and that
Anna was safe. This had become something personal.
"Is she all right?"

"She's great," Bjornolf said, not about to tell him that
she was a little woozy from the drug. She wouldn't appreciate it. And he didn't tell Hunter that *he* was the one
who was feeling shaken to the core.

"I've got paramedics on the way. And I'm talking
to the feds. Making arrangements for new parents for
Jessica also, pronto. See you in a sec."

"Okay," Bjornolf said. He pocketed his phone but
couldn't quit thinking about how she hadn't been disarmed. "He didn't remove your gun?"

She shook her head. "He must have thought the
chloroform would knock me out for good. He didn't use

enough to kill me, or he just wanted to incapacitate me. Either that or our *lupus garou* healing genetics helped me to overcome it better than a human would. I thought he intended to bury me alive." She shuddered.

"God, Anna." The thought gave him heart palpitations.

"But after he dumped me into the pit, he got off the backhoe and came around to the trench and aimed a gun at me." It had taken Everton a moment to realize Anna was standing, blanket tossed aside, gun in hand, ready for him. Before he could overcome his surprise, she fired first and hit him in the chest. "I recovered his weapon and it's in my jacket pocket," Anna said.

Bjornolf was still tense. He couldn't shake the fear that he could have lost her. He realized then just how much Anna meant to him.

They heard sirens and Anna pressed harder against him as if she was ready to collapse. The drug hadn't quite worn off. "The police and the feds will take it from here," he said, lifting her off her feet and carrying her away from the pit and into a section of Douglas firs.

Three police officers hurried in their direction: Wes Caruthers and his mate, Greta, and Allan Smith, all wolves from Portland but now residing with Hunter's pack on the Oregon coast. Caruthers had been a Texas Ranger when the unit first started out. Most of their kind had to change occupations or locations, or find a way to "die" and be "reborn," to keep up appearances for living so long. Often, they continued to work in the kind of jobs they'd been trained for and just updated their skills as needed.

The three Portland wolves had all joined Hunter's pack when he desperately needed loyal police officers to keep his pack members out of trouble.

Allan, with his salt-and-pepper hair, round and jovial cheeks, and green eyes, looked more like the fatherly type than a cop. But he was all business when he was doing his job.

His sandy hair graying at the temples, Caruthers said, "Finn and Hunter will be here pronto." He looked Anna over, concern etched in his face. "You okay?"

She nodded.

He looked at Bjornolf as if getting a second opinion, probably knowing Anna wouldn't admit she was hurt.

"She'll be fine. Everton's in a pit, gunshot wound to the chest, about three hundred yards that way."

"We'll get on it," Caruthers said.

The three officers hurried in the direction of the pit.

In their wolf forms, Nathan and Jessica came running to join Anna and Bjornolf.

Bjornolf started issuing orders, not wanting anyone who wasn't their kind to see them as wolves. "Nathan, go to the Land Rover and shift and get dressed. Jessica, run to the house, shift, dress, and join Nathan in the Land Rover. Until your mother comes home, you'll stay with us."

Bjornolf knew the paramedics would take Everton to a hospital and patch him up, and then the police would incarcerate him. The feds would investigate now because the two men murdered were DEA officers.

Jessica and Nathan raced off together. Bjornolf thought of how they were starting their new life as mated wolves amid a world of turmoil. He carried Anna back toward the Land Rover. God, he was glad to have her tightly in his grasp, alive and well.

They'd have to answer questions. She'd have to

hand over her gun and Everton's, and show the feds her credentials.

A federal officer approached them. He eyed Bjornolf with his dark brown eyes for a moment before he said to Anna, "See you're up to your old tricks."

Bjornolf smelled the man was a wolf and instinctively tightened his hold on Anna.

She smiled. "Yeah. Well, someone had to do your job, Yale." She handed over her gun and Everton's.

The guy grinned, gave her a small salute, took the guns, and waved her and Bjornolf on. "I'll talk to you later after the drug Everton gave you wears off. In the shape you're in, no sense in asking what went on here until later."

Hunter finally arrived at the scene and hurried toward them, Finn in tow, looking like they were ready to take care of Anna, too.

Anna quickly said, "I didn't need rescuing."

Finn and Hunter looked at Bjornolf as if confirming her claim.

"Don't look at him. I shot Everton." She sounded proud of herself.

He was proud of her. "She did," Bjornolf said. "We're going home. We'll take the kids with us."

"One of the other families is taking them to their place so you can... get some rest." Hunter tried to hide a smile but wasn't accomplishing the task.

"We were going to have dinner," Anna said, as if she'd been programmed and couldn't think of changing plans at this late date. "Jessica needs to have the pregnancy test."

"You're in no shape to have dinner guests tonight.

Someone else can take her to the drugstore and pick up the test." Bjornolf wanted to spend time alone with her after nearly losing her. He would have provided moral support to the teens if needed, but he knew others in the pack would help out. "The kids will understand."

She finally sighed and nodded.

Hunter got the door of the Land Rover for them.

Bjornolf set Anna in the passenger seat. "Thanks."

"Take good care of her, Bjornolf." Hunter headed off toward the crime scene.

"I'll fix a nice dinner and you can take a shower," Bjornolf said as he climbed into the Land Rover. "Then if you're not too sleepy, we can curl up on the couch and watch a movie."

"Hmm," she said, "I'd love that."

As soon as he'd put the Land Rover in gear, she was sound asleep.

When they finally pulled into the driveway of the cottage, Anna raised her head and turned to look at Bjornolf, her expression saying she was ready for something more than just a movie and rest. No sparring, though. Tonight, he wanted to take it easy with her.

"Did you see the hot tub in the bathroom?" he asked.

Chapter 19

AFTER THEY PARKED AT THE COTTAGE, BJORNOLF LIFTED Anna from the vehicle before she could attempt to climb out. "I can walk," she said, more amused than annoyed.

"You're all muddy. You'll get the carpet dirty." He gave her a devilishly raised brow, as if he was waiting for her to argue with him.

"That *better* be the reason," she said in her most serious voice. "What about you?" He was all muddy, too.

He smiled and lifted her out of the car. "*I* wasn't in a mud pit."

She unlocked the front door for him and he carried her inside.

He set her down on the tile floor, then crouched to remove her boots while she rested a hand on his shoulder to keep her balance. He leaned down to untie his boots and pulled them off. Standing, he reached over and locked the front door, and then he said, "Ready?"

Smiling, she hadn't moved an inch from the tile floor, hoping he'd carry her. She kind of liked this treatment.

Amusement lit up his face. "Good." He lifted her in his arms and headed for the laundry room.

Laundry room. She hadn't thought of that. "Good thinking." They could ditch their filthy clothes there, and *then* retire to the bathroom.

He flipped on the light.

A mint green, navy blue, and white braided rug ran

the length of the terra-cotta tile floor. Windows made the room seem bigger. A slate hand-painted sign hung over the washer and dryer, picturing a pair of jeans, a sock, and a teddy bear drip-drying on a clothesline and proclaiming: "Everything eventually comes out in the wash."

Yeah. Except for *this* time, she was afraid. She fretted that they'd get mud all over the place in here, too. And then there was all the stuff they were dealing with— Jessica and Nathan's mating not the least of it.

A braided country rug of a goose and a gander eyeing each other sat on top of the dryer. White cabinets hid laundry detergents and bleach and the like. A shelf holding baskets to sort clean clothes sat above the washer and dryer and sink.

He set her down on the rug, and she was glad at least her socks were clean. Her pant legs were another story.

He stripped off his black sweater and threw it in the washing machine. "Are your jacket and sweater machine washable?"

"Yeah, delicate cycle for the sweater, regular for the jacket, and neither can go in there with your black sweater. They'll need tons of bleach. Even then I'm not sure bleach will get the mud stains out."

"Okay." He fished his sweater out and tossed it in the sink between the washer and the dryer.

She pulled her phone out of her jacket pocket and placed it on the shelf above. Thankfully, she'd found it in the blanket that she'd dropped in the muddy pit.

Bjornolf took her jacket and slipped it in the washer.

She removed her holster and set it on the shelf with her phone. "We could clean yours in the machine and soak mine in the sink for a while."

"Ladies first."

"Hmm," she said, biting her tongue.

He slipped off his charcoal gray shirt and hesitated.

"Sink," she said.

He tossed it in there.

She sighed. "We could have washed more at one time if we'd taken care of my sweater and jacket later."

He shook his head and considered her sweater again. "I love it on you."

"Thanks. It *was* my favorite." She appreciated the way he had observed her in the sweater, like he wanted to get his hands on her and kiss her all over.

He helped pull it over her head and added it to the jacket in the washer. He touched the dirt streaking her skin. His touch was gentle, his expression dark and contemplative.

Suddenly, she didn't really care if she was squeaky clean or not. Or if Bjornolf was. She didn't want to think of what might have happened. Only of where they were now. Muddy, sure, but alive and well. And hot for each other in the laundry room of a cabin retreat. That's all that really mattered.

Before they could focus on keeping things clean, they were kissing, tongues and lips colliding. He fumbled with the fastener on her white bra while his tongue was teasing hers and her fingers were unbuckling his belt. The bra went sailing and ended up inside one of the sorting tubs on the shelf above.

His large warm hands slid over her breasts, making them swell, her blood heating. Her hands took measure of his chest, feeling the ripple of muscles, his nipples hardening, his stomach tightening. Somehow they managed to get out of their jeans. She thought her white panties went into the sink when they were supposed to go into the washing machine, but when she glanced in that direction, she saw them hanging off the sign, the teddy bear peeking through the silky fabric.

His white boxers landed on the floor. He lifted her onto the top of the dryer. They weren't going to make love in here, were they?

He saw the hesitation in her expression, and he spread her legs and moved in close to her. His gaze held hers, and she swore his amber eyes were a little misty. Dark with lust, but misty.

He took her face in his hands and rubbed her cheeks with his thumbs. "I thought I'd lost you today, Anna."

She thought of making a smart-ass reply because she didn't want to feel the emotions that were swirling through her—the fear of losing him, of leaving him behind—but she knew what he must have suffered.

She took his hand and kissed the palm. "I wasn't giving up."

"Yeah, I know. That's what I love about you. If I'm not there to protect you, you're going to do it yourself." He smiled slightly. She could tell he was damn proud of her for being able to stay alive on her own.

She smiled. That was the end of the serious discussion as far as she was concerned. "Here… or in the bath… or in the bed?"

"In the living room," he said, his hands stroking her breasts, his eyes focused on them now. He looked up at her to see her expression when she didn't say anything.

"With the Christmas tree lights on, a fire going, and a wild sword fight on the TV. What could be better?" he asked. "When I saw you standing in front of the

Christmas tree after we'd hung the lights, that's all I could think of. If Nathan hadn't been in the guest bedroom, I would have made love to you next to the fire."

She loved the idea. "Sounds like a deal."

He went over to the sink and took a cloth from the cabinet, then warmed the water and added a little hand soap to it. "We'll clean up a bit first."

The cleaning up involved a lot of kissing, her mouth on his and on his neck and shoulders and throat. His mouth kissing her back, then moving down her throat to her breasts. Her hands combed through his hair, while one of his hands massaged a breast and the other ran the wet cloth over the streaks of mud on her belly. Cleaning off dirt had never taken this long or been this erotic, she thought as he rubbed his stiff cock against her leg.

After they'd cleaned themselves, he tossed the rinse rag into the sink, lifted her off the dryer, and was about to carry her into the living room when she said, "No. Go get the fire going, and I'll start the wash."

He sighed and set her on the floor. "Don't take too long."

She wrapped her arms around his neck. "Keep it warm for me. All right?"

"I'll be ready." He gave her another searing kiss and then took off as if he was in a race. She started the wash and then filled the sink with water to soak the rest of their garments. She snagged her underwear and his, tossing them into the machine. Their jeans had managed to land on each other—his on the bottom, hers on top, pinning his to the floor. She smiled at the image that brought to mind. She threw them into the sink.

By the time she was finished and walked into the living room, the dark room was filled with the soft twinkling lights on the tree, the reflection sparkling on the round, multicolored Christmas ornaments. The fire had just begun at the hearth, but what really stole her attention was that he'd moved the coffee table out of the way, and sitting in its place was the sofa's foldout bed.

He was bent over the bed as he covered it in red-and-white, candy-cane-striped bedsheets. She studied his gorgeous ass. Perfectly muscled like fine art. "Are you going to climb into bed, or just ogle me?" He looked over his shoulder at her with a smug smile.

She laughed, gave him a pat on the butt, and meant to climb onto the bed, but he tackled her. In that instant, the imagery of her jeans straddling his faded and a new one came into mind—his hot, naked body straddling hers.

She grinned. "I thought we were going to do it on the floor."

"You deserve soft."

"I want hard." She stroked his cock, as aroused as before. "What made you so hard?" She was curious, not thinking he could have remained that way all that time.

"You," he said, "just thinking of you on the sofa bed with me like this."

There were no more words after that, just the sound of the wood crackling in the fireplace, their hearts beating wildly, and their breaths ragged. The lights sparkled softly in the room, and the scent of the sweet-smelling soap they washed themselves with filled her senses.

Everything else was touch.

The heat from Bjornolf and the fire warmed her as his fingers stroked her clit, making her hot, wet, and eager to have him finish her off. His tongue teased a nipple, his other hand cupping a breast. *Faster*. She wanted him to stroke her faster. She touched him, too, wanting to reciprocate the pleasure he was giving her. She caressed his buttocks, loving the hard feel of him. She reached between them and stroked his cock. He was rigid, throbbing, engorged, and ready for her. He groaned and rubbed her faster.

"Yes," she said in a hushed voice, as if anyone would hear them out here on the coast. Only the sounds of the ocean waves striking the beach and the wind blowing snow off the pines were audible. No other cottages were close by—just wild nature and two hot wolves.

She arched as he dipped a finger inside her, then continued to assault her senses with his strokes. Her breathing grew shallow as she felt herself lifted heavenward. So close, so close, she was almost there as he pulled at her nipple with his teeth in a gentle tug.

The climax hit, sending her senses reeling, and she loved him with every cell in her body.

"OhGodIloveyou," she said in one string tied together, trying to capture her breath. Was that the first time she'd made the declaration of love to him?

She saw the expression in his lust-filled eyes change a little. Surprise, she thought.

Hell. She loved him.

——◦◦◦——

Blood had rushed straight to Bjornolf's loins as soon as he had carried Anna into the house. She needed tender, loving care, and all he could think of was getting her naked and making love to her. He'd craved having her from the moment he got up that morning and saw the way she was snuggled under the covers.

After nearly losing her, nothing else mattered but loving her, feeling her in his arms, all around him, while he buried himself deep inside her.

She came and exalted in it, and he wanted her to come again, only this time while he was submerged in her sweet, wet heat. Her declaration of love smacked him right in the solar plexus, and he couldn't have been more surprised or happy about it.

Anna clearly worked out. She had well-toned muscles and used them to her advantage during lovemaking, arching her pelvis to capture him more deeply. She wrapped her legs around him as if she wasn't about to let her prisoner go no matter what, tightening them like a glove around his cock. He couldn't get enough of her. She was hot, wet, and snug. Her tongue played with his in a loving, fun-hearted way as her hands traveled all over him... first on his ass, then digging into his back and his shoulders, and then combing through his hair.

He suckled on a nipple and enjoyed its rigid contour. He treasured the way he made her gyrate underneath him and moan. He massaged the other breast, loving the softness, the size, the sexiness. All the while his cock penetrated her deeper, plunging, the couch bed squeaking as it rocked with his thrusts.

Through a haze of passion, he felt her come again, her inner muscles clenching in climax, her soft moans driving him on. She buckled underneath him, and he couldn't hold off any longer, the pleasure sucking him in. At the breaking point, he held his breath, and then he came inside her, thrusting until she'd milked him for everything he had.

"Anna," he breathed against her hair as she wrapped her arms around him, keeping him on top of her.

"I've changed my mind," she whispered.

He studied her for a moment, not knowing what she meant.

"Let's skip the movie and just... cuddle, like this."

"I need to feed you."

"You'll cook?"

"Of course."

"I'm glad you cook." Then she sighed. "But I'm not hungry right now."

He was, but he wouldn't leave her for the world if she didn't want him to. Instead, he rolled off her and tucked his arm under her head, his hand caressing her breastbone as he stared up at the ceiling. He kissed her forehead, then said quietly, not wanting to disturb her if she was falling asleep, "It's nothing we have to decide anytime soon, but..."

She took a deep breath. "We have to decide where we're going to live."

"Right."

"What do we do about Nathan and Jessica?"

Chapter 20

BJORNOLF WASN'T SURE WHAT TO SAY TO ANNA ABOUT Nathan and Jessica. He enjoyed cuddling with her now as mated wolves in the privacy of their own place, and he knew they needed the time to get to know each other like this. Having Nathan and Jessica living with them with babies on the way?

He let out his breath and continued to stroke her arm as the fire crackled in the hearth and the Christmas tree lights lent a holiday ambience to the sofa-bed play they'd just experienced. "When it was just Nathan, I considered his staying with us. Now that he's got a mate and maybe babies on the way, he'll have the help of the whole pack behind him. I'm thinking that they might need a place of their own, close to pack members who can assist them," Bjornolf said.

Anna turned and snuggled her soft cheek against his chest and didn't say anything.

"What do you think?"

He thought she'd fallen asleep when she didn't respond, and he began to caress her bare shoulder again.

"What about us and the pack?" she asked.

He looked down at her. She turned her chin up and met his gaze.

"Hunter's pack?"

"Maybe it's time for us to join one," she said. "Like Hunter's. Here on the Oregon coast."

He went back to rubbing her arm. "Yeah, maybe it is. Hunter wouldn't be too bad as a pack leader. He might consider letting us join."

"He's good. And I'm sure he'd jump at the chance to have us in the pack."

"You're not thinking I should join his team as well, are you?" Bjornolf was ready, but he had to hear what Anna thought first.

"We couldn't handle missions without you."

He nodded.

She chuckled. "Glad you're not conceited or anything."

He smiled and kissed the top of her head. "So what about the kids?"

"We can't stay here. This is one of Meara's cabins to rent. So I'm thinking we'll need a house."

"Okay," Bjornolf said.

"On the coast."

Bjornolf nodded. "I like the area. Close to other pack members. Finn's got that property farther south of here. He's trying to sell the land. Maybe we could make an offer he couldn't refuse."

She smiled. "I like that idea. Beautiful vista. What do you think about us having a garage apartment? Or a mother-in-law house behind ours?"

"Nathan's got money, you know. His parents left him money and a home that he also sold."

"Okay. So he could buy his own place," Anna said.

"But you want him close by." Bjornolf studied her expression, noticing that even though she didn't want to let on that she had a mothering instinct, she had one.

"Yeah," she said softly. "He reached out to us first. He made me view Christmas in a different light and brought us closer together. How long would it have been if you had continued to ghost missions before we got this far on our own?"

Bjornolf snorted. "Not long."

She looked up at him, brows raised quizzically.

"I seriously contemplated changing cabana arrangements when we stayed at that jungle town."

She laughed. "You know Allan and Paul were trying to get a reaction from you."

"That's why I whispered in your ear. I was dying to kiss you."

"And you did. Some kiss." She licked his nipple and snuggled tighter against him. "Nathan made us recognize how important the pack is. I want to see him and Jessica do well."

"We'll discuss it with them and see what they want to do." Bjornolf wasn't sure he was ready to be a surrogate grandfather when he hadn't even had his own kids yet. He ran his hand over Anna's belly. He was working on that, though.

"We haven't even talked about our schedule for after this business is finished," she said.

"Schedule?" he asked. He hadn't found anything in her profile that indicated she was fanatical about scheduling herself for anything on a regular basis.

"Sparring practice," she said.

"Every day of the week," he wholeheartedly agreed. He definitely would ensure that they had one room for sparring in their new home—and whatever else came up in the process. "And massages."

"You had regular masseuses rubbing your muscles down after a workout?" She looked cynically at him.

"No, but now that I'm going to have a regular sparring partner and she's you, I'm adding massages to the schedule. After the workout. Maybe before… to loosen us up a bit."

She chuckled. "Yeah. Like we're going to get any workouts done then."

"Oh, I'll guarantee you that we'll get workouts. Plenty of them."

Still grinning, she shook her head. "And weekly trips to the firing range."

"Gotcha," he said.

"If I get a mission that you *aren't* invited to go on, then what?" she asked.

"I'll go. Just ghost you."

"Okay. If you get a mission that I can't go on?"

He hesitated to answer. If the job was too dangerous, he wanted her home. He was certain she wouldn't like that answer. He'd even thought of saying she could go on a different mission without him. But he couldn't go along with it. For one thing, he didn't want her anywhere on a dangerous job without him watching her back. For another, he was certain she wouldn't appreciate that he'd sound like he was telling her what she could and couldn't do.

He smiled and kissed her head. She was watching him, observing him as if she could read every thought going through his mind. He finally said, "If someone asks me to take on a job that's too dangerous for you to go on, it's most likely too dangerous for me."

He loved the way she smiled up at him, and that led to him kissing her all over again.

———

The fire had gone out, but the Christmas lights were still twinkling on the tree when Bjornolf's phone rang in the laundry room around two that morning. He carefully replaced the cheery, yellow-and-red quilted comforter over a sleeping Anna and then sprinted for the room.

He missed the call but saw the text. Call me. Nathan.

Bjornolf hit autodial as he pulled Anna's white sweater out of the washing machine and laid it out gently on top of the dryer to dry. He stared at the streaks of light brown and frowned.

The phone was asking him to leave a message, so he did. Then Bjornolf pulled her jacket out of the wash. Pale mud stains streaked the front and the back. He checked the labels on the jacket and sweater, and decided it was time for some online shopping. He left the jacket to soak some more.

He opened a browser on his phone and began searching for a replacement for Anna's lacy white sweater. Elated to find the online version of the store, he clicked on the link for sweaters and saw hers on the first page.

He glanced at the color selections. Ice white! Yes! He began to click on the links to the other colors just to see what they looked like. Stunning Black. Ecru. Royal Blue. Red Hot, Pleasing Purple. Hell, yeah, he'd have to get them all. She'd look amazing in any of the colors. Then he looked for white fleece jackets, found one, and ordered it, too.

In the meantime, he tried calling Nathan again.

"Bjornolf," Nathan said, his breath short as if he'd run to get the phone.

"Yeah, what's up?" Bjornolf let the water out of the laundry sink, squeezed the excess water out of each article of clothing, and then threw them into the washing machine.

"Jessica and I couldn't sleep. She told me there's a safe in her parents' home where they keep important papers. She thought it might help us find some answers about the DEA agents or maybe even about her birth."

"The feds will have a search warrant and investigate the deaths," Bjornolf said.

"Yeah. If they can find the safe—it's hidden. Even if they do, would they be looking into her birth records? What if they open the safe and just take everything? Then we've lost the chance to learn who her parents were."

"There might not be any record of her birth. We make up our own birth records when we need to because we live so long that we have to change our records from time to time. We homeschool our children so they don't go to public school."

"She did."

"Okay, so she would have had some records. Falsified maybe. It might not help."

Nathan didn't say anything.

Bjornolf said, "What's going on, Nathan? Why do you really want to go to the house?"

"Jessica says that they've got some evidence against the Wentworths," Nathan said. "She heard her parents talking about it. Her dad knows William Wentworth is up to his eyeballs in illegal stuff in Colombia. Everton's mother died two years before his father. Before that, the will stated that if both parents should die, the estate would be divided equally between William, Jeff, and Roger. If either parent died first, the will remained the same. After Everton's mother died, the will was changed.

"William coerced their father to alter the will. When their father died, all the money was left to William and Jeff. Roger got a dollar from the estate, showing that the father hadn't left Roger out of the will by accident. That was all he got. He and Dottie talked about it a lot. A year has passed and they are still mad that William cheated him out of the estate."

Bjornolf frowned. "So he had evidence to blackmail William."

"That's what we figure. Hunter said your team might have been set up. What if the evidence is in the safe?"

"All right. I'll check it out."

"We're coming with you." Nathan sounded both eager and adamant.

"No." Bjornolf didn't need the kids getting in trouble if he and Anna get caught trying to get into a safe in the Evertons' home.

"We have to. Jessica's the only one who knows where the safe is hidden. And I'm not letting her go alone."

Bjornolf suspected that if she told him where it was located, he could find it. He couldn't fault Nathan for wanting to help. Or be first on the scene if Bjornolf and Anna did learn the truth about Jessica. "Can she get into the safe?"

"She thinks so. You're bringing Anna, aren't you?"

Bjornolf would rather let her sleep, but he wasn't leaving her behind. "Yeah."

"We'll meet you there in half an hour."

"I'll let Hunter give the family you're staying with a heads-up that you'll be meeting us there. If you get there first, wait for us before you enter the house."

"Will do."

They ended the conversation and Bjornolf called Hunter.

"Yeah," Hunter answered the phone, sounding half asleep.

Bjornolf relayed the information to him, though normally he would have just done his job and not informed anyone he was doing it. He kind of liked the idea of having backup and not being out on a limb all by himself for a change.

Now, Hunter was fully awake. "Who do you need?"

"Jessica and Nathan are meeting us there."

"I don't really care for that setup," Hunter said, but he didn't object. He trusted Bjornolf to do what was right.

"I know. Me, neither. If she's the only one who can show us where the safe is and can get into it, I'm going to let them go along to help out."

"I'll send Finn and our police officers for backup. They'll keep perimeter watch in case anyone comes snooping around."

"All right. We're on our way." Bjornolf ended the call, saw a shadow move into his space, and glanced at the entryway to the laundry room. He smiled to see Anna dressed all in black. Boots. Jeans. Turtleneck. And jacket. Her hair was tucked into a bun.

He took her into his arms and kissed her. "Good morning."

She slid her hand down his naked chest. "Are you going as a wolf, or are you getting dressed first?"

"If we had time, I'd take you back to bed first."

"Promises, promises." She glanced at the mud left in the laundry sink. "Thanks for taking care of the rest of the clothes. I'll just clean this out while you get dressed."

Then she looked at her sweater and jacket laid out on top of the dryer. She didn't say a word, but he could see by her expression how disappointed she was. He wanted to tell her he'd bought replacements, but he also wanted them to be a surprise.

"Sorry for the late-night clandestine operation," he said, trying to cheer her up.

"All in the job." She smiled up at him. "We can make up for it when we get home."

"Too bad we couldn't get started on making up for it *before* we go."

Chapter 21

WHEN THEY REACHED THE TREE FARM, ANNA COULDN'T help but look in the direction of the pit Everton had dumped her into. She'd felt the cold seep into her bones as soon as she and Bjornolf arrived.

"You alright?" Bjornolf reached for Anna's hand, giving it a squeeze.

"Yeah. I'm okay. I worry about Jessica's frame of mind, though. The only father she knows is in jail, and no one's been able to reach her mother. Now she has all these other issues to deal with… I wonder how she's handling it."

"She's lucky to have Nathan to help her through it. Can you imagine if we'd had each other when we were teens to deal with all our issues?"

Anna couldn't even imagine having hooked up with Bjornolf as a teen. "We would have been a mess. Getting into all kinds of trouble."

He laughed. "Yeah, you're probably right. But we would have had fun. There they are," Bjornolf said as Nathan and Jessica moved out of the darkness.

Except for their blue jeans, Anna noted, they were dressed in all black just like she and Bjornolf were, as if they were teen versions of undercover operatives.

Jessica was a pretty blonde with dark brown eyes, and Anna thought she looked sweet and innocent, except for the fact that she was a mated wolf and could be expecting.

Jessica was tucked under Nathan's arm as if he was protecting her. Jessica's gaze settled on Anna. From the intense look Jessica gave her, Anna knew she wanted to say something to her.

"Jessica," Anna finally said, her voice hushed, as if giving her permission to ask whatever she wanted to.

"I didn't... use it yet." Jessica's gaze remained steady on Anna. "The directions said to use it first thing in the morning."

"Ah." *The pregnancy test*.

Nathan took a deep breath.

"I want... I want you to read the results with me when I do it." Jessica was still watching Anna, studying her reaction.

"Sure. I will." Anna suddenly had a frog in her throat.

Jessica swallowed, her eyes shimmering with tears. "I... I can't tell my mom about this. I mean, about any of this. Nathan, the wolf stuff. Not any of this." She said it as though she was asking a question.

"No, you can't. Do you have any clue where your mom would have gone?" Anna needed to have a heart-to-heart talk with Jessica. Having to keep the werewolf part of their existence secret from humans was essential.

"I think my Aunt Helen had to speak with her. But I called there and no one was answering the phone. I'm kind of worried about her. Nathan told me that he saw my uncle kissing my mom, and... I just figured it was family stuff. But... Nathan said it wasn't that kind of kiss. What if Aunt Helen found out about it? I'm just glad my dad wasn't here at the time. He probably would have killed Uncle William." Jessica took a deep breath, thinking about how her father had tried to murder Anna.

"Hunter's looking into it."

Anna wondered how Jessica was dealing with her dad's actions. In that instant, Anna saw herself as a teen again. No way did she want Jessica to have to carry this burden all on her own. She wanted Jessica to know she could speak with her about any of it. After what Anna had been through, if Jessica was pregnant, she'd refer her to Tessa in the matter. Gladly.

Jessica didn't look happy, but nodded and then motioned to the house. "I'll show you where the safe is. We'll go in the back way through the kitchen."

Anna's phone rang, and when she answered it, Finn said, "We're in place on the perimeter of the tree farm. Yale's on his way to give us more backup if we need it, since he's handling the case."

"Good. We're about to enter the house."

Anna relayed the news to Bjornolf that backup was in place.

"Who is this Yale guy?" Bjornolf sounded very much like a jealous mate.

"He's got a mate, Bjornolf. Don't worry. I met him on an assignment in Washington, DC. He went to Yale, so that's what we call him. Smart as can be."

"Too bad he isn't on Hunter's team."

"Some of us need to be in the field with humans. Like I was. Like you and Hunter and his team were."

"Agreed." Bjornolf unlocked the door to the kitchen with the key Jessica provided, gun readied, then pushed the door open with a squeak. "You stay here with the kids, and I'll check the house out."

Anna nodded. She could easily check the house while Bjornolf stayed with the kids, but she knew it wouldn't have looked right. Nathan would expect Bjornolf to protect her and the kids. Even as highly trained as she was, the perceptions still reigned—big bad he-wolf protects she-wolf and offspring.

"Clear," Bjornolf said after several minutes, then ushered them inside. He took Anna's arm and pulled her aside and whispered, "Gray wolves, old scent."

Anna stared at him, uncomprehending.

"Don't you smell it?"

She took a deeper whiff and frowned. "Man and woman's."

Bjornolf nodded.

"The safe is in the basement," Jessica said as she walked into the posh kitchen, everything crisp, clean, and white—cabinets, ceiling, tile countertops, blue and white chairs—with a warm golden floor and table, and big windows overlooking a field of evergreens covered in white.

She led the way down the stairs. "It's a rec room. Pool table, exercise room."

A massive, gray slate fireplace took up one wall, sooty and full of ashes, giving off a smoky smell. Dark wood paneling covered two walls, the ceiling, and the floor. A large TV sat against one wall, brown leather couches configured around it. Two narrow windows were situated high above, evergreen shrubs blocking what little light might have come through the windows on a day that wasn't overcast.

The smell of bleach and lemon-scented wax cleaner masked the odor of smoke from the fireplace that would have dominated the room.

Jessica headed past the billiard table, a rowing

machine, and a treadmill sitting against the opposite wall. A dartboard in a cabinet took center stage against a corkboard wall, perfect for really lousy shots.

"Do you come down here a lot?" Anna asked.

Jessica shook her head. "I don't like it." She shuddered.

Bjornolf noticed her trembling a little.

"I've never seen a dartboard like this," Anna said.

"It's one of those electronic ones." Nathan motioned to the scoreboard. "It keeps score on an LED screen and has voice commands and makes sound effects."

Anna shook her head. What happened to doing things the old-fashioned way?

Jessica unhooked the dartboard and set it on the floor to expose a wall safe. "He figured if anyone ever searched for his safe, they'd look in his office or bedroom. Maybe the living room. But a basement? Behind a dartboard? No one would think of that."

Heavy-duty gray wall safe. Standard dial combination.

"You don't happen to know the combination, do you?" Bjornolf asked Jessica.

"I only know one of the numbers is six. I was watching him when he saw me and told me to run back upstairs. He was angry, but I'm sure he didn't think I could ever figure out the other numbers. That was the only time I ever got close when he was unlocking it."

Bjornolf got on his cell phone to Hunter. "Okay, we've got six as the first number of the combination. Any ideas for the rest?"

"Give me a sec." Hunter started talking to someone nearby. "Rourke, in your investigations, have you come across any numbers that might have been used on a safe?"

The speakerphone was on as Rourke responded.

"Yeah, often wedding dates or birth dates. Sometimes owners won't change the combination on a safe after it's installed and it'll be all zeroes. You said the first number is six?" Rourke paused. "Bingo. Try one and then five. The numbers correspond to the month and day that the Evertons' daughter was born."

Click.

"It worked," Bjornolf told Hunter. He pushed the lever down and pulled the safe door open.

Inside the safe, bundles of money were stacked on one shelf. A huge stack of papers rested at the bottom of the safe. Bjornolf pulled out the papers and said to Hunter, "Thousands of dollars' worth of cash stashed in the safe. I can't imagine why someone who owns a Christmas tree farm would have this much cash on hand."

The papers included birth certificates, a marriage certificate, titles to vehicles—including the work vehicles used by employees at the farm—and the deed to the tree farm.

Bjornolf said to Hunter, "Just going through the papers now." He handed some of the documents to Nathan and Jessica.

They carried them over to the pool table, spread them out, and began concentrating on the birth certificates and the Evertons' marriage certificate. "Everton was Roger Wentworth, married to Dorothy Slade on the marriage certificate. And here's a birth certificate for Angela Wentworth. Then a death certificate dated three years later for Angela Wentworth," Jessica said, her voice soft and upset.

Anna looked at the death certificate. "She died when you would have been just a toddler. Did your adoptive mom ever talk to you about it?"

Everyone looked up from the documents they were reading and studied her. Jessica took a deep breath and nodded. "Just once. I was looking through some pictures my mom had taken of me at Christmastime with Santa, and I came across some photos of Mom holding a toddler I didn't know. I asked who she was. My mom said she was her daughter born three years before they adopted me. It happened when they lived in Portland. Mom was at the mall shopping. A nanny was watching Angela and she got away from her. She ran out into the street and a car hit her. My mom gave me a sad smile and said then they adopted me. She wouldn't talk about it after that."

Jessica sorted through the papers she'd been looking at. "No birth certificate for me. No adoption papers. Nothing. I don't even know if my first name is really Jessica."

Nathan looked unsure. Anna joined Jessica and pulled her into an embrace. "We're all trying to learn the truth. You're not alone in this."

Jessica nodded and gave her a hug back. "Thank you." Then she wiped her eyes and went back to looking at the papers with Nathan. She paused and glanced at Anna and Bjornolf. "Nathan talked to me about the dead men."

Anna and Bjornolf looked at him.

He let out his breath and shrugged. "She smelled the dead bodies, too. Like we did. I told you. When she and I went on that walk that time. I thought she might have been here at the time. Heard something. No one has asked her."

"And?" Bjornolf asked.

Jessica sighed. "I overheard a couple of men talking

with Dad. I stayed home from school because I had a bad cold that day and was in my bedroom playing a video game, but you know how our hearing is. They asked Dad how well he knew my Uncle William. He said he was his half brother. They asked if he knew anything about Uncle William's business.

"He said sure, Uncle William was into pharmaceuticals. They wanted to know if he was involved in anything illegal. My dad said for them to follow him outside because he had to get some work done, and they could talk while he worked on some new plantings. That was it. He must have gone to get his coat and gloves and stuff, and then left with them, shut the door, and was off."

Stuff? More like a gun, Anna suspected.

"When was this?" Bjornolf asked.

"It was a Monday morning. We're closed on Mondays to give the farmhands a break for working over the weekend. Dad catches up on work even when we're closed. So we didn't have any customers."

"How did your dad and William get along?" Anna asked.

"It was weird. They hated each other but needed each other for jobs... somehow. Not sure. Dad worked for Uncle William before he got the tree farm. So they were kind of okay back then. But then Uncle William cut Dad out of their father's will, and Dad said he wasn't going to work for his older half brother any longer. I... don't think he knew William was having an affair with my mom. If he knew, I'm certain that Dad would have killed Uncle William."

Anna nodded. "I'd have to agree with you there." She examined the deed to the farm while Bjornolf was searching through some old papers having to do with plants in the Amazon. They were dated thirteen to fifteen years ago, shortly before Jessica was adopted by the Evertons. After comparing handwriting on documents written, signed, and dated by Everton, Bjornolf could tell Everton was not the same person who had written the list of rainforest plants.

Anna touched Bjornolf's arm and he saw the worried look in her eyes. "The Everton farm belonged to an Oliver and Jenna Silverstone," she said quietly.

Silver. Gray wolves. They often used gray, grey, or silver in their names.

"The deed's old," she said.

He scrutinized it. "It is. But why would Everton have this old deed and not the one that shows he and his wife now own the property?" The situation looked more sinister than he had first suspected. "Hunter," Bjornolf said over the phone, "I'm scanning the deed and sending it to you." He waited.

"Got it. We'll check into the deed as soon as the county courthouse opens this morning," Hunter said.

"Sounds good. What do you make of this?" Bjornolf asked Anna, showing her the papers listing the rainforest plants and their chemical properties.

"What if the Silverstones were doing research on plants in the Amazon?"

Bjornolf agreed. "Hunter, we've got more. Listen to this. In the documents we found, someone made a detailed report of plants in the Amazon. Chemical properties, common plant names and botanical names, what they might be used for. There are weeks of detailed reports collected over two years, with breaks in between dates for several months, and then more reports as if the researcher left the Amazon, then returned and continued with the studies for another few months."

Bjornolf read a small portion of the notes to Hunter to give him an idea.

"*Amor seco*, a dense leafy perennial grass, rich in flavonoids and alkaloids.

"*Ajos sacha*, leaf power, calming effect for some, not sure of effectiveness, causes thirst.

"*Uncaria tomentosa*, cat's claw vine bark and root powder, strengthens immune system, similar to a wolf's.

"*Bauhinia forficate,* or *pata de vaca*, leaves of a flowering tree in the pea family used for diabetes mellitus."

"Hmm, sounds like we have another mystery," Hunter said.

Bjornolf took pictures and then emailed them to Hunter.

After a few minutes, Hunter said, "I'll have a research botanist I know look these over and see if she can come to any conclusions."

"Good," Bjornolf said. "I'll take pictures of the rest of these documents, then return the papers to the safe."

"Do you mind if I grab a bag of a few more of my things? Some more of my clothes?" Jessica asked.

"No, go right ahead." Bjornolf put away the papers as Nathan and Jessica went upstairs.

When he thought they were out of earshot, Bjornolf said to Hunter, "Something else that seems strange. Both Anna and I detected a very faint scent of gray wolves in the house. I checked out the whole house and found their scent in every room. It appears they were here years ago. A man and a woman."

"Like maybe fifteen years ago or so? When Jessica was a toddler?" Hunter asked.

"Possibly." Bjornolf glanced at the stairs. "Do you think maybe her parents actually owned this house? That this was her home all along?"

"Could be. My uncle lived here for many years, deeding the cottages along the coast to me and Meara this past year. He's living in Florida now, but he might know something about them. I'll call him."

"Something else to consider," Anna said. "What if it was combination of things? Something the Silverstones were looking into in the Amazon that the Wentworths wanted, and Dottie had seen the Silverstones' toddler and wanted to replace the toddler she'd just lost?"

Bjornolf swore under his breath. Then he told Hunter about what Jessica had revealed to them about the family dynamics. "We're finished here. We're taking the kids to our cottage for a bit, then they'll go back to the family they were staying with until the open house tomorrow night." Bjornolf grimaced as he realized it was later than he'd thought. "Actually at this rate, it'll be tonight. Talk to you later."

He took Anna's hand and walked up the stairs with her to the first floor.

Nathan and Jessica met them at the landing, two bags in hand. Nathan was smiling at them. He was glad when Bjornolf invited them to the cottage.

Jessica looked upset as she wrung her hands, then caught Anna's eye and quickly shoved her hands in her jacket pockets.

Anna said to Jessica, "It'll be all right. It's not going to be the end of the world, no matter what the results show."

Bjornolf realized it was probably getting to be time for Jessica to take the pregnancy test. They could feed the kids breakfast, see them on their way, and spend the rest of the day in bed while Hunter learned what he could about the situation.

"What do you think of all this?" Anna asked, climbing into the Land Rover with Bjornolf. Nathan was loading Jessica's bags into his truck.

"Seems odd that Everton was getting a lot of cash for Christmas tree sales and stuffing it in a safe. The list of rainforest flora doesn't make any sense unless it's something that's making them money."

"Like illegal drugs," she said.

"Yeah. And the deed? I'm wondering if Everton came by the property in the same way they came to *adopt* Jessica."

"He murdered her parents and raised their daughter," Anna said, believing just what Bjornolf had been thinking.

How could they prove it, and how would Jessica take the news if they learned the truth?

Chapter 22

HUNTER GUESSED IT WAS ABOUT SIX IN THE MORNING when he settled on the couch in his living room to make some more phone calls. Tessa was finally sleeping soundly after another restless night, the babies kicking in her belly and giving her fits.

Hunter dialed his uncle's number.

"Hunter. This must be important if you're calling me at this ungodly hour. Babies come early?" Hunter thought his uncle sounded hopeful.

"No, not yet. Knowing you, you're sitting on your porch watching the waves roll onto the beach while eating grapefruit with your highly sweetened coffee."

Hunter could envision his uncle smiling at that. "All right, here's a question for you. Did you know a couple of gray wolves who ran the Christmas tree farm near here? Everton's Christmas Tree Farm? They would have been a family—a man, woman, and baby."

"Hmm, yeah, now that you mention it. Long time ago, though. Twenty years maybe? Fifteen? They were off to the Amazon on trips all the time."

"How do you know that?"

"They told me. They were an odd couple. They had some notion they could control a wolf's need to shift. For those who were newly turned or who had a lot of human roots in their lineage. I bought a Christmas tree from them once. Mr. Silverstone was excited about some new finds, chemical properties of the rainforest plants he thought might help some of our kind. He told me because he recognized I was a wolf and might be also interested in a 'cure.' Blamed fool notion if you ask me. We are what we are. Instead of trying to change our nature, revel in it, I say."

"So they must have been fairly new wolves. What happened to them?" Hunter asked.

"I really never thought of them after that."

"Did any wolves work at the Christmas tree farm?" Hunter asked.

"No. All humans. The couple was kind of like me. They enjoyed not being part of pack life. So what's this all about?"

"Looks like we've got a case of humans taking over the farm, due to foul play, and *adopting* a wolf baby."

Hunter's uncle didn't say anything for a moment. When he did, he said, "Hell."

After ending the call, Hunter called Shelley Campbell, a wolf botanist he'd located when he was trying to learn something about plants for a mission he'd been on. "Hey, Shelley, Hunter Greymere here. I'm looking into a situation out here on the Oregon coast that I thought you might be able to shed some light on. I've got some plant names and their properties I want you to look over and see if you recognize any of them. You're not too busy, are you?"

She gave a heavy sigh. "No. Let me turn on my computer if my Highland hero will let go of me."

Duncan grunted. "No man should be calling you at this hour, lass, unless I know him personally. Even then, he's walking on thin ice."

"Whatever," she said, and Hunter listened, smiling as she left the bed, the mattress squeaking slightly.

Her computer signaled it was waking up, and he heard the Highlander with the distinctive Scottish burr say to her in a hostile throaty voice, "Who… is… he?"

She laughed. "A mated wolf friend who has twins on the way. He's a Navy SEAL who sometimes asks me to look into botanical questions relating to his missions."

"Tell him to hurry it up, then."

Hunter emailed her the images of the handwritten notes about the plants.

She gasped and said to Hunter, "Where did you get this information?"

"A couple of gray wolves living out near me were investigating plants in the rain forest, and—"

"Jenna and Oliver Silverstone? The initials in the margins look like theirs. She'd make notes and he would also, both documenting who had done what by initialing them. That way if one of them made a mistake, the other didn't get blamed for it. I haven't seen them in years. How are they?"

Hunter nearly stopped breathing. "You knew them?"

She paused and he wondered if she realized he'd referred to them in past tense. She took a moment to collect herself and said, "Yeah, I knew them. They were the ones that first got me interested in plant biology. They were trying to find a way to stop our kind from shifting. Not so much that we wouldn't shift ever, but just be able to control it. Especially for newly turned wolves. They had only been turned for a couple of years. Before that, they had trained and worked as a plant biologist team. Instead of continuing to look for new cancer cures, they began researching remedies for werewolves." A heavy pause ensued. "What happened to them? They had a daughter—Jessica. She was their angel."

"It seems they've disappeared. The new owners had a young daughter die, and the toddler they raised was named Jessica," Hunter said, confirming a piece of the puzzle. "Had you ever been to their house?"

"Yeah, while they were in the Amazon, I lived there and even managed their Christmas tree farm for a few months. They had the technology down to an art. The business fascinated me."

"The couple took their daughter with them when they visited the jungle?"

"They always took her with them. I saw them at a plant biology conference and they had the baby with them then, which is where they talked to me about taking care of their tree farm. They didn't belong to a wolf pack. They adored their daughter. As much as they loved plants, they would never have left her with strangers. She's okay, then?"

"She is, although it's going to be some adjustment for her as we try to teach her our ways and how to get along in a wolf pack. Are any of these plants something that might be turned into illegal drugs?"

"One of them can intensify the effects of some kinds of illegal drugs, but neutralize others. Otherwise, no."

"Thanks. If you think of anything else, let me know."

"If Jessica wants to learn anything about her parents that I might know, she can call me."

"Will do. I'm sure she will. Thanks."

Hunter ended the call with Shelley and stared at the floor for a moment, gathering his thoughts. Then he called Bjornolf back and gave him all the details. Next, Hunter contacted Rourke. "I need you at the courthouse as soon as it opens. Let me know if anyone bought this property from the Silverstones." He sent an email of the deed.

"Get right on it first thing in the morning."

Soft footfalls padded down the carpeted hallway to where Hunter was standing in the dining room. He smiled to see Tessa wearing her gown with the woolly lambs on it.

"It isn't even light out, you know," Tessa said, running her hand over his chest. "You're not micromanaging again, are you?"

He smiled and turned off his phone, then took her hand and led her back to bed. "What else did you have in mind?"

Chapter 23

WITH APPREHENSION, ANNA JOINED JESSICA IN THE guest bathroom of the beach cottage to study Jessica's pregnancy-test results. If the test was accurate, Jessica wasn't pregnant. Anna knew teen pregnancies were risky at best, and the young couple needed to get to know each other better, so the results were good news. But she wasn't sure how Jessica felt about it.

"As long as the test worked, it says you're not pregnant," Anna finally said, a sense of disquiet filling her.

Jessica had been tense, but she looked ready to collapse at learning the news. Anna took her in her arms. "Are you going to be okay?"

Jessica was crying softly but nodding her head.

Anna rubbed her back in a soothing manner. "Shh, it's going to be all right. Really."

"Nathan kept telling me he's happy to have the babies. He's going to be upset with me."

"No. You're both going to be fine. You'll share mated life together. Enjoy being a couple before the kids come. Learn all about each other and about being one of us, and get to know the pack."

Jessica sat down on the side of the bathtub as if she couldn't stand any longer. "Nathan told me all about you. About how you ran away from home. How you never had a Christmas."

Anna's throat tightened at the memory. Jessica

couldn't know. Bjornolf... Anna should have told him already.

"I... I don't know how you could have managed. Yet now..." Tears filled her eyes again and Anna grabbed a box of tissues and sat beside her.

"My father isn't my father," Jessica continued. "I think... I think he murdered my real parents. But he was good to me growing up. And now he's in jail. I... I don't know what to feel. Should I hate him when all I can do is think of the time he got me my first bicycle for Christmas and taught me how to ride it? How he taught me to drive my first car?"

She sniffled, took Anna's hand, and squeezed hard. "But I saw what he tried to do to you. We thought he killed you. Suddenly my adoptive father became a monster. Did he kill the DEA agents? Others?"

"We don't know for certain." Anna handed her a tissue.

"But he did try to kill you. And what about my mother? Was she in on all of this?"

Again, Anna said, "We don't know. She might have been."

Jessica nodded, tears still streaming down her face. "I'm glad I'm not pregnant yet. I can't imagine dealing with that when I still haven't come to grips with being..."

Jessica bit her lip. Then she looked at Anna. "A werewolf. Nathan said that some are royals who have been werewolves for generations. They can control when they shift. I'm not one of those," she said glumly.

"Rourke is newly turned. So is Hunter's mate, Tessa. You're a first-generation-born pure werewolf."

Jessica's expression brightened a little. "Tessa isn't a royal?"

"No. She has trouble with having to shift, just like any of the newer wolves."

Jessica nodded, looking as though she was at least farther along than that. She waved her hand. "I have to deal with all of this stuff about my parents, too."

"I understand. You know what, though? You don't have to do it alone."

Not like Anna had to.

Jessica blotted her eyes, then her teary gaze met Anna's. "Not like you did."

A teen alone, pregnant, and bereft.

Something in the way Jessica said it again made Anna feel as though the teen knew about her horrible past. She couldn't, and yet Anna felt swamped with guilt.

She should have already told Bjornolf. But it happened so long ago. Maybe he didn't have any need to know. It didn't have anything to do with their relationship, she told herself.

And yet what if she couldn't have babies of her own? She knew he was looking forward to having his own offspring. She felt terrible, small, and unworthy of his love.

Bjornolf knew something was wrong when Anna and Jessica left the bathroom. Anna wouldn't meet his gaze. Jessica gave Nathan a small smile, her eyes blurred with tears, and said, "I don't want breakfast. Can we go now?"

Pregnancy? No pregnancy? What had happened?

Anna's distressed expression shook Bjornolf up the most.

"You'll be back later? For the open house?" Bjornolf asked Nathan and Jessica, unsure what was going on.

Jessica nodded, and she and Nathan left the house hand in hand, cuddling together. He was glad to see that Jessica seemed to be all right with whatever the results were. Anna was a different story.

As soon as Bjornolf watched Nathan and Jessica leave, he locked the front door and turned to question Anna, but he heard the back door close. He thought she'd gone outside to get some fresh air until he saw her clothes lying on the kitchen tile floor, scattered as if she'd been in a rush to escape the confines of the house, her human form, and *him*.

He should have left her alone, let her sort out her feelings, and then comforted her if she still needed a shoulder to lean on. He was quickly coming to the conclusion that he couldn't do it. He had to take measures to help her in any way that he could, but waiting for her to resolve her own issues wasn't his way.

First, Bjornolf punched in Reid's number. He needed to know what Anna was hiding, and he couldn't wait any longer.

"Time's up, Reid. What have you learned about Anna? Anything?"

"Hell, Bjornolf. Ask her yourself if you want to find out quicker! Okay, this is what I've learned so far. She was born and raised in New Jersey. She moved around a lot. I haven't found any clue that would indicate why she would have an aversion to Christmas. I've questioned a friend of a friend of a friend, and I think I've got a lead. But damn it! I'll call you. I promise. Okay?"

"Yeah, all right."

"Hell, you're mating with her, aren't you?"

"Done."

"Why didn't you tell me? Son of gun. Congratulations. I would never have thought it. I swear I'll get the info to you as quick as I can."

"Thanks, Reid. Gotta go."

Bjornolf stripped as fast as possible and hurried outside. He slammed the door closed and shifted before the frigid air chilled him too much. He could have used the wolf door, but he needed the cold for a moment to cool his heated blood.

He took off running, following her scent down the stairs to the pebble beach. To his guarded relief, he found her sitting next to a boulder, staring out at the ocean. She looked as though she wanted to be alone.

He wanted to hold her close like a human would. He wanted to ask her what the matter was.

She turned her head to see who was coming, her ears perked, her greenish amber eyes studying him.

Anna's not wanting to share what was troubling her was killing him. But as a mate, he nuzzled her face in friendship and love, then lay down on the rocky beach next to her.

He tried to clear his mind of all the worries rushing through it, and then finally decided he wasn't getting anywhere. He licked her face, snuggled next to her, and when she laid her head on the beach and closed her eyes, he laid his head across her neck and did likewise.

Whatever the matter was, they'd deal with it together when she was ready.

A noise woke Bjornolf up. Realizing that he and Anna were still on the beach in their wolf forms, he looked back at the house, wondering if he'd just imagined hearing a suspicious noise.

A crash that sounded like glass shattering had him on his feet in an instant. Anna was beside him. He was across the beach and up the stairs in several quickly pounding heartbeats. He heard the front door slam as he reached the back patio. Bjornolf raced around the house to see who was there.

A red pickup truck barreled out of the driveway, but he got the license plate number before it took off. He came back around the house as fast as he could to check on Anna. She wasn't on the patio. He dove through the wolf door, ran across the kitchen, and saw her standing in the living room as a wolf. She was panting, her tail drooping, as she stared at the Christmas ornaments smashed all over the floor, bits and pieces of colorful chips of glass everywhere.

She looked back at him. Her eyes were so sad that he wanted to kill the bastard who had done this.

She shifted, walked back into the kitchen, and dressed as he hurried to turn into his human form and join her. Naked, he took her into his arms and said, "Anna."

She was always so on top of everything. If one thing didn't work, she tried something else. He'd never seen her look so devastated. He didn't want to leave her alone for a second, even though he didn't want to cancel the open house over this.

He had a million tasks to accomplish to set things right, and if it wasn't for her shattered expression, he would have taken over and set matters in motion to fix everything immediately.

But no matter what, he couldn't leave her like this.

He hugged her tighter and kissed her cheek, wanting to cheer her up in any way that he could. He noted the popcorn garland was unharmed. The tree was fine. The copper angel and wolf treetop ornament was still standing tall on the tree, watching over their little cottage. "The angel and the wolf are just fine."

Anna burst into tears.

When Hunter got the distress call from Bjornolf, he didn't know what to think. Hunter and Tessa were putting the finishing touches on their place before the open house, and *now* this. Bjornolf was ranting in a whisper. The waves were hitting the shoreline with such ferocity that Hunter could barely hear what Bjornolf was saying.

"Where *are* you?" Hunter asked.

"The beach down below the cottage," Bjornolf said.

"Okay," Hunter said, not used to a SEAL falling apart on him. "Say again."

Bjornolf took a deep breath. "Someone trashed the tree decorations. Red Ford pickup." He gave the license plate number as Hunter quickly jotted it down. "The ornaments are ruined. Anna's shook up, and you know she doesn't shake up easily. I'm really worried about her."

"We'll be right there. All right, Bjornolf? We'll tend to it. You take care of Anna."

"She's cleaning. Not speaking to me."

"Take care of her, Bjornolf. We'll be right there. Ten minutes tops."

Hunter ended the call and called his sister. Meara and

Finn would meet them there. Then he called Caruthers with the truck description. The police officer would get right on it.

Hunter turned to see Tessa waiting anxiously to hear what he had to say about it. "Will you be alright alone?"

"I'm going with you. I may be having these babies any second, but I'm part of the pack, and we all help each other out during a crisis. If nothing else, I can pat Anna's hand or something."

"Who's going to take care of me if you have your babies prematurely in the middle of that mess?" Hunter asked. He was serious. He didn't know why Bjornolf was so rattled, but hell, if Tessa had her babies at a disaster scene? Hunter would have a stroke.

He kissed her and pulled her into his arms. "You can't go like this." He ran his hand over her flannel nightgown.

She gave him an exasperated look and sighed. "I planned to get dressed."

Bjornolf was glad when the troops arrived. The women took Anna aside, and Tessa was talking to her softly. He was about to ask the cop Caruthers what he'd discovered about the license plate when Jessica spoke up.

"I know you all are looking for whoever was driving the red truck. Whoever that person was wrecked the decorations. It was Dottie Everton, aka Dorothy Wentworth, my adoptive mother," Jessica said, both angry and upset. "I know her scent. It was her."

Bjornolf had wondered when Jessica would finally realize she was part of the pack, even though it had to be hard for her to give up her mother like that. The woman must have followed the kids here when they left the tree farm after searching the safe.

While Anna and Bjornolf were at the beach, they'd left the back door unlocked. Neither of them thought anyone would come around the back to break into the house and destroy their Christmas.

Bjornolf had smelled the woman's scent earlier at the Evertons' house, but he didn't know who the woman was. He was glad Jessica had revealed the truth. It would take time for Jessica to feel wholly part of the pack, but she'd made a nice start.

"The truck is registered to her husband, but with that additional information, we'll know to arrest her for breaking and entering and destroying private property," Caruthers said, taking pictures of the damage.

With that settled, Bjornolf and Rourke cleaned up the rest of the mess. Hunter was in the kitchen preparing wassail and apple cider. The police officers—Allan Smith and Caruthers's wife, Greta—were busy trying to track down Everton's truck.

Nathan and Finn had gone to the store to pick up more Christmas decorations that would match the ones that were ruined. With the Christmas tree lights and the outdoor lights on, a fire flickering at the hearth, and the smell of apple cider and wassail simmering on the stove, the place was soon ready for the open house.

Meanwhile, Anna, Jessica, Tessa, and Meara were all clustered in the master bedroom, talking behind closed doors. Except for Anna, who was still wearing all black from the clandestine visit to check out Everton's safe, all the ladies were dressed in sparkly Christmas sweaters, ready for the open house. They were just a little early before the rest of the pack members arrived.

Bjornolf was dying to know what was going on. In the meantime, Rourke began laying out the case they were building on the coffee table. Copies of everything they'd found in the safe and other documents that Rourke had brought with him, including a transcript of his interview with Helen Wentworth, were spread out for everyone's perusal.

With one more long glance toward the master bedroom, Bjornolf began to look over the documents again to see if he'd missed anything.

"Courthouse records show the tree farm still belongs to Oliver and Jenna Silverstone," Rourke said. "Roger and Dottie Wentworth didn't purchase it."

Bjornolf nodded, concentrating on the paperwork when he heard the women laughing in the bedroom. He glanced up at Hunter, saw a hint of a smile in his expression, and realized then that everything would be all right.

He'd never known how truly important a pack could be in a crisis until now. He still didn't know what had upset Anna, but he figured once she discussed the matter with the women, she'd share the truth with him. He loved her, and he had to let her know that every day of their lives.

He sighed heavily and looked at some of the papers concerning the planting of trees. One of them in particular caught his eye. He began thinking—if the DEA bodies had been buried at the farm, it would have been either where new seedlings were growing or on some spare acreage. He started looking at dates of plantings and found that the schematics showed a detailed planting regimen. And identified some places that might just yield a couple of bodies.

"Hunter," he called out. "I have an idea where the DEA agent bodies might be located."

Chapter 24

THE WOMEN WERE ALL TALKING TO ANNA, TRYING TO bolster her while she sat quietly on the edge of the bed. She had never been a member of a pack or truly belonged to a family, so she wasn't expecting them to rally around her. She was stunned.

Anna had never talked to anyone about her past. She'd buried it, but it was there—always there. Deep. The first Christmas she'd thought she'd enjoy, one that she'd believed she could get through and forget the past, had been destroyed. She was numb all over.

To lighten the mood, Tessa said, "Hunter was ready to expire on the spot when I insisted on coming to Anna's open house, afraid I'd have the babies spontaneously once we arrived."

Everyone laughed. Anna could just envision Hunter, who was always so in charge, being distressed over the pregnancy.

Then Tessa said, "Bjornolf was just as bad when you were upset, Anna. Hunter said he'd never seen one of his fellow SEALs crash that hard. That was before Hunter was having a stroke over my coming here."

Anna wondered how Bjornolf would react if he ever made her pregnant. Then she let out her breath. She didn't know if she could ever have babies again.

Greta said, "When I had my babies, Caruthers threw up. Worst of it was, he got my overnight bag in the car and was backing out of the drive before he remembered to take me! I was moving kind of slow with triplets at the time."

The ladies laughed.

Meara glanced at Anna, then took a deep breath. "Maybe we shouldn't tell all these stories in front of Tessa. She's due any second."

"Nonsense." Tessa looked at the sweater that Meara was wearing and frowned. "Are you gaining weight?"

Every eye turned to stare at Meara's sparkly Christmas tree sweater. "Twins, next spring."

"Ha!" Tessa said. "Does Finn know?"

"I told him right before we came over here. He's thrilled."

Everyone congratulated her and then grew quiet.

Tessa said to Anna, "Maybe you need to talk to Bjornolf about what's troubling you."

Anna was tough. She had to be. She'd worn a coat of armor for years. But this was the hardest thing she'd ever have to do.

"You have to trust him," Tessa said. "He's your mate."

Anna nodded.

"We're leaving and sending him in here. Okay?"

"Okay."

"If someone will help me up from the bench," Tessa said.

Anna could not imagine being that full of babies again, and when she cast a look at Jessica to see her take on it, she looked like she was thinking the same thing.

Meara said, "I'll get Hunter." She hurried out of the room and quickly returned with both Hunter and Bjornolf.

He looked worried. Anna hated how she'd hit such a low spot and he was the one who had to put up with her.

Hunter helped Tessa up and escorted her out of the bedroom.

The other ladies left the room, and Meara shut the door behind her.

"Some potentially good news," Bjornolf said as he sat on the bed and put his arm around Anna. "If the plans for the tree plantings are any indication, we might be able to pinpoint the location of the bodies. Hunter's going to have the police get on it."

"That's good," she said, genuinely meaning it. For a moment, she thought she might just skip telling him about her past.

"You know you can tell me anything, Anna. You're the most important person in the world to me."

She took a deep breath. This was it. She had to get it off her chest. He deserved to know. Maybe… he could help her deal with it. "I haven't told anyone this… since it happened. Years and years ago."

He kissed her cheek. "You're the first one I confided in about the bear killing my friend."

She nodded. He was right. He'd bared his soul to her and it was time for her to do the same. She took a deep breath. "Okay. I was fifteen the first time I kissed a wolf. He was…" She paused. "Older. Cocky. I really liked him. All alpha. I had these notions that if I loved him and he loved me, we'd become mated wolves."

She felt Bjornolf stiffen a bit.

She shook her head. "My parents were never nurturing. I needed somebody to love who would love me in return. I thought he could be that someone."

She harrumphed. "My past was so gray and murky that I don't remember a time when I ever received a

Christmas gift. My parents should never have had me. I always suspected I was a fluke, unintentional. I even had the notion that they weren't my real parents. And then they were murdered."

Bjornolf rubbed her arm. She appreciated his comforting touch, when she would have pulled away in the past.

"So when I met Rory, I thought he would be good for me. He even gave me a gift. New hair ribbons. I was so naive. He forced himself on me. He didn't want me. He left, and... I learned I was pregnant."

"At fifteen," Bjornolf said, his voice quiet.

"With twins. A boy and a girl. I was too young to have babies. They arrived seventeen weeks early on Christmas Day. Even today, many premature babies die. Back then, they had no chance of survival. I was devastated." She took another deep breath and expelled it.

"I used some of the money I received after my parents' deaths to buy a small child's coffin and headstone and buried them together, just as the twins had been snuggled next to each other in my womb. A minister spoke last rites for that young girl's twin babies—that's how I looked at it. Like I wasn't even there. And then I buried the recollections as best I could." She glanced up at him and saw the look of love in his eyes.

"I should have told you earlier, Bjornolf. I'm sorry."

He pulled her into his embrace and held on tight, kissing her hair and keeping her close. "I'm sorry you had to go through that alone. You know you can tell me anything. I'm always here for you."

She nodded.

"You're not worried about what I think, are you?"

She didn't say anything.

"You thought I wouldn't still love you? God, Anna, I do love you, no matter what."

"What… what if we can't have children?" she asked, softly.

He hugged her. "That's nothing to worry about. If we have children, that's great. If we don't, that's fine, too. Besides, we're kind of busy taking care of two nearly grown kids anyway."

She smiled a little at him. "Yeah, we are."

He cleared his throat and seemed to want to say something else, but was afraid to.

"What?"

"Is the wolf dead?" he growled. Gone was the soothing, caring Bjornolf. And in his place was a retired SEAL wolf who was ready to mete out justice on her behalf.

"Yeah, he is. The minister's brother killed the wolf right after I'd buried my babies. I love you, you know?"

"Yeah. And the feeling's mutual." He gave her a knowing smile.

They heard more voices in the living room. The open house had begun.

"I've got to get dressed," Anna said, sighing. She was ready to have a new outlook on the holidays. She was ready to truly forget the past. But she knew she couldn't. Some memories never went away.

"Are you going to be all right?" he asked, concerned, running his hand soothingly over her back.

"Yeah, thanks."

"Need any help?"

"Dressing? Or undressing?" she asked, moving to the closet. He was good for her.

Bjornolf chuckled. "If I help with either, we'll miss

the party. I'll just enjoy the show. Are you ready for us to tell Hunter we want to join his pack?"

Anna slipped into her black dress, the back cut low and sexy, and black heels. She smiled when she saw Bjornolf's tongue practically hang out, and held out her hand to him. "Yeah, I am. Ready to join the party?"

"If we weren't hoping to join Hunter and Tessa's pack, I'd skip the party."

She smiled and kissed him thoroughly, his hands stroking down her naked back and over her buttocks, the silky fabric sliding with his touch. She finally sighed and said, "Let's go before we decide we don't need a pack."

"I've been thinking," Bjornolf said, her hand in his, "it's time I saw my brother again. It's been years. I'd… like to take you to meet him."

She snapped her gaping mouth shut and smiled at him. "I'd like that."

The decorated homes for the pack's open-house parade were lovely. Bjornolf kept Anna tucked under his arm for most of the night as they visited one house after another, meeting each of the pack members. Nathan was as proud as could be and kept his arm around Jessica's waist the whole time.

Bjornolf thought Anna was more beautiful than any sparkly lights or glamorous Christmas decorations. She seemed like a whole new person in the sexy black dress that caught everyone's eye, along with her long legs, high heels, and low-cut bodice. She smelled sweet and delicious—of oranges and cinnamon, and of the apple cider she'd been drinking. And they had a wonderful time. He couldn't wait to get her home and spend the rest of the night making love to her if she was up to it.

He managed to walk outside at Tessa and Hunter's home and sneak a call to Reid while Anna was talking to some of the women.

"Hey, Reid—"

"Bjornolf—"

"I don't need the information. Okay? Don't look anymore."

"Okay. The guy's dead."

Angry that a wolf could have done what he did to her, Bjornolf clenched his teeth. Reid had found the information. But like him, that's the first thing he had wanted to know—*was the bastard who'd taken advantage of Anna still alive?*

"Thanks," Bjornolf said. "I owe you—"

"Lots," Reid said. "Give that little wolf of yours a hug and a kiss for me. Merry Christmas."

"Yeah, same to you."

Bjornolf let out his breath, frosty mist in the cold air, and headed back to the house. Everything was going to be all right.

As soon as he walked inside, Anna frowned a little at him. He quickly joined her and said, "Come on, before we chicken out. Let's tell Hunter and Tessa the good news."

She smiled. "Maybe they won't see it that way."

He chuckled. "His pack will be lucky to get us."

They found Tessa and Hunter pouring more wassail. Both turned to see what they had to say.

"We've got good news," Bjornolf said. "Well, unless you don't want us to join your pack."

Tessa hurried over to hug Anna. "Thank God it

worked. Hunter's been trying to figure out a way to get the two of you together since the last mission here on the Oregon coast."

Anna and Bjornolf looked at Hunter. He smiled a little, then shook Bjornolf's hand and gave Anna a hug. "I didn't know that Meara had the same idea. That was why she sent Bjornolf to watch our backs in the Amazon."

Bjornolf grinned. "I should have known."

"This means the two of you are also going to be on the team for missions, right?" Hunter asked.

"Bjornolf told me only if it's not too dangerous for him," Anna said, smiling.

Bjornolf slipped his arm around her waist and pulled her tight. "She's right."

"Having well-seasoned wolves who could help us with pack issues and on covert missions, too? The scenario couldn't be better," Hunter said. "I was worried about Anna being alone, and now..." Hunter breathed a sigh of relief. "I'm glad for you, Anna. And glad for you, Bjornolf. I'm pleased you're no longer a ghost. That you want to be part of the team. Not just on the outside looking in." Hunter saluted them with a cup of wassail. "Welcome to the pack."

When Bjornolf, Anna, Jessica, and Nathan arrived back at the house later that night, Jessica and Nathan wanted to talk to them about future living arrangements. Bjornolf wanted to take Anna to bed, but he knew this was important, too.

They all sat down on the couch, and Jessica started

the conversation as they sipped eggnog. "We've been thinking. Nathan sold his house, and he's got money so he could help with the cost. And I could sell the Christmas tree farm…"

"It's not in your name—yet. Your adoptive parents claim it's theirs," Bjornolf warned.

Jessica's eyes narrowed a little. "But we know it *isn't*. It's my parents' house. And they're *dead*." Jessica spoke as if she was coming to grips with what had happened. That under all this other talk, she was hurting, angry, and wanted to settle things a bit. "I think I know where they're buried."

Anna should have been shocked at Jessica's revelation, but she wasn't. She guessed that Jessica was compartmentalizing things. Taking care of one major issue at a time. Jessica had been worried about being pregnant. Now she was concentrating on something else.

Her parents' deaths.

Jessica loved the people who raised her, and she was struggling with giving them up, too. No teen should have to deal with issues like this.

"How do you know?" Anna asked.

"I started analyzing the sections of trees and the years they were planted. We have tons of records dating back some years before that. I was trying to match up when my parents might have been buried on the farm."

"I've been pondering that same thing about the DEA agents," Bjornolf said. "Hunter's police officers are going to look into it."

"What if your parents died in the Amazon, Jessica?" Anna asked, trying to be realistic. If they'd died there, no one would ever discover what had happened so long ago.

"Sure, I considered it." Jessica folded her arms. "When I was little, maybe five or so, I was playing in the basement, and I smelled blood."

"Your parents would have been gone about three years by then."

"Yeah, I don't know. I never really gave it any thought until later when I fell and split my forehead open. I was six at the time. Head wounds bleed a lot. The doctor couldn't find the cut in my hairline so they couldn't stitch it. I remember smelling all that blood. It reminded me of the blood I'd breathed in earlier in the basement."

A wolf's strong sense of smell.

"I don't recall getting a whiff of any blood when we were in the basement," Anna said.

"That's my fault. I told my parents I smelled it on one side of the basement, opposite where the dartboard was. They said that I was imagining things, but they used bleach to clean it up. I could only smell bleach after that."

"It's not your fault, Jessica. Forensic scientists can still discover bloodstains using luminol, which reacts by turning fluorescent."

Jessica nodded. She didn't look happy about the situation, but she appeared resigned. If her adoptive parents had murdered her own parents, they'd lost the right to be her family.

"Where do you think they were buried?"

"Two different areas. Seedlings were just being planted. The other trees were too mature."

Bjornolf had his cell out and was already calling Hunter. "We think we've got a possible location for Jessica's parents' bodies."

Chapter 25

AFTER NATHAN AND JESSICA RETURNED TO THE OTHER pack member's home where they were staying and Anna fell asleep, Bjornolf left the bedroom and went into the living room. He turned on his phone to check the order status on the clothes he had ordered for her. He smiled when he confirmed that they would arrive in time for Christmas. He couldn't wait to see Anna's face light up when she opened his presents. He would do anything to make her smile.

"What are you doing?" Anna asked as she walked into the living room, naked and mouthwatering.

He quickly turned off his phone. "Nothing. Did I wake you?"

"If you're not doing anything, why don't you come back to bed and do *something*?" she purred and slipped her hand around his arm. Her eyes took in his nakedness, giving his thickening cock a long, hungry look. She smiled as she gave her upper lip a little lick.

He couldn't help but give her a cocky grin. His mate was insatiable. So was he. Muscles tensing and ready for action, he swept her up in his arms and carried her back to bed. He was just glad the earlier upset was over.

His feet were soundless on the thick carpeting. When he dropped her on the bed, she bounced and gave a little "oh." As he joined her, he looked into her eyes, their gazes locking, and she teased, "So who were you texting? Old girlfriend?"

"Are you kidding? Mated to a she-wolf with lethal moves, I'd never be *that* foolish." He raked her from head to toe with his gaze, and then he ran his hands over her feet. She gave him a look that was particularly devilish, as if she wanted to try her moves out on him right then. Instead, she waited to see what he was going to do next, hands behind her head.

He settled his cock against her nest of curls and lifted her legs around his waist. He ran his hands over her hips and waist, caressing her breasts while her smile broadened. He shrugged. "And these? A total distraction when I'm trying to take you down."

He slid his hands over her silky arms. "You're all I ever wanted in a woman in one heavenly package."

"Hmm," she said, her fingers sliding down his back and making him want to plunge into her. The moment he'd lifted her into his arms and carried her to the bed, he'd been ready.

He kissed her long and hard, their tongues tasting of cinnamon and oranges. He shifted his attention to that sweet spot that had her writhing beneath him and begging him to finish her off.

His cock was rock hard, throbbing with the need to find release, as her fingers dug into his shoulders. Every muscle in her body was toned to perfection as if she was meant just for him. For his pleasure. For his touch.

She smelled of she-wolf and peach shampoo, of sweet wassail and sex and desire. Her heart was racing to the moon, and her breath caught when he sensed she was close to climaxing. He pushed her over the edge by pressing his cock between her folds. She cried out, not needing to hide their lovemaking from the teens tonight.

He joined her, pressing hard and deep, surrounded by her hot, wet heat, as her muscles contracted with thrilling little ripples of climax. He told her he loved her and stretched her as he deepened the penetration.

Her fingers were all over him—clawing at his back and ass, pulling at his shoulders.

He wanted to hold on to the peak, wanted to make it last even if it killed him, but he couldn't. He reminded himself that as needy as she was, they could do it again after a little bit.

And he let go.

"You're so hot," she murmured.

"Hell, you make me hot."

Satiated, he pulled out of her, rolled onto his back, and moved her over to cuddle with him. No matter what happened, he would always love her.

The next day, several investigators gathered at the Christmas tree farm, searching for bodies. Yale, Hunter, Finn, Anna, and Bjornolf watched the proceedings as teams of men dug up the areas that most likely held the bodies of Jessica's parents and the DEA agents who were murdered.

"Over here," a man shouted, and they all moved to the area of freshly planted seedlings only a couple of weeks old. "Two bodies."

The bodies hadn't decomposed much. Bjornolf was able to ID the first man as Montoya Sanchez.

One of the men on the scene located an ID in the pocket of the other dead man. "Thomas Cremer," he said.

"The missing DEA agents," Yale confirmed.

A man hurried to speak with Yale and said, "Second dig site yielded the skeletal remains of a man and woman."

"If the young girl will agree to it, we'll get DNA samples and see if we have a match."

―⁓―

After the day of excavating the bodies at the tree farm, Bjornolf got a text message from Nathan.

Can we see you tonight?

Bjornolf was afraid they'd already heard about the bodies being found. Then again, the feds might have contacted Jessica for DNA samples, so she probably knew.

He showed Anna the text message. "Invite them to dinner," she said.

Come for dinner.

They were early, and Bjornolf suspected they were really worried about something. Everyone was quiet as they ate the spaghetti and meatballs he'd made from scratch. He half expected someone to bring up the weather—they were going to get a snowstorm—but no one even mentioned that.

They finally cleaned up the dishes and retired to the living room. Jessica and Anna turned on the outdoor lights and Christmas tree lights, and he and Nathan started a fire.

Nathan and Jessica cast glances at each other, then Jessica finally said, "About Christmas—Hunter said he wanted us to give you both time alone together and time to investigate the murders…" She bit her lip.

"The other family we're staying with is great…" Nathan said.

Bjornolf knew what Nathan was getting at, but he felt it was up to Anna. This was her first Christmas. *Their* first Christmas together.

"Yeah, really loving and all… you know, worried that we're not going to have fun at Christmas because of… well, you know," Jessica said.

"They have five-year-old quadruplets." Nathan looked like that was all he needed to say.

"All boys," Jessica added.

Bjornolf waited quietly for Anna to take the lead.

She glanced at Bjornolf, trying to read his expression. She appeared willing if he was. He should have known she would be. All that camouflaged armor she'd worn for missions was gone now. He gave her a ghost of a smile, telling her it was all right with him.

"We have a guest room that's all yours," Anna said decidedly.

"I'll go get our bags," Nathan quickly said, as if he was afraid Bjornolf would contradict Anna.

He was amused that they were packed and ready to move in without even knowing they were welcome to stay.

"I'll help you." Jessica beamed, mouthing a *thank you* to Anna and hurrying after Nathan.

Shaking his head, Bjornolf snuggled closer to Anna. "Do you think we're doing the right thing?"

Anna rested her head against his chest. "It might be just what we all need."

"You're right." Even though he'd wanted Anna all to himself over the holidays.

The kids were back in the house again soon afterward, and they headed for the guest room.

When they returned, Jessica glanced at Anna and asked, "Can we make Christmas cookies?"

Bjornolf suspected Anna hadn't made them before, so he helped her out. "I've never made them." He felt Anna's eyes on him and added, "I'm game if you can teach me."

"Me, too," Nathan said, coming out of the bedroom. "I've never made them, but I'd sure like to eat them." Nathan gave Anna a wicked grin.

Jessica dumped her bags in the room before joining them, slipping her hand into his. Smiling, she headed for the kitchen. "How about pfeffernusse cookies?" She started pulling open cabinet drawers. "What are your favorites?"

"Shortbread cookies?" Nathan asked.

"Sugar cookies?" Bjornolf added, as they all followed Jessica into the kitchen, getting into the spirit of baking cookies. They all looked at Anna to see what she preferred.

"They're not really Christmassy." Anna looked a little like she was unsure how to join the party.

"What are they?" Jessica asked.

"Chocolate chip cookies. Double the chips."

Jessica grinned, looked at Nathan, and said, "We'll need some ingredients."

"We'll go get them."

Before Bjornolf knew it, the kids were off again.

Anna slipped her arms around Bjornolf's waist. "Yeah, I think this was just what we needed."

The last of the cookies were made, and several of the cooled ones had already been eaten. They were in the middle of cleaning up the mess when Jessica gave them all a funny look, then ran for the guest room.

Nathan quickly followed her to see what had happened. Anna and Bjornolf continued to sweep and wipe up spilled flour and sugar. They were washing mixing bowls when Nathan returned.

"She had the sudden urge to turn wolf. She's upset that she can't control the shifting, but... well, we're going to take a run in the woods tonight."

Anna said without hesitation, "We are, too."

Nathan looked a little startled.

"We don't have to run with you, but..." She patted Bjornolf's stomach. "He needs to keep in shape."

Bjornolf pulled her into a hug and kissed the top of her head. "I recall seeing *you* eating your fair share of the cookies."

"*More* than my fair share." She hugged his arms as he wrapped them around her waist.

Nathan grinned. "Jessica will be thrilled to have you guys tag along."

He rushed back to the bedroom.

"Ready for a run?" Anna asked Bjornolf.

"We forgot to add that to our schedule. Running."

"As wolves."

"As wolves," he said, and she was glad. That was her favorite kind of running.

Anna and Bjornolf and the teens ran through the chilly woods. The snow was falling in huge, fat flakes, and the waves crashed against the boulders below in a steady rhythm.

Anna nipped at Bjornolf's neck in fun-loving play. He licked her nose back, his eyes flashing with a predatory gleam. She was bound for more fun later tonight. The kids ran with them, sometimes a little ahead. Anna noticed the way Jessica studied her while Anna was sniffing the ground and the trees, nuzzling up to Bjornolf, licking his cheek, jumping at his back, playing.

Anna realized that Jessica was learning what it meant to be a wolf. She hadn't grown up with wolves, didn't know how to play as one, and needed guidance and inspiration.

After Anna nipped Bjornolf twice more, he finally caught her off guard and pinned her to the snow. She growled playfully while Jessica and Nathan watched. Anna loved this part of a wolf's nature, though she'd never done this with an adult male before. Sparring with men in training was as close as she'd come. For her, this was all fairly new, too.

Bjornolf still had Anna pinned down when she quit struggling to get up. He licked her face. She licked his in return. His eyes were dark with lust. She imagined hers were, too.

Time for them to head back to the house. This part they didn't need to teach to the teens.

He let her up and she shook off the snow sticking to her fur. They both looked at Jessica and Nathan.

In wolf language the teens knew what Bjornolf and Anna had in mind. Nathan bowed his head a little in acknowledgment, and then Anna sprinted for the cottage. Bjornolf chased after her with a *woof*, like two teens in the race for the finish line. She hoped Jessica and Nathan would take a nice long run before they returned to the house.

Chapter 26

A WEEK LATER, YALE CALLED ANNA AS BJORNOLF AND she were getting ready to prepare Christmas Eve dinner. Bjornolf knew at once that Yale had some forensic results. Anna put him on speakerphone so Bjornolf could hear.

Jessica and Nathan were out doing some last-minute Christmas shopping. Bjornolf was glad they weren't here at the moment.

"I know this is bad timing with it being Christmas Eve. But the DNA test results came back and I wanted to let you know they were positive," Yale said. "The young lady is Jessica Silverstone, daughter of Jenna and Oliver Silverstone. The blood we found using the luminol in the basement of their home proved to be both Jenna and Oliver's blood. And… some of Roger Wentworth aka Roger Everton's blood. He was probably wounded when he killed the couple. Their daughter was right."

Anna listened, not saying a word, her jaw clenched tight.

Bjornolf wrapped his arm around her shoulders, grateful that Yale hadn't revealed the gory details in front of Jessica. "What about the DEA agents? Any word on what happened to them?"

"They were checking into allegations that William Wentworth was dealing in illegal drugs. Their investigation led them to the Christmas tree farm. They were in the house at some point or another. We didn't find any of their blood there, but they appeared to have been caught as soon as they entered the house. The only place they had been was the front foyer. I almost missed smelling a vague hint of their scent there. If you came in the back door, you might have missed it, too."

"We did. Did Hunter tell you what Jessica heard when she was home sick from school that one day?"

"Yes. The time corresponds to the approximate time of death. Both of them were shot several times. They bled out before their wolf's healing abilities could come into play."

Anna took a deep breath.

"I've informed their families. Not the kind of news anyone wants to hear at Christmastime, but they need closure. William and his family had an alibi for that time. They were with you in the Amazon." He took a deep breath. "You have the hardest job—giving the news to Jessica."

"What about Everton's condition? Any word?" Anna asked.

"Intensive care still. He had a heart attack. He's in a coma. So no questioning him yet."

They said good-bye, and Anna looked at Bjornolf. "I should have aimed better."

"Hell, Anna," Bjornolf said, taking her into his arms. "You were drugged, and he intended to shoot and bury you. If you'd hit somewhere less vital, I might not be holding you here now."

"You're right. I just wish they could have interrogated him and learned what all this was about. As to Jessica, she has to be told. I hate being the one to tell her. She'll want to know the truth, but it comes at a price."

"If you want me to…"

Anna shook her head. "She knows my parents were murdered. So I kind of have a connection." She hesitated, her gaze drifting to his chest.

He kissed her and hugged her tight. "I know, Anna. I don't want you to be sad about any of it any longer."

She sighed and gave him a small smile. "I don't want to be, either. I want this first Christmas to be really special. And it will be," she said with determination, dragging him into the kitchen. "If we get to cooking."

They should have known that something was wrong when the kids didn't come home for dinner on time. Not when Jessica and Nathan had proved how responsible they could be. Not when they were just doing some last-minute shopping and most places were already closed for Christmas Eve.

"I'm worried about them." Anna turned off the oven.

Bjornolf glanced outside at the dark and the snow falling. "The mall's closed by now." He tried to get hold of Nathan by phone again.

Anna left another message on Jessica's phone. A text message back from Jessica made Anna's heart leap.

At farm. Getting stuff. Be quick and home soon.

What would they be doing at the farm? Getting more of her clothes? Or something else?

Dottie, Jessica's adoptive mother, was still unaccounted for.

Concerned that someone else was using Jessica's

phone, Anna called Jessica and got her message machine. "Jessica, answer the phone." Jessica had to hear her voice and know it was Anna.

But Jessica didn't respond.

Anna shook her head at Bjornolf's quizzical look.

"Maybe they're just fooling around," Bjornolf said, rubbing Anna's arm. "Nathan told me he'd meet her at the house when her parents were away. They might have wanted to get away from us for some privacy. They're young."

"Maybe," Anna said, but she still didn't think they'd be that irresponsible when they all had planned on having a nice dinner together.

"If we go to the house to check up on them, there's no telling what we might find. On the other hand…" Bjornolf said, his words trailing off.

"They could be in trouble," she finished for him.

"We'll leave a message to let them know we've gone out to the farm in case they arrive here, and we miss them somehow."

Anna was already headed for the bedroom. "We're going armed," Anna said, breaking into his thoughts as she jerked on a white turtleneck and switched her blue jeans for white to blend in with the snow.

"Absolutely." Bjornolf called Hunter to give him a heads-up in case there was trouble, while he and Anna strapped on knives and guns and headed out to the Land Rover. "We don't know if there's any problem. We're on our way to check out the farm." Anna had already called Hunter about Yale's conversation, so he knew what was up with that.

"I'll get Finn to notify the troops. Don't get yourself

and Anna killed, Bjornolf," Hunter said with a stern warning. He meant for them to wait for backup.

"There may be nothing to it. Just a couple of parents worried about their teens," Bjornolf said as he glanced over at Anna.

She was tense and ready for a fight.

"I hope so. But wait for backup," Hunter said again. But he knew that Bjornolf and Anna couldn't wait. Not if the kids were in danger.

They drove a little slower than they wanted because the roads were icy. Anna kept trying to call Nathan and Jessica with no result.

Bjornolf said, "We'll park outside the fence."

"We'll keep to the trees until we reach the back side of the house. You got your lockpicks?" she asked, but then patted her pocket. "Forget it. I have mine."

"Text Jessica and tell her the food's getting cold, so we're going to go ahead and eat. If someone else has her phone—"

"Incoming," Anna said as he parked the Land Rover next to the fence. She read the message: Flat tire. Tow truck coming. Later.

"They're in trouble," Anna said.

"Or this is a setup, figuring we'll assume they're in trouble and come to help them."

Anna texted back. Got a flat where? At farm, or on the way back?

They answered. Farm. We're fine. Take 2 hours. Roads bad. Get there when can. Eat.

She called Hunter and told him the messages they'd received. "We're going in."

Bjornolf leaned over and kissed her mouth. "Keep low until we get close to the house."

The chain link rattled as they climbed the fence. They both ran at a crouch through the trees.

Gunshots rang out inside the house, and Bjornolf and Anna forgot stealth. At a dead run, they headed for the back of the house.

When they reached one of the basement windows, Bjornolf made Anna stand back while he got a look.

Helen Wentworth looked like a crazed woman as she waved a gun at Dottie Everton, who was seated on one of the couches. Dottie was glowering at Helen, her face splotchy with anger. The kids were sitting nearby. Nathan's arm was wrapped protectively around Jessica. There were small-caliber holes in the sofa only inches away from Dottie. Helen started to pace. The kids looked pale faced.

Nathan saw Bjornolf out of the corner of his eye, turned his attention more fully on him, and sat up a little taller. Bjornolf shook his head, indicating for him to look away. Nathan did and squeezed Jessica a little. She looked up at him as if trying to read some message in his action.

Bjornolf and Anna were going to have a devil of a time getting to the kids and Dottie without Helen witnessing their arrival on the basement stairs.

Bjornolf was concentrating so hard that he didn't realize Anna wasn't close behind him any longer. He turned and saw she was gone. *Shit*.

Then he saw her inside the house at the top of the basement stairs. The wall hid her from everyone in the room, but Bjornolf had a clear view of her. "Shit," he said again, this time under his breath.

Weapon ready, Anna was already moving down the stairs. She carefully placed a boot on one step after another, using Helen's screaming and Dottie's crying to cover her approach.

Bjornolf's heart was racing as he held his weapon. He was preparing to shoot through the window and target Helen, but he was afraid the bullet might hit someone else, since she was pacing in front of Dottie and the kids.

Helen shrieked, "I can't believe it was you who had the affair with my husband the first time. And then started it back up! But that wasn't enough, was it? No... you had to be in on this scheme to get rid of me and the kids. You couldn't just divorce Roger. And William couldn't just divorce me. You had to plan my murder! And the kids'! How could you? After you'd lost your own baby!" Helen choked up.

Dottie wiped away tears. "You're wrong. William said he'd ask you for a divorce."

"You weren't mall shopping that day when your daughter was killed," Helen said as if she hadn't heard her. "William said he was on a business trip. But you were together. He arranged to have your baby murdered because it was his baby, too."

Dottie sobbed. "He wouldn't have."

"If I had learned he was having an affair with you, I would have taken him to the cleaners. He knew that. His father loved Roger and would have cut William out of the will if he'd known he was screwing you. William had to get rid of the baby. The proof you two were having an affair. He arranged for the nanny, didn't he?"

Dottie just stared at her as if she was in shock.

"He cut off the affair. Or you did after you lost the baby. Then last year you and he started it back up again. Right after William cut Roger out of the will. That's when William starting acting cold toward me again. Being married to Roger was fine until the will was read, and he only got a dollar from his father. You wanted what William got. You think he would have let her live?" Helen asked, motioning the gun at Jessica. "He never wanted kids."

Dottie quickly looked at Jessica and shook her head. "No. She was going away to college."

"You think so? You think that if William had no trouble having his own kids killed, he wouldn't have Jessica murdered once he got rid of me? He only had to get rid of Roger. He'd used him to kill the couple who owned the tree farm. Once Roger killed the DEA agents, if he got caught, he'd permanently be out of the picture this time."

Four more steps. The stair Anna stepped on creaked. With their wolf hearing, both Jessica and Nathan turned their heads slightly toward the stairs. Anna immediately stopped.

Dottie and Helen were too wrapped up in their own drama to hear her. *Thank God.*

"Roger tries to kill a woman. The two dead DEA agents are unearthed. Another couple was killed, the owners of *this* farm. Coincidence that your adopted daughter came to you at the same time? You murdered her parents and raised the baby. You didn't buy this place."

"William said the baby needed a home. I took her in. That's all!" Dottie shouted.

Bjornolf heard a truck pull up out front.

Helen turned her head toward the stairs. "Showtime."

Bjornolf frowned. His people wouldn't drive up that close to the house, alerting Helen that they had arrived and set her off.

"Front door's locked, Jessica. Get it, won't you? Don't think of running or telling anyone what's going on here or your boyfriend gets it. Okay?" Helen said.

Jessica looked at Nathan. He nodded, kissed her cheek quickly, and let go of her.

Her whole body trembling, she headed for the stairs. As soon as she turned the corner and put her foot on the first step, she covered a startled gasp and froze, staring up at Anna.

Bjornolf prayed she wouldn't give Anna away.

Then, as if she realized her mistake, she dashed up the stairs, gave Anna a really quick hug, then slid past her to the landing.

Bjornolf didn't want Jessica to get hurt. But he didn't want to leave Anna, either. He had no choice. Anna was trained for this kind of work and was armed. Jessica wasn't.

He raced for the front of the house.

William was at the front door, gun in hand, finger on the trigger, safety off, waiting like a wolf who was about to pounce on the unsuspecting.

Bjornolf slammed into him. William fired off several rounds as he went down. Bullets hit the door, the door frame, and the siding of the house before Bjornolf wrested the gun away.

Gunshots rang out inside the house at the basement level, and Bjornolf's blood went cold.

Chapter 27

SHOTS RANG OUT AT THE FRONT DOOR, AND HELEN turned toward the stairs. Nathan jumped up from the couch, tearing her attention away from there.

"You want to be shot? Just pull that again…" That's all Helen got out as Anna leaped from the stairs.

Anna tackled her so hard that Helen's gun went off, a bullet striking the ceiling. The weapon went flying. Dottie dove for it.

Nathan scrambled to get it. He fought her over it and socked her in the jaw, apologizing as he did: "My mother taught me never to hit a woman, but if you go for the gun again, I'm going to have to forget that lesson."

"Don't get up," Anna ordered Helen, as she pinned her to the floor. Anna held her arm against her back, threatening to break it if she moved. "Everything's under control down here!" she shouted up to Bjornolf, hoping he was all right.

"We're good up here!" Bjornolf answered from the front porch.

Anna let out her breath with relief.

"I don't understand why my parents had to die." Jessica raced down the stairs and glowered at Helen.

"A long time ago, I overheard William talking to Jeff about a new find in the Amazon that they'd gotten from some people in Oregon," Helen said. "Shortly thereafter, Dottie and Roger moved to the Christmas tree farm and had a new baby. I didn't think anything of it. I never connected the dots. Not until the trip to the Amazon, the so-called kidnapping, and then Roger's arrest."

The Silverstones were only trying to find a werewolf cure, Anna thought grimly.

"What about the DEA agents?" Anna asked.

"They had been snooping around William's businesses for some months. He swore he wasn't doing anything illegal. I believed him. Or… at least I wanted to. They must have visited Roger to learn if he knew anything about William. Big mistake." Helen let out a breath. "Dottie had to be in on it. She wanted the baby."

"I was not," Dottie screamed at her, but she was seated again on the couch.

Nathan watched her closely with the gun in his hand. "Why wreck the Christmas decorations? That's what I don't get."

Dottie pointed at Anna. "She and that man were trying to take Jessica away from me."

Well they did do that, but not for a reason Dottie could ever guess. As a she-wolf, Jessica had to be with a pack.

Vehicles roared into the parking area next to the house and Anna sighed. The cavalry was a little late, but they had arrived.

───※───

"I've decided," Jessica said as she and Anna, Bjornolf, and Nathan sat down for their reheated Christmas Eve dinner. "I don't want to do the kind of work Anna does. It nearly killed me to see her standing on the stairs. I can't believe they didn't hear my muffled shriek. I was so afraid Helen would shoot Anna before she was able to disarm her."

Nathan shook his head. "Amen to that."

Except for a few bruises, Anna was fine. She was satisfied with the way things had gone down.

"So why was William at the house?" Nathan poked the serving fork into another yam and loaded it onto his plate.

"He really did care about Dottie and had planned to come to her rescue," Anna said. "Helen thought we'd believe the kids had a flat tire while they took care of it."

"Only we wouldn't have made it home," Nathan said.

"No," Jessica said. "Helen would have killed everyone if she could have. She was furious with her two-timing husband and Dottie. If William had made it down the stairs, he would have shot us to get rid of all the witnesses."

Nathan selected another yam. "If Dottie had gotten hold of the gun, William and Helen would have been dead." He looked over at Jessica. "I don't know about us."

Jessica shook her head. "She wouldn't have shot us. I don't think. I think she truly did love me. I was the child who replaced the one she lost. I think my… Roger really loved me, too. Maybe he knew Dottie had the child with William. Maybe he felt sorry for my parents being murdered and he wanted to protect me. Maybe William really killed my parents."

They all sat in awkward silence for a bit. Then wanting to lighten the mood and share in some Christmas spirit, Anna said, "Did anyone want some dessert?"

"I'm full," Jessica said.

"I'll pass until later," Bjornolf said.

Nathan grinned. "I guess I'll wait."

Anna nodded. "It's Christmas Eve, and I've never had one before so let's have some fun after we put the food away."

Nathan squeezed Jessica's hand and smiled at her. She smiled back at him. It was their first Christmas Eve together, too.

Jessica and Anna put away the leftover food while Bjornolf and Nathan set up a board game.

"Thank you for coming to our rescue." Jessica put down the platter of ham and crossed the floor to give Anna a hug. "Thank you for everything."

"We knew you kids were too responsible, and it wasn't your fault when you didn't come home on time for Christmas Eve dinner."

Jessica's face flushed a little.

Anna studied her and smiled. "You… went to the farm to spend some alone time together?"

Jessica shrugged. "I wanted to get some more clothes. And we'd just gotten to fooling around when we heard Helen and Dottie come in the front door. We went down to see what was going on. That was a *really* big mistake. Helen took our phones away. When you started calling, she had to do something. So she tried to get you to stay away. She hoped William would arrive before anyone came looking for us."

Anna shuddered and hugged Jessica again. "I'm glad we were there in time."

After cleaning up the kitchen, they made hot chocolate and went into the living room, where the guys had set up a murder-mystery board game. "We choose teams and play against each other to solve the murder," Nathan said, eager to begin.

Her brows raised, Anna looked from the board game to the guys. "You're kidding, right?" She motioned to the packages under the tree. "Why don't we each open a gift tonight instead?"

Nathan and Jessica's eyes lit up, and Anna thought they looked like kids for an instant.

Bjornolf had gotten Anna a fluffy red sweater. It was beautiful and soft and thankfully wasn't covered in Christmas cheer. She gave him a big hug and kiss.

"It's really for me," he said, "because I get to hold all that softness up close and very personal."

Jessica was smiling and said to Nathan, "Why don't you say things like that to me?"

"He's a SEAL. He can get away with it."

Anna watched as Bjornolf opened his present from her. A pair of cobalt Speedos. "They're for me because I get to enjoy them when you wear them," she said.

He smiled at her, telling her he was willing to wear them whenever she wanted him to.

Nathan was blushing. Jessica was grinning. "We're going to learn a lot from the two of you," Nathan said.

Nathan gave Jessica a new smartphone so that she could give out the number to only those she wanted to. "Thanks, Nathan. Now I can find my way places, too. He knows I get turned around in Portland whenever I go there." She handed him his present and waited, smiling.

He opened the envelope and inside was a Christmas card. Inside that was a receipt for a year of martial arts training. He laughed.

"He kept saying he wanted to learn all Bjornolf's moves, so I was afraid he'd be bugging you to death about it. I got him a year's worth of martial arts training instead. If he likes it, he can keep it up," Jessica said. "It cost a lot and took most of my earnings at the Christmas tree farm, so no skipping lessons."

"This is great," Nathan said. "And I can teach you some of this stuff for self-defense."

Anna stared dreamily into the fire, then said, "It's time for bed, kids. You know *who* will be coming down the chimney soon, and you don't want to catch him in the act."

Everyone looked at the flames shooting up the chimney and chuckled. All the Christmas presents were already under the tree. Santa had already come.

"Yeah, let's go to bed." Nathan helped Jessica up from the couch.

"Ready?" Anna asked Bjornolf.

"Yeah. What I want to know is, when do you expect me to wear this?" He held the suit against his crotch.

"When you take me to an island somewhere."

He smiled. "I'll have to do that soon."

They went to bed and settled down, kissing and snuggling when they heard something on the roof.

Bjornolf slipped on a pair of boxers and was nearly into his jeans when he heard a "Ho-ho-ho!" from the rooftop. He looked at Anna, and she started laughing. "That's Nathan and his reindeer. I mean, Santa and his reindeer."

Bjornolf had to look anyway. The kids weren't in the guest room, and he saw Nathan and a she-wolf walking across the snow-covered roof. On the patio out back, he saw angel figures made in the snow. He smiled, then went back inside, not recalling ever having done anything so crazy in his life. Well, maybe he had.

"You were right, Anna." Bjornolf crawled back into bed.

"Did you put out cookies and milk for Santa, and carrots for his reindeer?"

Bjornolf groaned, shook his head, got back out of bed, put on his boxers, and left the bedroom.

Bjornolf and Anna didn't get up early for Christmas Day. Neither did Nathan or Jessica.

After grabbing some hot tea and coffee, they all sat down on the couches while Jessica handed out gifts with "All I Want for Christmas is You" playing in the background. Every time they all had a present, she sat down to unwrap hers while everyone else opened their own.

Anna couldn't help it. She was in tears most of the time while she unwrapped one after another of the crocheted sweaters that Bjornolf had given her—black, white, ecru, blue, and purple, and a white fuzzy jacket to replace the one ruined in the mud pit. Nathan and Jessica had bought her a dozen boxes of dark chocolate thin mints.

She smiled at them. "How did you know?"

Nathan looked at Bjornolf, who nodded. "When Roger Everton grabbed you in the drugstore, we found you had touched several boxes of thin mints."

Anna smiled through her tears. "I didn't want you to know that the thin mints had distracted me so much that Everton got the drop on me."

"It can happen to the best of us." Bjornolf winked at her. He admired the small arsenal of weapons she'd gotten him.

"To keep you alive if I'm not there with you," she said with a smirk.

"If you can't be with me, I'm not going. Haven't I already told you that?"

Jessica was smiling at them, nestled in Nathan's arms. "I love how they talk to each other."

"This was the best Christmas ever," Anna said, cuddling with Bjornolf. "The best ever."

It wasn't the gifts, but the thought behind them. She loved that Bjornolf was so concerned about her ruined clothes that he'd gotten her replacements, and in different colors, too. And that Nathan and Jessica wanted her to have the mints she enjoyed so much.

Who said you had to have little kids to enjoy Christmas?

"Yeah, it's been the greatest," Bjornolf said, kissing her head, "and the best is that it's only the first of many."

Nathan looked contemplative as he stared at all the discarded wrapping paper on the floor. "About the murder-mystery board game…"

Everyone raised brows at him.

"Okay, so is it time to eat?" he asked instead.

Later that afternoon, Bjornolf wrapped his arms around Anna, and they watched as Nathan and Jessica played tug-of-war over the dried-out wishbone.

Jessica won and Nathan swore she cheated because she'd been doing it more often than he had, but she had a gleam in her eye as she looked at Anna and said, "But I get my wish."

Then the call came from Hunter to Bjornolf. "I can't get hold of Finn to let him and Meara know. I'm on my way to the hospital with Tessa."

Tessa was having her babies on Christmas Day, and

Hunter was coming unglued. Bjornolf called the pack members, and Meara and Finn hurried over to the hospital, followed by Anna and Bjornolf.

Nathan and Jessica opted to stay home, and Anna knew what that was all about.

The twins were born half an hour after Hunter got Tessa to the hospital. No wonder he had been panicking!

Tessa was one tired momma, but the babies were crinkly and well, and Hunter was one proud wolf of a father. Little name tags on the bassinets declared that one was Ryan and the other Blaine Greymere.

Bjornolf stood with his arm over Anna's shoulder as they looked through the viewing window at the babies. She was happy for Tessa. Truly happy. Even if she couldn't have any children, she would love Tessa's like her own because of wolf-pack rules and a wolf's natural nurturing instinct. Maybe her parents had been the same with her when she was that little. If not, it didn't matter. She knew now *she* would be.

Rourke joined them to look at the babies. "They could have been mine."

Bjornolf and Anna looked over at him, wondering what he was talking about.

"I dated her once."

Bjornolf shook his head. "A SEAL *always* wins." He smelled a male red wolf approaching and turned to see a man stalk toward them that he didn't recognize. The man stopped to look at the babies and smiled. "Two boys." He looked over at Bjornolf. "Leidolf Wildhaven, pack leader of the red wolves of Portland."

"Bjornolf Jorgenson and Anna Johnson recently of the Oregon coast."

"Ah, a SEAL and a female undercover operative. Carver told me the teen giving him trouble mated with another teen she-wolf."

"Yeah."

"Hunter said you're both mated now and staying with the pack."

"Yep." Bjornolf and Anna continued to watch the babies.

"I'm not sure I like that."

They glanced at him.

Leidolf smiled. "Seems Hunter's bringing his whole SEAL team and a she-wolf operative into the pack. If I ever need your services?" Leidolf held out his hand.

Bjornolf shook it, then Anna followed suit. "You've got it," Bjornolf said.

"Good. Tell Hunter I'll check on him and Tessa later. I'll be shipping gifts for the babies tomorrow." Then Leidolf strode off.

Anna snuggled with Bjornolf. "Seems to me we had no pack and now we can be part of two."

"A red, a gray, and all we need is to belong to an Arctic pack."

"None around here."

Bjornolf didn't say anything.

Anna looked up at him.

"I've heard there's a pack of newbie Arctic wolves trying to find a home somewhere in the great Northwest."

She chuckled. "That would be the day."

------~~~------

Three months after Tessa's babies were born, the Wentworths were being prosecuted. All of them were being held without bond.

Anna was on the phone with Hunter and so thrilled that she could barely contain herself when Bjornolf came up from the beach with another stack of logs for the fire. She put the speakerphone on as soon as she shut the door for Bjornolf and he dumped the wood in the bin. "Hunter, go ahead. Tell Bjornolf the news."

"Roger Wentworth recovered enough from his injuries to give details about William's involvement in illegal drug shipments. He also told them about William murdering Jessica's parents when he thought they knew about a new species of plant that would make him even richer. Feeling set up by his older half brother, Roger murdered the DEA agents and tried to cover his tracks by attempting to eliminate Anna. You were next."

"And Dottie and Helen?" Anna asked.

"Verdict's still out on them. Dottie swears she didn't know that the couple was murdered. Only that she had to raise the baby. Sounds like a lot of BS to me. Helen is being charged with aggravated assault. But it appears she was clueless about William and Roger's business. Jeff's an accessory to the whole thing. DNA on Dottie's toddler proved William was the father, not Roger. They're still looking for the nanny who was involved when the toddler was killed by a hit-and-run driver. That's the end of our involvement until we get another mission."

"Sounds good," Bjornolf said. "We decided on a house plan for Finn's old property, and construction starts next week. Kids have picked out the style of place they want and it'll be built next to ours."

"We couldn't be happier for you," Hunter said.

"We've got to go," Anna said, all smiles, glad Roger had pulled through and would help to nail both his half brothers. "Give Tessa and the babies our love."

Wanting to shout to the world, she hung up on him and then put her arms around Bjornolf's neck. "Jessica's wish over the turkey bone has come true."

Bjornolf smiled down at her, his hands stroking up and down her back. "That we'd have the houses started by this time?"

Anna gave him a devious smile. "No."

"Ah, yeah, that Roger made it. I told you that you weren't at fault for shooting him where you did. You were drugged and barely able to—"

Anna shook her head, smiling even more broadly now. "We're having triplets."

Bjornolf looked stunned, and then he grinned. He grabbed her up and swung her around and howled for the whole Oregon coast pack of wolves to hear. He was one happy SEAL wolf.

The rest of the wolf pack would be just as thrilled. Sometimes belonging to a pack and not being a lone wolf was worth everything in the world. With babies on the way, missions would be close to home, but if Bjornolf and Anna had an assignment later, they had tons of wolves who would step in and help out.

"Triplets," he said, looking all misty-eyed.

And Anna knew she was just where she belonged—with her sparring partner and lover, who was one sexy SEAL wolf.

HAVE YOU MET THEM ALL?

READ ON TO DISCOVER THE ULTIMATE ALPHAS FROM
TERRY SPEAR'S SIZZLING PARANORMAL ROMANCES

AVAILABLE NOW FROM
SOURCEBOOKS CASABLANCA

From *Heart of the Wolf*

BELLA STOPPED PACING AND TURNED TO LISTEN.

Thompson placed his hands on his hips. "Now isn't it interesting how she listens to our conversation?"

"She seems to sometimes. She's really gentle."

You should see me on a bad day.

Thompson shook his head. "A wolf is a wolf, still wild at heart. Anyway, a man was interested in transferring her to another zoo. But. . . ." He looked at his feet. "I don't know. I didn't trust him. He seemed to have something else in mind."

When he looked up, his blue eyes widened, and he straightened his back. He motioned with his head toward the railing. "In fact, there's the man, right there."

She turned to look at the railing, and her heart nearly stopped.

"See what I mean? It's like she understands everything we say."

Staring at Devlyn, she couldn't unlock her gaze from him. So many lonely years, dreaming of his hard embrace, and now he stood across the moat from her in the flesh. Her heart beat so hard it was sure to bruise her ribs. Adrenaline coursed through her body at breakneck speeds, the thought that he'd come to free her giving her hope. What she wouldn't give to nip him in the neck, to tackle him and force him to the ground. To have his heated kisses, his firm touch embracing her with wanton desire.

She took a steadying breath. She couldn't deny he still held her heart captive.

Like before, a strap tied his shoulder-length dark brown hair back. A black leather jacket fitted over his broad shoulders, and denims stretched comfortably down his long, muscular legs to his well-worn western boots. He was every bit as handsome as she remembered him, only much taller and more imposing and real than the photos Argos had sent her.

She focused on Devlyn's mouth. How many women had he kissed since he'd kissed her? Her veins turned to ice as an uncontrollable jealousy washed over her.

Was he already mated? Her gut tightened with the idea. She shifted her gaze back to his eyes. His dark brown eyes turned into black quartz, angry with a hint of concern.

Did he recognize her? Sure he did. If she caught him in his wolf suit, she'd know him any day. But how had he found her?

Unless . . . unless . . . somehow the fact that a red wolf was living in the Cascades, when none should, got big-time media. *Great*. That's how he'd found her. He must realize the predicament she faced and the danger to all of them. That's why he'd tried to move her from the zoo. If she turned into a human by the new moon, she could be used to prove legendary werewolves truly exist.

Did he have a plan? He moved his hands over the black wrought iron posts, up and down. His actions hypnotized her. What was his plan?

"What's he doing?" Thompson asked.

"I don't know, but he sure has her attention. You think maybe she belonged to him once?"

"Hmm, now that sounds like a distinct possibility. And he wants her back so he can release her to the wild again. I want him checked out and watched. He's probably one of those crazy animal rights activists. Doesn't he realize she's safer here, with a good diet, and no one to hunt her down? Besides, where can she find a male red to mate? She'd be stuck with scrawny coyotes."

Joe laughed. "Guess it wouldn't matter to her, as long as the deed is done."

She emitted a low growl.

"Don't think she likes your suggestion," Thompson joked.

She turned her attention back to Devlyn. He looked kissable. He'd filled out into a man-sized hunk, but his eyes remained dark and foreboding—even more so now.

Devlyn tilted his chin up as if taunting her to tell him what she thought of him, but he continued to stroke the bars. She realized then he smelled she was in heat. The urge to mate with her would be as natural to him as breathing the air or blinking an eye.

Her gaze met his, the depths of his eyes smoldering with lust. Then he scowled and turned away. He strode off, his long gait taking him away from her within seconds. She wanted to scream at him to set her free. But in the worst way she wanted him to mate with her, to fulfill the unquenchable craving that the sight of him sparked, to take her for his own, his mate forever.

From *Destiny of the Wolf*

LAUGHING AND BOISTEROUS, THREE MORE MEN BARGED into the tavern, glanced to where Jake and Tom sat, then shifted their attention to Lelandi. Which meant what? That Jake and Tom normally sat with Darien at the table where she was now sitting?

Terrific!

"Howdy, boys," the older bearded man of the group said, nodding a greeting. The other two were nearly as old, gray streaking their brown beards, their gazes pinned on her. "Bring us the usual, Sam." He turned to Jake and pointed his head at her. "*He* know about this?"

"Still giving orders at the factory, Mason," Tom said.

The bearded man grumbled, "Fourth of July's coming for a second time this year."

Figuring she'd be better off sitting next to the restrooms to lessen the chance of creating *fireworks,* Lelandi grabbed her purse.

The door banged open again. The chatter died.

As soon as she saw him, she knew it was *him*—not only because silence instantly cloaked the room and every eye in the place watched Darien Silver's reaction. His sable hair curled at the top edge of his collar. Brooding dark eyes, grim lips, features handsomely rugged, but definitely hard, defined him. Wearing a leather jacket, western shirt, jeans, and boots, everything was as black as his somber mood. He looked so much like Tom and Jake, she figured they must be triplets, and he was the leader of the gray *lupus garou* in the area. Had to be, the way everyone watched him, waiting for the fireworks.

Something about him stirred her blood, something akin to recognition, yet she'd never seen him before in her life. It wasn't his face, or clothes, or body that stimulated some deep memory—but the way he moved—commanding, powerful, with an effortless grace.

He glanced at the barkeep and gave a nod of greeting—sullen, silent, still in mourning for his mate? If he discovered why Lelandi was here, he'd be pissed.

A shiver trickled down her spine. She released her purse and kept her seat, for the moment. Everyone was acting so oddly, she imagined *that* was the reason he quickly surveyed the current seating arrangement. When his eyes lit on her, incredulity registered.

Crap! He recognized her; she just knew it. Didn't matter that she had dyed her hair this horrible color that didn't do anything for her fair skin, or that her eyes were now blue. Didn't matter that the heavy padded leather jacket gave her broader shoulders and made her appear heavier, or that she wore her hair straight as blades of uncut grass, compliments of a hair straightening iron, when her sister's and hers was naturally curly. She couldn't hide the shape of her face or eyes or mouth. All of them mirrored her sister's looks.

Then again, his look was puzzled. The hat and glasses appeared to confuse him. Maybe the fact that she wore the faux pierced earrings that looked like the real thing did too.

She broke eye contact first, her skin sweaty, her

hands trembling. God, he was more wolf than she was used to dealing with—broader-shouldered and taller. His eyes locked onto hers with sinful determination, no backing down, no compromise. No wonder Larissa had fallen for the attention-grabbing gray. Lelandi couldn't help wondering how a romp with a virile wolf like him would feel. But damn if it hadn't gotten Larissa killed. Stick with your own kind, that's what her father would have said. No humans, *lupus garou* only… the red variety.

Everyone remained deathly quiet—no one lifted a mug to take a sip of a drink, no one moved a muscle. Swallowing hard, she forced herself to look at Darien, to see what he was doing now.

Still staring at her. She wanted to sink into the floor like mop water on a hot day. She gritted her teeth, lifted her glass of water, and took another swig, hoping she wouldn't inadvertently choke on the icy drink out of nervousness. But she wasn't leaving Silver Town until she avenged Larissa's death.

From *To Tempt the Wolf*

BEFORE TESSA REACHED THE MAN LYING DEATHLY
still on the beach, certain he was dead, she thought one
of his fingers twitched. Her heart went into overdrive.

Not dead. Ohmigod. He's alive. Maybe.

She rushed forward and pulled him onto his back.
Big. Naked. Blue—she reminded herself. And badly
battered—his face, body, limbs.

She yanked off her glove and held his wrist. No pulse
that she could feel, although her blood was running so
fast, she figured it overrode feeling his pulse, if he had
one. Not breathing, she didn't think, because her warm
breath was turning into puffs of smoke in the chilly air
and there was none escaping his parted lips, full and
sensual, but purple.

"Hello? Hello? Can you hear me?" She jerked
her glove on, and then fumbled to remove her parka.
Covering his torso with her heavy white coat, she tried
to remember her CPR training. "Fifteen pumps to the
chest. Breathe two times into his mouth. Then repeat.
No, clear his passageway first."

With hands trembling, she crouched next to his head.
His wet hair dragged the sandy beach, his eyelids sealed
shut. She tilted his head back and made sure nothing
obstructed his airway. Moving back to his torso, she
pushed the coat lower to expose his chest—muscled,
sculpted, dark curly hair trailing down to her parka,

speckled with sand, the best shape she'd ever seen a man in close up—which meant he was too hardy to die on her. She prayed.

She pressed her gloved hands together against his hard chest and began compressions. Counting under her breath, she hoped to God he didn't die on her. If the wind and cold weren't bad enough, sleet began sliding down in gray sheets, crackling and covering everything in a slick icy sheen, plastering her turtleneck and jeans against her frigid skin. She worked harder, faster.

The blood pounded in her ears, blocking the sound of the wind and sleet and waves.

"Fifteen!" she shouted, and then moved closer to his head, yanked off her glove, and felt for any sign of a pulse in his neck.

No pulse, or so faint she couldn't feel it. And no breath. He wasn't breathing.

Her heart in her throat, she pinched his nose shut and leaned down to cover his mouth with hers. Before she could blow air into his lungs, his eyes popped open. Amber, intense, feral. Her mouth gaped.

With a titan grasp, he grabbed her wrists, flipped her onto her back and straddled her, the parka wedged between them as the weight of his body restrained her.

"No!" she screeched, right before he kissed her—pressed his frozen lips against hers, his mouth firm, wanting, pressuring with uncontrollable need—like a man used to dominating—sending her senses reeling.

Instantly, the cold left her, his body heating every inch of her to the core, her heart pounding. And in that moment, she wanted him—as insane as the notion was.

He lifted his mouth from hers and glowered at her for a second, his eyes smoky with desire. Speechless, she stared back at his chiseled face, the grim set of his lips, his dark silky hair curling down, dripping water on her cheeks. Then his fathomless, darkened eyes drifted closed and his tight grip loosened on her wrists.

"No!" she shouted, right before he collapsed on top of her in a faint, his dead weight pinning her to the beach.

"Hey!" she yelled, her hands on his shoulders, shaking him. "Wake up!" She couldn't budge the muscled hunk, but if she didn't revive him and get him to some place warm, he would die for sure. "Hey! *Wake… up!*" She pushed and shoved, trying to roll him off her. But he was too heavy—solid muscle and bone.

"Get… off… me!"

He moaned and lifted his head, his glazed eyes staring at her, his beautiful white teeth clenched in a grimace, but he didn't seem to comprehend.

"Can you move? I'll… I'll take you up to my house and call for help."

For the longest time—although it probably was no more than a second or two, but with the way his heavy body pressed against hers, it seemed like an eternity—he watched her.

From *Legend of the White Wolf*

THE WOLVES' HOWLS FADED INTO THE MISTY SNOW and the moan of the wind returned. Cameron jerked awake, feeling strangely unsettled. Faith was curled up against his chest, her breathing light in sleep, her body soft and huggable. He held her with his good arm, reached over with his bad, and stroked her golden hair. But she was sound asleep, and he didn't want to wake her. His wounded arm didn't even give him a pinch of pain now. Maybe it hadn't been as bad as he thought.

But what he couldn't comprehend was the restlessness stirring deep inside him. He'd never felt that way before. On cases he was close to solving, he might not be able to sleep, his mind working overtime in solving the puzzle. But this was something more primal, more physical. He was torn between staying with Faith and enjoying her comforting heat, the sound of her steady heartbeat, and her subtle fragrance—and squelching the craving to ditch his clothes no matter how cold it was and run through the snow.

Trying not to disturb Faith, Cameron slipped out from under her, making sure his sleeping bag still covered her, and then he left the bed. He was surprised to experience no dizziness or fever from the wolf's bite. He stretched out his arm, but no matter how he moved it, the ache was completely gone.

After pulling the towel off his arm, he examined where the wolf had bitten him. Except for faded bite marks, dried blood, and light bruising, he was nearly as good as new, although it had seemed so much worse when he was first bitten.

He went to the door and opened it, stared out at the moonlight reflecting off the snow, the clouds having moved away, the storm spent and gone, leaving mountains of snow in its wake. It looked as though the day was already upon them instead of the dead of night. Mystical, magical, even romantic, if Faith had been awake and here to share it with him.

But the moon compelled him to do what no sane man would ever have done. He couldn't repress the urge he had to—well, he wasn't sure what he wanted to do. Leave. Maybe. But it wasn't exactly that either. Despite not being able to see the actual moon, he could feel its presence. Like the moon's gravitational pull on the tides, he felt an odd connection. A seduction, a caress of wills, his against the moon's. *Come to me, and I'll make your dreams come true. Fight me and you'll suffer.*

He was going mad.

Without another second's hesitation, he stripped out of his jeans and boxers, and stood watching the tree limbs stirring in the breeze. The bitter cold surrounding him shook him to the marrow of his bones, but then dissipated when a strange warmth quickly worked its way through every fiber of his being, his muscles twisting, bones reshaping, all painless, effortless, exhilarating.

He stood on four pads, a thick, double white coat covering his skin, making him impervious to the cold. He stared at his large front paws, black wicked-looking claws touching the wooden floor. He sniffed at his fur, which smelled of spicy aftershave.

The moon again called to him, the branches of the trees waving at him, beckoning him to join them. Without another thought, he lowered his forequarters, keeping his hindquarters straight and did a slight bow, then raced out the door, bounding over the piles of snow left by the storm and took off through the woods.

Cameron raced through the forest, brushing against the snow-covered branches of towering spruces, shaking loose torrents of snowfall. The snow falling down on him didn't touch his skin though. A thick coat of fur kept the snow from melting, and he felt toasty warm. He expected the snow and cold to chill his "bare" feet, but it didn't bother his paws, maybe, he thought, because of the fur between the pads.

He ran on the tip of his toes, which seemed weird, but it lengthened his stride, and he covered more ground that way. Whenever he began to slip on an icy patch, he instinctively spread out his pads, increasing the surface area that he stepped on, the additional friction preventing him from taking a spill.

A fresh coat of snow, looked to have been a foot or more, covered everything, but he found that he didn't sink into the fluffy white stuff as he would if he was running as a human. The freedom this gave was exhilarating as he raced through the trees, only stopping momentarily to smell a whiff of a rabbit or bird and fresh clean air.

From *Seduced by the Wolf*

TAKING A DEEP BREATH OF THE COOL AIR, CASSIE didn't catch the scent of anyone or anything else. Either she was imagining things, or whatever-it-was knew to keep downwind of her. She hoped it wasn't Alex Wellington, trying to track her down again. Letting out an exasperated sigh, she swore she'd never convince him she strictly worked alone. And then she thought of Leidolf and those of his pack. She stood very still, listening, not hearing anything further. That's all she needed. Leidolf or one of his people tracking her.

She brushed aside the soft needle-covered branches of a hemlock blocking her view of the source of water and… *gasped*.

Not at the spectacular sight of the dark blue lake, still closed for visitor day use until May, but at the naked man standing mid-thigh in the cold water, his back to her as he stared out across the region.

She didn't see anything to garner his attention but the beauty and serenity of the vista. Picturesque Mount Hood, the snow-covered volcanic mountain in the distance, the focal point of the whole landscape, so prominent that it could be seen from a hundred miles away.

Well, it would have been the prominent feature if a naked man hadn't been standing in the lake in front of the view, taking center stage instead.

Chestnut hair curled about the nape of his neck,

shorter than she thought a reclusive mountain man would wear it. His backside was pure delight to look at, from his broad and muscled back down to his narrow waist and a toned butt a girl could die for. Muscular legs disappeared into water that rippled in the slight breeze.

She sniffed the air but couldn't catch his scent. Being a *lupus garou*, she could smell the mood of an individual like any wolf could—whether he was fearful, aggressive, cowed, or sexually aroused. The way the man was standing so peacefully, she assumed his scent would be a mixture of woods, water, musky male, and blissful serenity.

Before she could back up and leave, he dove into the lake with a splash and, with a powerful momentum, began swimming freestyle. Fascinated, she watched his compelling overarm strokes and legs slicing the water, wondering how he could stomach the cold. Unexpectedly, he plunged beneath the surface. Forever, it seemed, she watched the dark blue waters, the building clouds making it appear blacker. And no sign of the man. He remained under so long that she finally took a step forward in rescue-mode when he suddenly rose up like Poseidon, Greek god of the sea, took a deep breath, and dove under again. She half-expected him to be wielding a trident while porpoises swam alongside him.

Frozen in place, she continued to watch where he'd disappeared, when he abruptly shot up again. Only this time, he headed for the beach. She frowned. Leidolf? She couldn't be sure with the way he dove in and out of the water so quickly and the distance between her and the beach. Waiting for him to dive again, she didn't move. This time, he remained on the surface and kicked vigorously with his legs, his arms plying the water, his head mostly submersed under water as he swam toward the shore and a pile of clothes she hadn't noticed before.

To her relief, his focus remained on the beach whenever he turned his head to take a breath of air. She was afraid that if she backed into the woods, he would notice her movement and, *God forbid*, realize she'd been a voyeur spying on him. Not that spying on him bothered her overly much. If he was going to run around naked at a closed park, it was *his* fault that she caught him at it. She still didn't want him catching *her* spying on him. Especially, if the man *was* Leidolf.

So the plan was that as soon as he concentrated on dressing, she'd slip away.

Upon reaching the shallows, he stood, and she swallowed hard. He looked different naked, his hair dripping wet. It *was* Leidolf.

His strong legs plowing through the water, he waded toward the shore. The lake rippled at his navel, water droplets raised like translucent pearls all over his golden skin, his nipples crisply pebbled. *Beautiful, powerful, tantalizing*. Poseidon in the flesh, just as masculine and intriguing to women as the god who had exerted his power over them, just like his brother, Zeus.

At least that's the effect Leidolf had on her. And she wasn't easily swayed by men's appearances. In or out of their clothes.

From *Wolf Fever*

"BUT YOU TRULY BELIEVE OTHERWISE," RYAN finally said.

This time Carol's smile was bright and true to her feelings. She couldn't help liking Ryan, despite his denial of her abilities. He had an easy but determined manner about him, not brusque like Darien or teasing like Jake or afraid to make waves like Tom. His determination was matched only by her own.

She glanced at the men standing about, including both Tom and Jake. Which made the situation worse. Why couldn't any of the alpha males show any real interest in her? She was not a beta kind of girl. She supposed that was because her father had become so downtrodden by her mother's treatment of him. She couldn't see being married, um, mated to someone like that.

"Carol?" Ryan said, his deep baritone voice again yanking her from her faraway thoughts.

She really needed to get more sleep. She turned her attention back to Ryan. He thought *she* wasn't being honest with him about her abilities, when *he* wasn't honest about why he had been lurking in the woods last night, watching her window. She didn't have to be psychic to know something more was going on between them. Time to turn the tables. Throw him off balance.

Trying to look like this was a perfectly natural way for her to act, she smiled, wrapped her arms around his neck, and leaned into the soft sweater covering his hard body, which instantly reminded her just how hard his body was when he wasn't wearing a stitch of clothes. She only meant to give him a slow kiss on the mouth, just to prove to him that he had another agenda that he wouldn't admit to. Or if not, then maybe Tom or Jake would finally show some interest in her. But more than anything, she wanted to get Ryan off the subject of her abilities before she said something in anger that she shouldn't.

To her surprise, he eagerly captured her mouth with his. Not cautiously, building up the desire in slow careful increments, but judiciously, as if he had been starved for affection for a very long time. His hand cupped the back of her head, his free hand drifting lower on her back and holding her in place.

She hadn't meant to respond so fully to the kiss either, but his unbridled need fed into hers. Forgetting they had an audience, she parted her lips to accept him, to open an intimate path between them, their tongues dancing, touching, exploring. Her hands fisted in his soft sweater at the back of his neck and held him even tighter. She pressed her body against his hard muscles, and shamelessly she wanted more.

But then he released her and unwrapped her arms from around his neck, his eyes smoky and dark, his expression otherwise unreadable, his hands still securely holding her wrists. Their breaths came quickly as their hearts thundered at a runner's pace. He opened his mouth as if he was going to say something, but she didn't want to hear the apology she figured he would offer or another word about her abilities, if that's what he had in mind.

She quickly spoke instead. "I accept. Come pick me up for a date at six o'clock. Promptly."

She'd show him he wasn't as much in control of the situation as he might think.

Then she winked, pulled free, and stalked off toward the house without a backward glance, her blood sizzling with arousal and irritation.

She harrumphed under her breath. All the idiotic romantic notions she had been harboring for Ryan McKinley… and all he really wanted was for her to confess she wasn't psychic?

She doubted Ryan would take her on a date, and she doubted even more that Darien would allow it. But if the date did come to pass, she would get out of the gathering of bachelor males tonight, and she'd give Ryan McKinley a piece of her mind.

From *Heart of the Highland Wolf*

"A WARM BATH WILL DO YOU A WORLD OF GOOD, LASS. But I wondered what you'll be doing during the filming."

Julia loved his brogue. She could soak it up all day long as she listened to the way he rolled his *r*'s and twisted his tongue around in ways she couldn't even imagine, her gaze focused on his sensuous mouth all the while.

Ian touched a piece of her hair tickling her cheek and moved it behind her ear. "Lass?"

"You asked?"

He chuckled. "Either you're too tired to think straight, having been through too much in the last several hours, or…" He smiled, and the intimation was that she was too wrapped up in him to think clearly. "Water should be ready." He rose from the sofa, and without waiting for her to say she could walk, he scooped her up and headed for the bathroom.

She didn't need blankets or hot baths or anything of the sort to heat her up. His body did the trick—his hot, hard body pressing against hers, his arm securely around her waist, his hand resting beneath her breast, his other arm cupped under her legs. She was feeling incredibly warm.

"It's jet lag," she finally said, looking up at him, her head tilted back, her hair tumbling backward. "You're right. I'm exhausted, and I'm not thinking clearly." It had nothing to do with Ian being an incredibly hunky Highlander. Or that she was imagining the virile warrior wearing a kilt and a sword as he carried her into the bathroom instead of the wet clinging trousers that showed just how hot and sexy and intrigued he was with her.

He hesitated to set her down on the floor or the edge of the bathtub, staring into her eyes as if she had mesmerized him and momentarily made him forget his mission. But then he did the unexpected and set her on the marble sink countertop. She thought he meant to offer to help her further with undressing and intended to quickly decline his generous offer. Instead, he leaned his face down to meet hers and kissed her! Full on the mouth with a sensuous, hot-blooded kiss that would have knocked her stockings off if she'd still been wearing them.

She didn't even object or pull away like she should have done. What would the Scotsman think of American women if she didn't? But she couldn't, not when his lips were caressing hers in such a sexually charged way, warm and soft and needy and in control. *Very* much in control. She loved the feel of his mouth on hers, the desire sparking between them, the heat that chased away the chill.

Enjoying the feel of his masculine lips on hers, she wanted more. She wrapped her hands around his neck and parted her lips just enough to give a hint that she wanted him to deepen the kiss, but not too much to make it seem she was desperate for more. *Even if she was*.

His mouth smiled against hers as his eyes grew smokier with desire. And then he obliged. His hands shifted to her hair, stroking and grasping handfuls as he poked his tongue between her lips, drew her body closer to his, and then pressed deeply into her mouth with his tongue.

She gave as good as she got, shifting her hands from around his neck to his hips and pulling him in even closer, settling him against the heat between her legs. Felt his rigid erection against her. Rolled her tongue around his in a lover's intimate dance.

But he suddenly went very still and then groaned, pulling his mouth from hers. He wanted more. She could tell from the way his body was still pressed against hers, the way he was fighting with himself to let go, and damn if she didn't want him to keep kissing her. A wolf had never kissed her before, and she wondered if it was just Ian or if all wolves were this hot.

He gazed into her eyes, his own filled with lust, his body hard and ready for more, but he cleared his throat and said, "Welcome to Scotland, lass."

From *Dreaming of the Wolf*

IN A TANGLE OF LEGS AT THE ICE-SKATING RINK, ALICIA laughed out loud as she found herself on her butt on the ice again with Jake. His eyes were bright with laughter as he pushed her hair out of her face and grinned at her. She hadn't laughed this much in forever.

"I haven't fallen this many times in an hour on the ice since I was a little girl. And I was a *lot* lower to the ground then. But then again, I haven't had this much fun in years."

And she meant it. She had applauded every wobbly bit of success Jake had accomplished. And when they'd fallen, she'd laughed and enjoyed his good-humored responses. She wasn't the only one who was interested in Jake, though. From older teens to college-aged women, he had their undivided attention. She was certain they wished they were entangled with the hunk on the ice instead of her and laughing their heads off. She had to admit, they looked fairly risqué at times with his leg wedged between hers and her short flare skirt thrown back, exposing the panties of her leotard.

If Jake hadn't had such a difficult time staying on his feet and keeping from tripping Alicia up, she figured he would have been more hot and bothered in an intimate way by their close proximity. But he hadn't let on, and for that, she was grateful.

Two of the women watching him with hungry,

desirous gazes had been bold enough to come to speak with him when he told Alicia he wanted her to demonstrate how she did the figure eight and other ice skating maneuvers. She hadn't wanted to leave him for a second, and now she knew for certain what a mistake that could be.

Even though she had wanted to chase off the voluptuous blond and striking brunette, she concentrated on her performance and gave Jake the show of her life as if she were trying out for the Olympics while he stood propped against the railing, smiling at her with admiration. She loved him for it because no one had ever cared how she skated except for her mother and her grandmother. But this was different, seeing the look in his eyes as she skated for him—a sexual attraction, a feral desirous look in his gaze—and his lips curving upward as if he was thinking sinful thoughts about some of her sexier moves.

When she was through with the last jump, she skated back to Jake. He pulled her into his arms, holding her tight, and gave her a kiss that could have melted the ice. It certainly warmed her from the tip of her cold nose to her cold toes, and he made her feel special all over again.

"You're beautiful, you know?" he murmured against her ear.

His two new fans gave her simpering smiles, but their smiles were designed to get his attention. He ignored them, thankfully.

She smiled up at him. *He* was beautiful and fun and the best thing that had ever happened to her. "You make me feel beautiful." She leaned against him, loving the heat and hardness of his tall body but knowing they needed to skate or leave. Before they got kicked out of the rink for too much sexy cuddling. "Do you want to ice skate some more?"

"I need to drop by the art gallery and sign some consent forms. And it's past time for lunch. If you've had enough fun and are ready to go. I'm afraid watching you skate is getting harder and harder for me." He cast her a wickedly salacious grin.

She chuckled, wanting to check out his package, but... what the heck. She glanced down at his crotch, saw the rigid bulge in his stonewashed jeans, and was ready to ease his discomfiture anyway that she could.

"All right." She gave the women a smile that said, "He's mine, so hands off," and then skated slowly to the exit with him so that he could keep up with her. "You were gathering quite a fan club."

"I was the only male on the ice, and I looked a bit needy," he explained.

"You looked anything but that. I think the idea of you getting tangled up with one of them was more what they had in mind."

He laughed. "I wasn't interested in getting tangled up with anyone else, believe me."

Discover a new LOVE

Are You In Love With Love Stories?

Here's an online romance readers club that's just for YOU!

Where you can:
- **Meet** great *authors*
- **Party** with new *friends*
- **Get** new *books* before everyone else
- **Discover** great *new reads*

All at incredibly BIG savings!

Join the party at DiscoveraNewLove.com!

About the Author

USA Today bestselling and award-winning author of urban fantasy and medieval romantic suspense Terry Spear also writes true stories for adult and young adult audiences. She's a retired lieutenant colonel in the U.S. Army Reserves and has an MBA from Monmouth University. She also creates award-winning teddy bears, Wilde & Woolly Bears, that are personalized and have found homes all over the world. When she's not writing or making bears, she's teaching online writing courses or gardening. Her family has roots in the Highlands of Scotland where her love of all things Scottish came into being. Originally from California, she's lived in eight states and now resides in the heart of Texas. She is the author of the Heart of the Wolf series and the Heart of the Jaguar series, plus numerous other paranormal romance and historical romance novels.

Acknowledgments

Thanks to my fans who make writing the books possible! When I see all the interest on Facebook once I mention a new release or share a new cover, I'm so inspired to get to work on that next book and the next. I can't tell you enough how much it means that you are loving the wolves and now the jaguars, too!

I also want to thank my editor, Deb Werksman, for being such a great help over the years in assisting me to see a dream come true. Thanks to Danielle Jackson for being a fun publicist and keeping me straight on blog tours and giving me other opportunities to shine. And to the artists who create the covers that make the world in my books come alive.

And thanks to ELF who dropped by the RWA Conference in Anaheim and supplied me with the heroine's favorite-in-all-the-world dark chocolate thin mints because I share that obsession with Anna!

her gaze on his. But the way that his mouth curved up and his wickedly darkened eyes smiled back at her meant he knew the truth. She couldn't get her fill of him.

"Go. I mean it. I'll stay here," she said to Finn, nearly forgetting what he should be doing.

Seemingly reassured that she'd stay put, Finn loped out of the bedroom, and she went for her rifle.

As soon as Finn made certain the house was clear and no one was lurking inside, he used his nose to push through the wolf's door to check the perimeter of the house and its surroundings. Outside, he smelled Joe's scent coming from the direction of the blue cabin. Finn raced through the woods to the first of the cabins, circling around the outside, but he didn't see or hear any signs of life. Where was Joe?

As he made a broader search, Finn smelled that a male werewolf had been in the vicinity, but he saw no sign of the unknown wolf. He continued to search around each of the empty cabins but found nothing. The faint smell of gunfire rippled through the breeze, though. He hadn't been wrong about that.

So she really didn't know Finn well, except that she'd had words with him on more than one occasion when the team returned from a mission. She was angry that he was always getting Hunter involved in something that could prove fatal. They had left the Navy once their commitments were up. Enough was enough. Hunter had done his duty for God and country.

Finn would listen patiently to her tirade and cast Hunter surreptitious looks as though commiserating with him for having a sister who couldn't leave well enough alone—and that had irritated her to no end.

Then Finn would depart and, several months later, turn up for another secretive mission, and they'd do what they intended without paying her any mind… *again*. She hoped that Hunter would give up the clandestine operations all together, now that he was mated.

But God, Finn had a body that wouldn't quit. If there was a werewolf calendar, he could be featured on every month—and women would be even more apt to buy it if he was featured for an additional couple of months the following year. A natural Scandinavian blond with hazel-green eyes, he was a real looker.

She thought of him without the towel, the way he had been drying his hair so *innocently*, acting as though he'd forgotten to cover himself in front of her. He'd only done that to pretend he'd been her lover the night before. And she had been determined to pretend right back that his nakedness had no effect on her, not wanting him to think he'd not only shocked but intrigued her. No matter how much she told herself she shouldn't, she couldn't quit giving his physique a few gaping looks. Even though she'd tried damn hard to refocus

From *A SEAL in Wolf's Clothing*

ONCE FINN HAD SHIFTED INTO HIS WOLF FORM, HE CAST a long, hard look at Meara, as if he was trying to tell her to stay put. He was a beautiful, big gray wolf with a tan face framed by fur in a mixture of browns and black, giving him a distinguished appearance.

Exasperated, Meara waved her hand toward the wolf door. "Go. Protect me, oh hero of mine." She couldn't help it if her words sounded faintly sarcastic. She'd never gotten herself into a bind she couldn't get herself out of, given enough time. And she didn't feel this would be an exception.

Finn hesitated and even looked a little surprised.

She smiled, liking that he seemed a bit unsure for the first time since she'd met him six years earlier. Not that she had seen much of him since Hunter and the rest of the team had left the Navy. Most of the time, Finn would come to the door, usher Hunter outside for a super-secretive conversation, and then vanish without a word. Hunter would make arrangements with his sub-leaders, leaving shortly after that with duffel bag in hand.

Sure, she'd seen all of them together when they were still members of the SEAL team, but they were mostly part of the background. The guys aimed a few sly smiles in her direction, but none of them ever spoke to her except to greet her by name. They had remained subdued, standoffish, and secretive.